James Rodway

The West Indies

and the Spanish Main

James Rodway

The West Indies
and the Spanish Main

ISBN/EAN: 9783337316051

Printed in Europe, USA, Canada, Australia, Japan

Cover: Foto ©Andreas Hilbeck / pixelio.de

More available books at **www.hansebooks.com**

THE WEST INDIES.

THE STORY OF THE NATIONS.

Large Crown 8vo, Cloth, Illustrated, 5s.
The Volumes are also kept in the following Special Bindings :
Half Persian, cloth sides, gilt top ; Full calf, half extra,
marbled edges ; Tree calf, gilt edges, gold roll
inside, full gilt back.

1. **ROME**. By ARTHUR GILMAN, M.A.
2. **THE JEWS**. By Prof. J. K. HOSMER.
3. **GERMANY**. By Rev. S. BARING-GOULD, M.A.
4. **CARTHAGE**. By Prof. ALFRED J. CHURCH.
5. **ALEXANDER'S EMPIRE**. By Prof. J. P. MAHAFFY.
6. **THE MOORS IN SPAIN**. By STANLEY LANE-POOLE.
7. **ANCIENT EGYPT**. By Prof. GEORGE RAWLINSON.
8. **HUNGARY**. By Prof. ARMINIUS VAMBÉRY.
9. **THE SARACENS**. By ARTHUR GILMAN, M.A.
10. **IRELAND**. By the Hon. EMILY LAWLESS.
11. **CHALDEA**. By ZÉNAÏDE A. RAGOZIN.
12. **THE GOTHS**. By HENRY BRADLEY.
13. **ASSYRIA**. By ZÉNAÏDE A. RAGOZIN.
14. **TURKEY**. By STANLEY LANE-POOLE.
15. **HOLLAND**. By Prof. J. E. THOROLD ROGERS.
16. **MEDIÆVAL FRANCE**. By GUSTAVE MASSON.
17. **PERSIA**. By S. G. W. BENJAMIN.
18. **PHŒNICIA**. By Prof. GEO. RAWLINSON.
19. **MEDIA**. By ZÉNAÏDE A. RAGOZIN.
20. **THE HANSA TOWNS**. By HELEN ZIMMERN.
21. **EARLY BRITAIN**. By Prof. ALFRED J. CHURCH.
22. **THE BARBARY CORSAIRS**. By STANLEY LANE-POOLE.
23. **RUSSIA**. By W. R. MORFILL, M.A.
24. **THE JEWS UNDER THE ROMANS**. By W. D. MORRISON.
25. **SCOTLAND**. By JOHN MACKINTOSH, LL.D.
26. **SWITZERLAND**. By Mrs. LINA LU'G and R. STEAD.
27. **MEXICO**. By SUSAN HALE.
28. **PORTUGAL**. By H. MORSE STEPHENS.
29. **THE NORMANS**. By SARAH ORNE JEWETT.
30. **THE BYZANTINE EMPIRE**. By C. W. C OMAN.
31. **SICILY : Phœnician, Greek and Roman**. By the late Prof. E. A. FREEMAN.
32. **THE TUSCAN REPUBLICS**. By BELLA DUFFY.
33. **POLAND**. By W. R. MORFILL, M.A.
34. **PARTHIA**. By Prof. GEORGE RAWLINSON.
35. **AUSTRALIAN COMMONWEALTH**. By GREVILLE TREGARTHEN.
36. **SPAIN**. By H. E. WATTS.
37. **JAPAN**. By DAVID MURRAY, Ph.D.
38. **SOUTH AFRICA**. By GEORGE M. THEAL.
39. **VENICE**. By ALETHEA WIEL.
40. **THE CRUSADES**. By T. A. ARCHER and C. L. KINGSFORD.
41. **VEDIC INDIA**. By Z. A. RAGOZIN.

RECEPTION OF SPANIARDS BY ARAWAKS.

(From Gottfried's " Reisen.")

THE WEST INDIES

AND THE

SPANISH MAIN

BY

JAMES RODWAY

London

T FISHER UNWIN

PATERNOSTER SQUARE

MDCCCXCVI

INTRODUCTION.

THE story of the West Indies and Spanish Main is one to stir the hearts of many nations. The shores of the Caribbean Sea have been the scene of marvellous adventures, of intense struggles between races and peoples, of pain, trouble, and disaster of almost every description. No wonder that the romance writer has laid his scenes upon its beautiful islands and deep blue waters, for nowhere in the world, perhaps, could he find such a wealth of incident. From " Robinson Crusoe " to Marryat's genial stories, and down to "Westward Ho!" and "Treasure Island," old and young have been entranced for many generations with its stories of shipwrecks, pirates, sea-fights, and treasure-seekers. Yet with all this the field has not been exhausted, for hardly a year passes without a new romance dealing more or less with the " Indies."

Under this name of the Indies the islands and continent were first known to the Spaniards, and it was not until some years had passed that the mainland received the name of *Terra Firma*. The string of islands facing the Atlantic were the Antilles, so called from a traditional island to the west of the Azores, marked on maps and globes of the fifteenth century. This "Bow of Ulysses," as Froude called the islands, was divided into the Greater and Lesser Antilles, the latter being also known as the Caribbees, from their original inhabitants. Other divisions were made later into Windward and Leeward Islands, but these differed so much in the descriptions of different nations that it would be as well to leave them out of the question. Perhaps the best way would be to name the whole the Antilles or West Indian Islands and divide them, in going from north to south, into the Bahamas, the Greater Antilles, and the Caribbees.

When we think of these beautiful islands and shores they recall those of that other "Great Sea" which was such a mighty factor in the development of Greece and Rome, Phœnicia and Carthage, Venice and Genoa. As Ulysses and Æneas wandered about the Mediterranean, so the early voyagers sailed along the coasts of the Caribbean Sea and the Gulf of Mexico in fear of anthropophagoi, amazons, giants, and fiery dragons. As the Indies were the scene of struggles between great nations and the raids of buccaneers, so also was the Mediterranean a battlefield for Christian and Turk, and a centre for piracy.

Reports of golden cities, pearls and emeralds in profusion, and wealth that passed all description, led the Spaniards to explore every island and river, until the cannibals became less alarming. Yet their sufferings were terrible. Hurricanes sunk their frail craft on the sea and earthquakes wrung their very souls on land. Starvation, with its consequent sickness and death, destroyed one party after another, but they still went on. The discovery of the riches of Mexico and Peru led them to look for other rich nations, and to travel thousands of miles on the mainland, guided by the reports of the Indians. Undaunted by suffering and failure, they would often try again and again, perhaps only to perish in the attempt at last.

The treasures of the Indies made Spain the greatest nation in Europe. With her riches she could do almost anything. Other nations bowed down before her, and she became sovereign of the seas and mistress of the world. No matter how it was obtained, gold and silver flowed into her coffers; what did she care that it was obtained by the bloody sweat of the poor Indians?

Then came envy and jealousy. Why should Spain claim the whole of the New World? England, Holland, and France began to dispute her supremacy and determined to get a share of the good things. The "invincible domination" of Spain led her to declare war against England, with the result that the hardy sea-dogs of that time began to worry the fat galleons at sea, and to pillage the treasure depôts on the Main.

And here we must mention that there were two important places in the Indies where Spain was most vulnerable—the Mona Passage between Hispaniola and Porto Rico and the Isthmus of Darien. Through the first came the outward fleets with supplies, and on their return with gold and silver, while on the Isthmus was the depôt for merchandise and the great treasure store. At these two points the enemy congregated, either as ships of war, buccaneers, corsairs, or pirates, and in their neighbourhood some of the most bitter struggles took place. There was no peace in the Indies, whatever might nominally be the case in Europe. Englishmen's blood boiled at the atrocities of the Spaniards, but we are afraid it was not love for the oppressed alone that made them massacre the Spaniards whenever they got an opportunity. The poor Indian received but a scant measure of justice from these very people, when as a matter of convenience they required possession of the Caribbee islands.

Other nations took possession of smaller islands, unoccupied by Spain, and from these centres continued their raids, as privateers in war, and as pirates at other times. Sometimes they were united among themselves against the common enemy, sometimes at war with each other. France and Holland against England, England and Holland against France— nothing but quarrels and fighting. Now an island changed hands, and again it was restored or recaptured. The planters were never sure of being able to reap their crops, and often had literally to superintend the estate work, armed with sword and arquebuse, while their black and white slaves cultivated the soil.

Now the West Indies became the great training ground for three maritime nations—England, France, and Holland. Spain lost her prestige, and the struggle lay among her enemies for over a century. At first the three disputants for her place were equally matched ; then Holland dropped behind, leaving England and France to fight it out. The struggle was a very close one, which only ended with the fall of Napoleon, and it was in the Caribbean Sea where the great check to France took place. Here Rodney defeated De Grasse, and here Nelson and many another naval officer gained that experience which served them so well in other parts of the world.

Here also was the scene of that great labour experiment, the African slave-trade. The atrocities of the Spaniards caused the depopulation of the Greater Antilles, and led to the importation of negroes. Whatever may be said against slavery, there can hardly be any question that the African has been improved by his removal to another part of the world and different surroundings. True, he has not progressed to the extent that was expected by his friends when they paid such an enormous sum for his enfranchisement; still, there are undoubtedly signs of progress.

The white colonists in the West Indies never settled down to form the nucleus of a distinct people. Since the emancipation the islands have been more and more abandoned to the negroes and coloured people, with the result that although the government is mostly in the hands of the whites, they are in such a minority as to be almost lost. In Cuba there appears to be such a feeling of patriotism towards their own island that probably we shall soon hear of a new republic, but elsewhere in the islands our hopes for the future must lie in the negroes and coloured people.

On the mainland the original inhabitants were not exterminated as in the large islands, and consequently we have there a most interesting process in course of accomplishment—the development of one or more nations. Here are the true Americans, and as the Gaul was merged in the Frank, and the Briton in the Saxon, so the Spaniard has been or will ultimately be lost in the American. At present the so-called Spanish republics are in their birth-throes—they are feeling their way. Through trouble and difficulty—revolution and tyranny—they have to march on, until they become stronger and more fitted to take their places among other nations. Out of the struggle they must ultimately come, and it will be a most interesting study for those who see the result.

In Hispaniola we have also a nation in the course of development—an alien race from the old world. More backward than the Americans, the Africans of Haïti are struggling to gain a position among other nations, apparently without any good result. The nation is yet unborn, and its birth-throes are distressing. We look upon that beautiful island and feel sad that such a paradise should have fallen so low. As a race the negro has little of that internal power that makes for progress—he must be compelled to move on. Some are inclined to look upon him as in the course of degenerating into the savage, but we, on the contrary, believe him to be progressing slowly.

In the islands belonging to European nations the influence of the dominant power is visible in the negro even when he has no trace of white blood. The French, English, or Dutch negro may be recognised by his manners, and even features. In some places

East Indians and Chinese have been imported, but these stand alone and make little impression. They are aliens as yet, and take little part in the development of the colonies.

Latterly the West Indies have sunk into neglect by Europe. Except for the difficulties of the planters their history is almost a blank sheet. Few know anything about the beautiful islands or the grand forests of the mainland. Even the discovery of gold in Guiana, which goes to confirm the reports of Ralegh, three centuries ago, is only known to a few. Ruin and desolation have fallen upon them since the peace of 1815 and the emancipation. Even the negro —the *protégé* of the benevolent—is no longer the object of interest he once was. Cane sugar is being gradually ousted by that from the beet, and hardly anything has been done to replace its cultivation by other tropical products.

Yet the islands are still as lovely as they were four centuries ago, and on the continent is a wealth of interest to the naturalist and lover of the beautiful. Now and again a tourist goes the round of the islands and publishes the result in a book of travel ; but the countries are out of the track of civilisation and progress. Possibly if the Panama or Nicaragua Canal is ever finished things may be a little better, but at present the outlook is very dismal.

In attempting to compress the story of the West Indies and Spanish Main within the covers of one volume we have undertaken a task by no means easy. Every island and every province has its own tale, and to do them all justice would require a hundred books.

Every West Indian will find something missing—some event unmentioned which is of the greatest importance to his particular community. This is only to be expected, yet we believe that the reader will get a fairer idea of their importance when they are comprehended in one great whole. The photo block illustrations are from negatives prepared by Mr. Thomas B. Blow, F.L.S.

CONTENTS.

I.

II.

III.

The Papal Bull of partition—English and French seamen in the Indies—Raids on the Spanish possessions—Master William Hawkins goes to Brazil—The Caribs friendly to the enemies of Spain—John Hawkins carries negroes from Africa—Francis Drake's attack on Nombre de Dios—The Simaroons—Drake captures the Panama train—John Oxenham — Andrew Barker — Drake's second voyage — He captures St. Domingo and Carthagena—Last voyage of Drake and Hawkins—Death of Drake—Exploits of other adventurers.

IV.

"Letters Patent" to Ralegh—"El Dorado" again—Ralegh's first voyage to Guiana—Keymis and Berrie—The Dutch in Guiana—Charles Leigh founds a settlement—Robert Harcourt's colony—Ralegh's imprisonment—He is released to again visit Guiana—Disastrous results—Roger North's colony—King James's want of policy—Changes after his death—St. Christopher's and Barbados—North's colony again—The Bahamas—The French and Dutch settlements—Rise of the Dutch—The French and English at St. Christopher's.

V.

The buccaneers of Hispaniola—Tortuga—Bay of Campeachy—Privateers turning pirates—Pierre Legrand—Captains de Basco and Brouage—Captain Lawrence—Montbar the "Exterminator"—Lolonois—Morgan storms and captures Panama—He settles down in Jamaica—Van Horn—Raid on the South Sea—Lionel Wafer's journey across the Isthmus.

LIST OF ILLUSTRATIONS.

THE WEST INDIES.

I.

THE SPANIARDS AND THEIR VICTIMS.

WHEN the early writers spoke of America as the new world, *mundus novus*, they could hardly have appreciated the full meaning of the name. True, it was a new world to them, with new animals, new plants, and a new race of mankind ; but the absolute distinctness of everything, especially in the tropical regions, was not understood. With our fuller knowledge the ideas of strangeness and novelty are more and more impressed, and we are ready to exclaim, Yes! it is indeed a new world.

Unlike those of the eastern hemisphere, the peoples of the West are of one race. Apart from every other, the development of the American Indian has gone on different lines, the result being a people self-contained, as it were, and unmodified until the arrival of the European. The American is perhaps the nearest to the natural man, and his character is the result of nature's own moulding. When compared with the European or Asiatic he seems to be far behind, yet the civilisation of Peru and Mexico was in some respects in advance of that of their conquerors. This was brought about by a dense population which forced men into collision with each other—in other parts of the continent and on the islands they were more isolated and therefore less civilised.

In the forest region of the Spanish Main, and on the West Indian islands, the communities were, as a rule, very small and isolated one from another. A kind of patriarchal system prevented much communication, and inter-tribal disputes were a bar to union. Every community distrusted every other, and even when one tribe fought against its neighbour there were few attempts to bring the sections together against the common enemy.

On the coasts and islands of the Caribbean Sea, at the time of their discovery, lived two distinct peoples, the Arawaks and the Caribs. There were also a few other tribes of minor importance, such as the Warrows, but these made little impression, and may therefore be left out of consideration. The remnants of the two great stocks still exist in Guiana and at the mouth of the Orinoco, living to-day in much the same manner as they did when the country was first discovered by the Spaniards.

Four centuries ago the Greater Antilles were exclusively inhabited by Arawaks, and the Lesser by Caribs. The Arawak, as his name implies, was more or less an agriculturalist—a meal-eater, a cultivator of vegetables, mainly cassava. From the poisonous root of this plant bread, drink, and a preservative sauce for meat, were prepared, so that, with game or fish, it formed the staff of life. The probable course of his migration was from Yucatan or Mexico to the south-east, terminating in Guiana, and from thence north through the whole of the Antilles. When Columbus arrived people of this stock filled the larger islands and the Bahamas, but along the coast and in the island of Trinidad they disputed the occupation of the territories with the Caribs. In Porto Rico also the Caribs had become aggressive, and even in Hispaniola the Arawaks had to defend their shores against that warlike people. If we believe the accounts of the Spaniards the inhabitants of the Greater Antilles were not altogether a savage people. Whether they had destroyed all the larger game, or whether they found none on their arrival, the fact remains that they were agriculturalists rather than huntsmen. They were, however, expert in fishing, and built great canoes with sails, in which they carried on their operations even in comparatively rough water. Their provision grounds were highly praised by the Spaniards in language that could hardly apply to little clearings like those in the Guiana forest. In them were grown, besides cassava, yams, sweet potatoes, and maize, while other things such as cotton and tobacco were also largely culti-vated. The natives had also acquired several arts besides that of canoe building, which, when we con-sider their want of proper implements, was almost wonderful. Cotton was spun and woven into cloth for their scanty garments, gold cast and hammered

into figures and ornaments, and wood and stone idols
and weapons were also carved. All this was done
with stone implements, even to the work of hollowing
great logs for their canoes, and shaping planks. We
read of axe-heads made of *guanin*, an alloy of gold
and copper, and also of attempts to make similar
tools of silver, but these were very rare, and could
hardly have been utilised to any good purpose.
When we appreciate the labour and pains taken in
excavating a large canoe, with only fire and the stone
adze, we can see that these people were by no means
idle. Nor were they altogether wanting in appreciation of art, for the figures on their baskets and pottery
were beautifully true geometrical patterns, and their
so-called idols, although grotesque and rude, often
striking.

On the mainland the Arawaks lived in small
communities, only electing a war-chief as occasion
required—in Haïti the Cacique seems to have been
leader and ruler as well. And here we must mention
the most striking characteristic of the American
Indian—his utter abhorrence of anything like coercion. Even in childhood his parents let him do as
he pleases, never attempting to govern him in any
way. It followed therefore that neither war-captain
nor Cacique had any real power to compel them to a
course they disliked, and that discipline was entirely
wanting. The traveller in Guiana at the present day
can thoroughly understand this trait of character, for
he has to take it into account if he wishes to get
their assistance. They must be treated as friends,
not as servants, and the greatest care taken not to

RECEPTION OF SPANIARDS BY CARIBS.

(From Gottfried's " Reisen.")

offend their dignity, unless he wishes to be left alone in the forest.

They quarrelled little among themselves, and only fought against the Caribs ; they were peaceable, kind, and gentle, so hospitable to strangers that Columbus could hardly say enough in their favour. " A better race there cannot be," he declared to his sovereigns, and this opinion was confirmed by all who came into contact with them. In fact if you do nothing to offend him, the Arawak of to-day is the same quiet and gentle fellow who met the voyagers on their arrival at Guanahani.

The Caribs were a stronger race, and had probably followed the same track as the Arawaks in a later migration. At the time of the discovery they appear to have driven the more gentle race from the smaller islands south of Porto Rico, and had taken their women as wives. All along the coast the two tribes fought with each other, but on account of the greater stretch of country there was nothing like the extermination which took place in the Lesser Antilles. The Arawaks retired up the rivers and creeks, leaving their enemies to take possession of the coast, which they did to such good purpose that the Spaniards were unable to get a footing in Guiana. All the early writers agree that the Caribs were man-eaters— in fact the word cannibal seems to have been derived from their name. In the smaller islands they had eaten all the men of the gentler tribe, and now made periodical raids on the larger, from whence they carried off prisoners to be cooked and devoured at leisure. These raids led to combinations on the part of the inhabitants of Haïti and Porto Rico, and hitherto they had been successful in preventing anything like an occupation of these islands by their enemies. Whether these successes would have continued is doubtful; the arrival of the Spaniards upset everything.

The Carib was not so entirely dependent on the produce of the soil as the meal-eater. He was a hunter and fisherman, but above everything else a warrior. His women had provision grounds like those of the Arawak, possibly because they came from that stock. The Carib's hunting grounds were circumscribed and poor, and his craving for meat could only be appeased in one way—by eating his enemies. Probably this made him all the more fierce and bloodthirsty, as a flesh diet is certainly more stimulating than one of fish and starchy tubers.

If the Arawak was impatient of control, the Carib was even more independent. The former would pine away and die under coercion, the latter refused absolutely to be a slave. He would die fighting for his liberty, but never admit that he was conquered. It was not he who welcomed the Spaniards to the West Indies—on the contrary, he did everything possible to prevent their landing on his shores. His so-called treachery caused many difficulties to the new-comers, but taken altogether he was much respected by them as a foe worthy of their steel.

These two peoples lived in a country which Columbus described as a veritable paradise—in fact he thought he had discovered the site of the Garden of Eden. Into this beautiful world he let loose a band of robbers and murderers, to depopulate and make it a wilderness. They were the product of an entirely different environment—a continent in which

A CORNER OF PARADISE. THE VICTORIA REGIA.

every man's hand was against that of his neighbour. For a long time Spain had been a battle-field, on which the most warlike instincts of mankind came to the front. Her soldiers understood the advantages of discipline, and would follow their leaders wherever anything was to be gained, yet at the same time they were individuals, and as such fought for their own hands as well.

Like the rest of Christendom Spain was very religious, and after treasure-seeking, the adventurers of that nation meant to convert the heathen. The cross was erected everywhere on landing, and religious services held to pray for help in their undertakings. If the cruelties that followed were not quite in accordance with Christ's teachings we must put it down to the manners and customs of the age. Ignorance was really the great characteristic of that period, and the brilliancy of the few only shone out the brighter because of the dark background. The majority were steeped in superstition, and almost entirely dominated by their passions.

Columbus was continually harping upon the desirability of making the natives of the new world Christians. "Your Highness," he said, in one of his letters, "ought to rejoice that they will soon become Christians, and that they will be taught the good customs of your kingdom." He took nine of them to Spain, on his return from the first voyage, who were baptized and taught the Spanish language. The king and queen told him to deal lovingly with those in the Indies, and to severely punish any who ill-treated them. More were sent to Spain and allowed to go back for the purpose of "gaining souls." Columbus, however, did not altogether agree with his sovereigns —his project was to send enough as slaves to pay the expenses of his expeditions, and he actually shipped

four lots for that purpose.   But Ferdinand and
Isabella would not have this, and even went so far as
to prohibit the deportation of the Caribs notwithstanding the admiral's argument that they were

EN ROUTE TO THE GOLDFIELDS OF GUIANA.   PASSING THE RAPIDS
OF THE ESSEQUEBO.

unworthy of the royal clemency, because they ate
men and were enemies of the friendly Arawaks.

How the new world was discovered in 1492 has
been told so often that it is hardly necessary to repeat
the story.   Haïti, named Hispaniola or Little Spain,
was chosen from the first as the island on which a
settlement should be planted.   Here Columbus left

thirty-nine colonists under the command of Diego de Arana, and under the protection of the great Cacique Guacanagari. He "trusted to God" that on his return he would find a ton of gold and a large quantity of spices, with the proceeds of which his sovereigns might undertake the conquest of Jerusalem from the infidels.

A ton of gold! This was the whole end and aim of his expedition. Everything else was subordinate to this. He had seen the natives wearing gold ornaments, and found that the precious metal could be gathered from certain streams on the island. But, could he estimate the amount of labour required to procure such an enormous quantity, by people who had no other appliances than baskets? This alone was enough to bring trouble upon the peaceful island.

But this was not all. The colonists quarrelled among themselves, interfered with the Indian women, went hunting for gold all over the country, took it wherever it could be found, and stole provisions when their friends did not bring them enough. Not satisfied with the district of the friendly Cacique, they ravaged that of Caonabo, the Carib chieftain of another clan, a man of a different stamp. He resented the insults at once by attacking the Spaniards, who, notwithstanding the assistance of their allies, were utterly exterminated. When Columbus arrived, instead of a ton of gold, he found nothing but the blackened ruins of the fort and houses.

This should have been a lesson to the Spaniards, but unfortunately it only led to further quarrels. The new-comers did not intend to cultivate the soil ; their main object was treasure, and they expected the natives to provide them with food. And here we must mention the fact that the people of tropical climes *never* have any store of provisions laid up— this is only necessary where winter prevails for half the year. It follows therefore that however liberal they may feel towards strangers, their supplies being restricted to their own wants leave little to give away. Up to a certain point the Indian gives freely, but when this means privation to himself he withholds his hand. The want of a full appreciation of this fact caused great trouble in many of the early settlements, and in some cases led to their destruction. The natives promised food supplies ; but when they found themselves starving, naturally withheld further assistance. The settlers considered this a breach of faith, and made incursions on the provision grounds, taking what they wanted, and seriously injuring the crops. This the Indians resented, and deadly quarrels ensued, which ended in their driving out the colonists or deserting the place altogether. In the latter case the food supply was necessarily cut off, and often led ultimately to the abandonment of the colony.

To the kindly people of Hispaniola the new-comers were gods, and their horses and cattle preternatural creatures. While wondering and admiring, they were at the same time frightened at these out-of-the-way men and animals, especially when the soldiers exhibited themselves on horseback. At first they thought them immortal, and were disagreeably surprised when they fell before the army of Caonabo. But even the proverbial worm will turn, and soon the

WORRYING THE NATIVES WITH DOGS.

(*From Gottfried's " Reisen."*)

oppressions of the second colonists drove the poor Haïtians to resist.   To labour in the field was beneath the dignity of the adventurous treasure-seekers—the natives must supply them with provisions.   What they had brought from Spain was soon spoilt in such a hot climate—no one had yet learned how to pack for long voyages.   They must get food, and what was the good of having thousands of people, and acres of cultivated land in their neighbourhood, if the natives did not bring in as much as was required?   At first they were supplied willingly, but when the results of this profuse hospitality began to tell upon themselves, the poor Haïtians withheld their hands.   Then the Spaniards began complaining to the Cacique, who, however, had no real authority over his people in a matter of this kind, and therefore could do nothing. Driven by want the Spaniards made incursions on the provision grounds, where they spoilt as much as they took away, and left a waste behind.   Sometimes they met with resistance, and the defenders were cut down without mercy.   The spoilers only wanted an excuse for fleshing their swords ; they were even anxious to show their powers, and make the natives feel that at last they had masters.

Before two years had passed the Spaniards were beset with difficulties.   The Indian looked despairingly at his wasted fields, and refused to cultivate them any longer.   Why should he plant for others when he himself was starving ?   Some fled into the mountains and forests of the interior, others died of want.   This naturally told upon the white men, who had not yet learnt that they must cultivate the soil if they wanted its produce. They could not demean themselves to this, but must have the power to compel the inhabitants and owners of this beautiful island to work for them.

The home authorities knew what was going on, and did their best according to their lights to provide a remedy. At first they gave large tracts of land to the settlers, *repartimientos* as they were called, but what was the use of these if their owners could get no labourers? Then to every grant was allotted a certain number of Indians as slaves, and thus the cruel system that ultimately depopulated the Greater Antilles and the Bahamas was introduced.

Those who were not allotted as slaves were compelled to pay tribute. In the neighbourhood of the gold-washings this was to consist of a little bellful of gold ; in other places of an arroba (28 lbs.) of cotton, once a quarter for every person above the age of fourteen. Metal tokens to hang upon the neck were given as receipts, and when these were absent the people were severely punished. Thus this gentle and independent race was enslaved.

Even with modern appliances and the use of quick-silver, gold-washing is a most precarious business ; what then could it have been here with nothing but a basket and gourd? Columbus had such exaggerated ideas that, when he saw the gold-washings of Cibao, he came to the conclusion they were the Ophir of the Bible ; from his reports the king and queen thought nothing of demanding this small tribute. To the Indian, however, the gleaning of the tribute meant the labour of days and weeks, and when there were so many seekers it was found utterly impossible for each to gather his amount. Then they ran away, and were hunted with dogs, brought back, and com-

A MODERN ALLUVIAL GOLD WASHING.

pelled to wash the gravel under surveillance, subject to the pricks of a sword if they were not active enough. But, even with all this, the returns were not equal to what was expected, and the tribute had

SUICIDES.

(*From Gottfried's " Reisen."*)

ultimately to be abandoned. However, it was stated that as much as the value of a million crowns per annum was extracted during the best years, at a cost of pain and suffering awful to contemplate.

The cotton tribute had also to be abandoned, and even the *repartimientos* were not a success. If they had been willing, the natives could hardly have performed steady work, and as slaves they were almost valueless. In their natural condition they laboured when they chose, wasting time as we should say with little good result. Now their masters demanded heavy tasks which prevented their working on their own provision grounds, and yet provided little or nothing in the way of rations. Hundreds died of starvation; thousands committed suicide. Some jumped from high precipices; they hanged, stabbed, drowned, and poisoned themselves; mothers destroyed their babes to save them from the misery of living. If caught in such attempts they were flogged, had boiling water or melted lead poured over them, and were otherwise tortured until death came to their relief. Their cruel masters, however, rarely wished to kill them outright—they were too valuable. No, they must break down this dogged, stubborn spirit—treat them as horses and mules, until they bent themselves to the yoke.

It was left for bands of soldiers on foraging expeditions to kill in mere wantonness. A company would be travelling through the island and come upon a village, where perhaps they stopped for a short rest. The people looked on, admiring their shining armour and weapons, wondering what sort of creatures these were that so quietly cropped the grass and shrubs. One of the soldiers would take out his sword, feel its keen edge, and think what a pity it was that the weapon should be used so little. Behind him comes a little boy. The temptation is great; in a moment the sharp weapon flashes and the child lies dead. The Indians fly, and the whole party follows, chasing and slaughtering to their heart's content, not knowing nor caring why. In a few minutes fifty are killed, the soldiers return to their bivouac, and if they inquire into the matter at all pass it off as a good jest.

Is it any wonder that the population decreased to a wonderful degree in a few years? The sugar-cane had been introduced by Columbus on his second voyage, and labour was soon required for cultivating this and other crops. As long as slaves were procurable the planters throve, and as by that time Hispaniola had become the great centre of the Indies, the settlers were in a fair way to make fortunes. But the decrease in the population became alarming, and something had to be done; then, new settlers were continually arriving who also wanted slaves. It followed, therefore, that some of the more audacious of the adventurers took up the trade of kidnapping the Indians from other islands and the mainland. A host of disappointed treasure-seekers had ransacked every shore, and were now well prepared for the business of man-hunting.

The first people to suffer were those who so kindly welcomed Columbus on his arrival — the gentle inhabitants of the Bahamas. They were even more peaceful than the Haïtians, because they had not suffered from Carib invasions. When the slave hunters told them to come to the south and live with their ancestors, they willingly allowed themselves to be carried off to suffer like their neighbours. Some ran away and got to the northern shores of Hispaniola, where they stretched out their hands to their beautiful homes and then died of grief.

Having entirely depopulated the smaller islands, and being prevented from kidnapping the people of Cuba, Porto Rico, and Jamaica, by the settlers on those islands, they tried the Caribbees. Here they met their match. No longer was it the gentle Arawak whom they encountered, but the ferocious cannibal. Like his foes he had been trained in war for many generations. Not only did he refuse to work for the stranger, but even went so far as to oppose his landing. On his islands was little to attract the treasure-seeker, and if he would not submit to be a slave, nothing was to be gained by interfering with him. This the Spaniard found out by bitter experience. A few vessels were wrecked on these inhospitable shores, the crews of which escaped to land only to be killed and eaten, after being tortured with all the ingenuity of the savage. Even a landing for fresh water had to be made in the most cautious manner, and the carriers protected by a strong guard. No doubt the Caribs had heard of the white man's cruelties from their Arawak prisoners, and were therefore all the more ready to repel their invasions. This was particularly noticeable later when the English and French arrived and found them by no means so ferocious as the Spaniards had reported. Possibly they knew these people to be enemies to their foes, and were therefore all the more ready to be friendly as long as no attempts were made to oppress them.

Hispaniola rose to some importance very quickly, and almost as quickly declined. The settlers depopulated the island, and then complained of the want of labourers. The gold-seekers went elsewhere, and Mexico and the isthmus of Darien became of more importance. Some writers have attempted to give the number of Indians exterminated in the early years of the sixteenth century, but little reliance can be placed on their statistics. Generally, they range from one to three millions, but it is doubtful whether even the lowest figure is not too high. Yet, when we read the statement of Columbus that crowds of people (in one place two thousand) came forth to meet him, and his description of the large area of cultivated land, as well as the broad and good roads, it is not difficult to conceive that a million people lived in these great islands.

With the destruction of the labourers down fell the plantations. Cattle had been introduced and throve wonderfully; now they ran wild over the islands, especially Hispaniola, until they became innumerable. On the abandoned provision grounds of the Indians they found a virgin pasturage. Hogs also took to the woods, and increased even faster than the cattle. At first there were neither huntsmen nor carnivorous animals to check this wonderful development. The once domesticated animals recovered some of the powers and capacities of their wild ancestors, and only required enemies to assist in bringing out other latent characters. And these were not long wanting. Large and powerful hounds had been imported from Spain to hunt the runaway Indians, and now that their occupation was gone, they also took to the woods and savannahs. Like their ancestors and cousins, the wolves, they combined into packs and fought the cattle and hogs. Both hunters and hunted became stronger and fiercer—the dogs learnt how best to attack, and their prey to defend themselves. It was a struggle like that between the cannibals and meal-eaters — nature's method of preserving the balance of life. This equalisation no doubt would have been the result had not man interfered; how this happened we must leave to another chapter.

II.

THE QUEST FOR "EL DORADO."

OPHIR was not found in the islands, and the bands of adventurers went over to *terra firma* or the mainland to continue the search. Along the coast of Guiana and Venezuela they again came across the gentle Arawak and ferocious Carib, the latter making himself respected everywhere, while his poor-spirited fellow-countryman was alternately caressed and plundered. In every place the Spaniards found gold ornaments, and every tribe told them that the precious metal was only obtainable in some far distant country. The Haïtians sent Columbus to the south in search of the *guanin* country, and it was there he discovered the coast of Paria and the delta of the mighty Orinoco. But he was not fated to come across the treasure cities of the Indies.

Others followed to at last conquer Mexico and Peru, but even then it was generally believed that nations existed who had more riches to be plundered than those of the Inca and Montezuma. To find these golden regions the voyagers wandered in every direction, contributing much to the knowledge of the

23

coasts and rivers, but always coming back disappointed.

The horrors of this search can hardly be appreciated nowadays. The ships were so small and ill-found that we should hardly care to use them for coasters, yet in them these pioneers crossed the Atlantic and encountered the hurricanes of the West Indies. Decked only at bow and stern, the waves dashed into the hold and wetted the provisions, while the sun poured down upon the water casks and burst their wooden hoops. The butter and cheese stank, the flour in sacks became mouldy, and the bacon and salt fish putrid. Then the hull of the vessel was unprotected, and the teredo, or ship worm, bored it through and through, until nothing but careening and caulking could save the poor craft from sinking. When we understand the privations and dangers of this navigation we are not surprised that the adventurers often came to grief, but rather wonder that any of them survived.

Living in the West Indies, we have often thought of the pain and suffering it would produce if we were compelled to walk or sit in the burning sun armed as were the soldiers at that period. We can hardly believe that they wore steel body armour, yet the evidence is too strong to be refuted. True, they gave it up afterwards in favour of quilted cotton, but before they did so how hot they must have felt! We can fancy the sentry standing exposed to the full blaze of the sun, his helmet and breastplate burning hot and his woollen underclothing saturated with perspiration. Then there would be the open boat ascending a river. The occupants dared not row in the shade for fear of cannibals shooting at them with poisoned arrows from the thicket, and out in the river they must have felt as if in a furnace. Even with our white clothing and light hats a long journey in an open boat when the sun is high often ends in fever, and almost invariably in a headache. The neck and backs of the hands get blistered, and become sore, the glare on the water dazzles the eye, and we feel faint.

In one of the accounts of such a boating expedition on a river in Guiana we read of the men finding some yellow plums floating on the water, and of their being much refreshed by them. We also have come across these hog-plums when almost exhausted by a long exposure on the open river, and when even our negro steersman was nodding as he held the paddle. Suddenly we came to our destination, the mouth of a creek, and were under an arcade of vegetation, beneath which the plums floated on the cool dark water.

The men of the sixteenth century must have been stronger than ourselves, or they could hardly have endured such pain and privation. They lay down on the bare earth night after night, and on board ship went to sleep on naked planks. As they could endure pain and discomfort, so also could they inflict it on others. The rough seamen learnt to bear hardships which blunted their feelings of humanity and made them inclined to torture others. When in the hands of the cannibals they were almost as stoical as the savage himself, their ruling passion being a desire for revenge. If cruelly treated by one tribe they retaliated on others ; in the same way the Indians killed one party of Spaniards to avenge the insults of their countrymen. This led to a great deal of trouble and

A GUIANA RIVER. THE TUMATAMARIFALLS.

made the voyages of the treasure-seekers dangerous to all. However free from blame one party might be, they were liable to suffer for previous wrong-doings and they in turn left behind them injuries to be avenged on the next comers.

And then, how very audacious these adventurers were! Alonzo de Ojeda was perhaps the most striking example of utter recklessness in face of danger. In 1509 he entered the harbour of Carthagena in spite of a warning that its shores were inhabited by a ferocious tribe who fought with palmwood swords and poisoned arrows. It was even stated that the women mingled in the battle, and could use the bow and a kind of lance.

These people had been irritated by another party of Spaniards, and on sight of the vessels were up in arms at once. However, Ojeda was undaunted, and landed at once with his men and some friars, who had been sent to convert the Indians. In front stood the enemy brandishing their weapons, and prepared for the first hostile movement. Yet, even under these critical circumstances, he ordered the usual proclamation to be read to the Indians in a language of which they knew nothing. He, Alonzo de Ojeda, servant of the most high and mighty sovereigns of Castile and Leon, conquerors of barbarous nations, notified them that God had given St. Peter the supreme power over the world, which power was exercised by the Pope, who had given all that part of the world to these sovereigns. They were called upon to acknowledge this sovereignty at once, which, if they refused to do, he would bring upon them the horrors of war, desolation to their houses, confiscation of their property, and slavery to their wives and children.

While one of the friars read this address the

INHABITANTS OF THE SPANISH MAIN.
(*From Colijn's "Reisen."*)

savages stood on the defensive, no doubt wondering what the delay meant. Ojeda knew not their language, and they took little notice of his signs of amity. As they still brandished their weapons, the intrepid adventurer led on an attack, calling the Virgin to his aid, and in a few minutes put them to flight, killing a few and taking others prisoners. Not content with this, he followed them through the forest to their village, and after a deadly fight, drove them out and burnt their dwellings. Still undaunted, he went on to another village, which he found deserted, but while his men were searching for plunder he was attacked by the enemy in overwhelming numbers. All his followers were killed, and he himself wounded with a poisoned arrow, yet he managed to escape into the forest to suffer hunger and thirst in addition to the pain of his wound.

Meanwhile his men on board the ships were wondering what had become of their leader and his party. They were afraid to venture far into the woods on account of the yells and shouts of the Indians, who were celebrating their triumph. At last, however, they commenced a search, and found their captain in a mangrove swamp, lying on a tangle of roots, speechless and dying of hunger, yet still clutching his naked sword and bearing his buckler. Notwithstanding all this, he ultimately recovered, to go on as eagerly as ever in making fresh conquests.

Later, the proclamation to the Indians was interpreted to them, sometimes eliciting replies very much to the point. When the Bachelor Enciso went in search of the country of Zenu, where gold was so plentiful that it could be collected in the rainy season in nets stretched across the river, he was opposed by two Caciques, to whom the paper was read. They listened courteously, and, when it had been expounded, said they were quite willing to admit that there was one God, the ruler of heaven and earth, whose creatures they were. But as to the Pope's regency and his donation of *their* country to the king of Spain, that was another thing altogether. The Pope must have been drunk when he gave away what was not his, and the king could only have been mad to ask him for the territory of others. They, the Caciques, were the rulers of these territories, and needed no other sovereign : if their king came to take possession they would cut off his head and stick it on a pole, as they did the heads of their other enemies, at the same time pointing to a row of grisly skulls impaled close by. Their arguments, however, were useless, for Enciso attacked, routed them, and took one of the Caciques prisoner.

The accounts of the early voyagers are full of such examples of audacity as well as of endurance of suffering. The perils of the sea were as great as those of the land, but few voyages were as disastrous as that of Valdivia, who in 1512 sailed from Darien for Hispaniola. When in sight of Jamaica, his vessel was caught in a hurricane and driven upon some shoals called the Vipers, where it was dashed to pieces. He and his twenty men barely escaped with their lives in a boat without sails, oars, water, or provisions. For thirteen days they drifted about, until seven were dead and the remainder helpless.

Then the boat stranded on the coast of Yucatan, and the poor wretches were captured by Indians, to be taken before their Cacique. They were now put into a kind of pen to fatten for the cannibal festival. Valdivia and four others were taken first, and the horror produced on their comrades led them to risk everything and break out of their prison in the night. Having succeeded in reaching the forest, they were almost as badly off, for no food could be had, and they dared not run the risk of going near the villages. Almost perishing with hunger, they at last reached another part of the country, to be again captured, and kept as slaves. Finally they all died except two, one of whom at last escaped to tell the tale almost by a miracle.

One of the stories is suggestive of "Robinson Crusoe." In 1499 Niño and Guerra sailed from Spain in a bark of fifty tons, and, while exploring the Gulf of Paria, came across eighteen Carib canoes filled with armed men. The savages assailed them with flights of arrows, but the sudden boom of the cannon frightened them away at once. One canoe, however, was captured, in which they took a Carib prisoner, and found an Arawak captive lying bound at the bottom. On being liberated, the Arawak informed the Spaniards, through their interpreter, that he was the last of seven who had been taken by the cannibals. The other six had been killed and eaten one after another, and he had been reserved for the next evening meal. The Spaniards, incensed against the man-eater, gave him into the hands of the Arawak, at the same time handing him a cudgel, leaving his enemy unarmed. Immediately the Arawak sprang upon him, knocked him sprawling, trod his breath out of his body, and at the same time beat him with his fist until nothing but a shapeless corpse remained. But, not yet satisfied, he tore the head off and stuck it on a pole as a trophy.

'After the conquest of Mexico and Peru had rewarded Cortez and Pizarro, others wished to be equally fortunate. From the Indians came reports of golden countries in the interior, and land expeditions were projected. These reports grew into shape, and at last a quest as romantic as that for the Holy Grail, led one adventurer after another on and on, to starvation, sickness, and death.

The germ of the story of "El Dorado," the lake of golden sands, and the glittering city of Manoa, appears to have first arisen in New Granada. Here was the Lake of Guatavita, and before the arrival of the Spaniards this was the scene of an annual religious festival. To the genius of the lake the Cacique of the neighbouring district offered a holy sacrifice on a certain day. In the morning he anointed his body with balsam, and then rolled himself in gold dust until he became a "gilded king." Then, embarking in a canoe with his nobles, he was paddled to the centre of the lake, crowds of people thronging its shores and honouring him with songs and the din of rude instrumental music. Offerings to the god of the lake were made from the canoe, gold, emeralds, pearls, and everything precious being scattered upon the water. Finally, the Cacique jumped in himself and washed the gold from his body, while the people shouted for joy. To wind up the festival a great drinking bout was held, when canoesful of piwarree, the Indian's beer, were drunk, and every one made merry.

Such was the tradition—for the ceremony had been discontinued half a century before—which had so impressed itself over the northern shores of South America, as to be told from the Amazon to the isthmus of Darien. " El Dorado " was gilded every morning, and his city was full of beautiful golden palaces. It stood on the edge of the great salt lake Parima, the sands of which were composed of the precious metal. Some went so far as to say that they had seen the glittering city from a distance, and were only prevented from reaching it by the peculiar difficulties of the way. Not to mention tigers and alligators, starvation and sickness, there were "anthropophagoi and men whose heads do grow beneath their shoulders," besides amazons and fiery dragons. Wherever the story was told the golden city was located at a far distance, and it seemed ever to recede before the eager seekers. They sought it in the forest and on the savannah, over the lofty peaks of the Andes, and along the banks of the mighty rivers. The whole of the Spanish Main was explored, and places then visited which have hardly been seen again by the white man down to the present date.

The quest began in New Granada, and from thence it shifted to Venezuela. The most daring seekers were German knights, the Welsers of Augsburg. They had received charters from Charles the Fifth, under which they were empowered to found cities, erect forts, work mines, and make slaves of the Indians. One of their representatives, Ambrosio de Alfinger, set out in 1530, accompanied by two hundred Spaniards, and a larger number of Indians, laden with provisions and other necessaries. On the journey the party committed such brutalities upon the poor natives that the reports afterwards helped to fire the blood of Englishmen, and make them bitterly cruel. To prevent the bearers from running away they were strung together on chains, running through rings round their necks. If one of them dropped from sickness or exhaustion, his head was cut off, the ring loosened, and thus the trouble of interfering with the chain saved. If he were to be left behind, it did not matter whether he was alive or dead. At one place on the river Magdalena the frightened natives took refuge on some islands, but the Spaniards swam their horses across and killed or took prisoners the whole of them. From their Cacique Alfinger got booty to the value of sixty thousand dollars, with which he sent back for further supplies. But, although he waited for a year his messengers did not return, and the company were reduced to such straits that many died for want of bare food. But the Indians fared much worse, for their provision grounds were utterly destroyed, and what with murders and starvation the surrounding country was quite depopulated and desolate.

Even Alfinger had to give up waiting for his supplies and move on at last, for these had been utilised by his lieutenant on an expedition of his own.

The party eked out a bare subsistence with wild fruits and game. If they found a village they plundered it of everything it contained, dug up the provisions from the fields, and left the survivors of the massacre to starve. Not that they themselves were in a much better plight ; fever, the result of want and exposure, carried them off in continually increasing numbers. At last they got into a mountain region, and the poor naked bearers were frozen to death. Descending again they encountered stronger and fiercer tribes, by whom they were defeated, the cruel Alfinger himself dying two days afterwards from his wounds. A small remnant only returned after two years' absence, leaving a track of pain and suffering to make their memory accursed for many generations.

George of Spires now fitted out a great expedition of three hundred infantry and two hundred cavalry, which started in 1536. They also went a long distance into the interior, braving hardships and dangers almost incredible. Jaguars carried off their horses, and even went so far as to attack and kill several of the Indian bearers and one Spaniard. Like their predecessors, they also encountered savage Indians, and died of starvation and sickness. After journeying fifteen hundred miles from the coast they had to return unsuccessful ; but as their leader was less cruel than Alfinger, the losses of the party were not so great. Instead of dying on the journey he lived to become Governor of Venezuela.

Nicholas Fedreman followed the last party with supplies, but took them to go treasure-seeking on his own account. He wandered about for three years, and at last returned with some wonderful stories which induced others to continue the search. Herman de Quesada also travelled about for a year, and returned like his predecessors. Then Philip von Huten, who had gone already with George of Spires, fitted out a great expedition. His party was at one time so utterly famished that they had to eat ants, which they captured by placing corn cobs near the nests of these little creatures. They travelled in a great circle without knowing where they went, and at the end of a year came back to the place from whence they had started. Hearing, however, of a rich city called Macatoa, Von Huten started again, and found streets of houses with about eight hundred inhabitants, but no treasure. The people here sent him on farther, with their tales of the Omaguas, a warlike people living away in the south. On he went for five days, and at last came upon what he thought must be the golden city. It stretched away as far as the eye could reach, and in the centre was a great temple. But, although the little party charged gallantly down a hill and into the town, the Omaguas came out in such force that they had to retreat, bearing their wounded leader in a hammock. Continually harassed by Indians, they at last got back, to tell such stories of the dangers of the quest that the Omaguas seem to have been afterwards left alone.

Our account of the search for "El Dorado" is necessarily short and imperfect, as it would be impossible even to enumerate all the expeditions. There is one, however, that was so tragic and awful, that, although it was fitted out in Peru, it must yet be mentioned in the story of the Spanish Main.

"EL DORADO."

(From Gottfried's "Reisen.")

Notwithstanding the enormous quantities of gold
and silver found in Peru, the crowds of needy
treasure-seekers who went to that country gave some
trouble to the Viceroy, who appears to have been
willing to get rid of them at any cost. Whether he
purposely sent them on a " wild goose chase," or
whether he really believed the " El Dorado " story, is
doubtful, but it is certain that he thought it prudent
to give them employment in some way, to prevent
mischief in his province.

The expedition was put in command of Pedro de
Ursua, and was intended to go down the Amazon in
search of treasure cities. Embarking on the river
Huallaga, in the year 1560, they had hardly passed
the mouth of Ucayali before Ursua found he had a
most unprincipled gang of scoundrels under his
command. A little farther down the river they
mutinied, under the leadership of Lope de Aguirre,
and murdered Ursua and his lieutenant, appointing
Guzman as captain. Being dissatisfied, however, with
their new commander, they also killed him a little
later, together with most of his adherents.

Now Aguirre became leader—a ruffian whose
character was of the blackest. Father Pedro Simon
delineates his features and character, making him
out to be a very devil. He was about fifty years of
age, short of stature and sparsely built, ill-featured,
his face small and lean, his beard black, and his eyes
as piercing as those of a hawk. When he looked at
any one he fixed his gaze sternly, particularly when
annoyed ; he was a noisy talker and boaster, and
when well supported very bold and determined, but

otherwise a coward. Of a very hardy constitution, he could bear much fatigue, either on foot or horseback. He was never without one or two coats of mail or a steel breastplate, and always carried a sword, dagger, arquebuse, or lance. His sleep was mostly taken in the day, as he was afraid to rest at night, although he never took off his armour altogether nor put away his weapons. Simon said he had always been of a turbulent disposition ; a lover of revolts and mutinies ; an enemy to all good men and good actions.

Such was the Tyrant or Traitor Aguirre—virtually a madman—who now became the leader of a band of wretches like-minded to himself. They journeyed down the mighty river, now and again murdering one or another of the party, on the least suspicion of their dislike to their proceedings, and ill-treating the natives everywhere.

Aguirre was not ashamed to boast that he had murdered a woman—not an Indian, but a beautiful Spanish lady, who had accompanied her lover on this arduous journey. Donna Inez de Altienza, a young widow, fell passionately in love with Ursua, who was brave, generous, and handsome ; and loath to part with him, she undertook the hitherto unheard-of journey of thousands of miles in a strange and savage country. No fears or terrors daunted this devoted woman until after the death of her lover. Aguirre then picked a quarrel on the ground that her mattress was too large for the boat, and she also was murdered. The Spanish poet, Castellanos, thus laments the cruel deed :—

> " The birds mourned on the trees ;
> The wild beasts of the forest lamented ;
> The waters ceased to murmur ;
> The fishes beneath the waters groaned ;
> The winds execrated the deed
> When Llamoso cut the veins of her white neck.
> Wretch ! wert thou born of woman ?
> No ! what beast could have such a wicked son ?
> How was it that thou didst not die
> In imagining a treason so enormous ?
> Her two women, 'midst lamentation and grief,
> Gathered flowers to cover her grave,
> And cut her epitaph in the bark of a tree—
> ' These flowers cover one whose faithfulness
> And beauty were unequalled,
> Whom cruel men slew without a cause.' "

Whether Aguirre reached the mouth of the Amazon
is doubtful—the evidence is in favour of his getting
out of that river into the Rio Negro, and from thence
into the Orinoco. However this may have been, he
arrived at last in the Gulf of Paria and proceeded to
the island of Margarita. Here, true to his character,
he and his men commenced to plunder and kill
the inhabitants, going so far as to defy the local
authorities and even the king of Spain himself. To
even enumerate the deeds of this band of outlaws
would fill a chapter, but we cannot omit giving an
extract from Aguirre's letter to his king, one of the
most curious productions ever written :—

" I firmly believe that thou, O Christian king and
lord, hast been very cruel and ungrateful to me and
my companions for such good service, and that all
those who write to thee from this land deceive thee
much, because thou seest things from too far off. I
and my companions, no longer able to suffer the

cruelties which thy judges and governors exercise in thy name, are resolved to obey thee no longer. . . . Hear me! O hear me! thou king of Spain. Be not cruel to thy vassals. . . . Remember, King Philip, that thou hast no right to draw revenues from these provinces, since their conquest has been without danger to thee. I take it for certain that few kings go to hell, only because they are few in number; if they were many, none of them would go to heaven. For I believe that you are all worse than Lucifer, and that you hunger and thirst after human blood; and further, I think little of you and despise you all; nor do I look upon your government as more than an air bubble. . . .

" In the year 1559 the Marquis of Canete entrusted the expedition of the river of Amazons to Pedro de Ursua, a Navarrese, or, rather, a Frenchman, who delayed the building of his vessels till 1560. These vessels were built in the province of the Motilones, which is a wet country, and, as they were built in the rainy season, they came to pieces, and we therefore made canoes and descended the river. We navigated the most powerful river in Peru, and it seemed to us that we were in a sea of fresh water. We descended the river for three hundred leagues. This bad governor was capricious, vain, and inefficient, so that we could not suffer it, and we gave him a quick and certain death. We then raised Don Fernando de Guzman to be our king. . . . Because I did not consent to their evil deeds they desired to murder me. I therefore killed the new king, the captain of his guard, his lieutenant-general, four captains, his major-domo, his chaplain who said mass, a woman, a knight of the Order of Rhodes, an admiral, two ensigns, and five or six of his servants. I named captains and sergeants, but these men also wanted to kill me, and I hanged them. We continued our course while this evil fortune was befalling us, and it was eleven months and a half before we reached the mouths of the river, having travelled for more than a hundred days over more than fifteen hundred leagues. This river has a course of two thousand leagues of fresh water, the greater part of the shores being uninhabited, and God only knows how we ever escaped out of that fearful lake. I advise thee not to send any Spanish fleet up this ill-omened river, for, on the faith of a Christian, I swear to thee, O king and lord, that if a hundred thousand men should go up, not one would escape. . . .

"We shall give God thanks if, by our arms, we attain the rewards which are due to us, but which thou hast denied us ; and because of thine ingratitude I am a rebel against thee until death."

He and his band of outlaws ravaged the settlements of Venezuela for some time, until at last, on a promise of pardon, all left him save Llamoso, the murderer of Lady Inez. Aguirre had a daughter, a girl of twelve to fourteen, and when he found that all was lost he resolved to kill her. They were living at a country house, and when Llamoso brought the news of the desertion of his men, he snatched up a loaded arquebuse and rushed into his child's room, saying, "Commend thyself to God, my daughter, for I am about to kill thee, that thou mayest not be pointed at with scorn, nor that it be in the power of any one to call thee the daughter of a traitor." A woman snatched the weapon from his hand, but, drawing his poniard, he stabbed the girl in the breast, saying, " Die ! because I must die ! " Rushing then to the door, he found the house surrounded by Spanish soldiers, who compelled him to surrender, and almost immediately took him out to be shot.

This put an end to treasure-seeking on the Amazon, but the search for " El Dorado " had been going on and was still continued along the banks of the Orinoco. The first attempt to reach the golden city by this river appears to have been made by Pedro de Acosta about the year 1530, but after most of his men had been killed and eaten by the cannibals, he was compelled to abandon his project. After him came Diego de Ordas, the following year, whose expedition became afterwards famous. He, however, found nothing himself, although he went as far as the mouth of the Caroni—it was from one of his men that the " El Dorado " story was gleaned. By some accident the whole of the gunpowder was exploded, and this being attributed to the negligence of the munitioner, Juan Martinez, he was sentenced to be put in a canoe, without paddles or food, and allowed to drift at the mercy of the current.

What became of the culprit was not known, but some months afterwards a strange white man was brought by some Indians to Margarita. He was wasted by sickness, naked, and apparently destitute, but, through the kindness of a ship-captain, he got a passage to Porto Rico, and was there placed in a religious house, under the care of some Dominican friars. Here he became worse, but when on the point of death he presented his friends with two gourdsful of gold beads to pay for the repose of his soul; he also declared himself to be Juan Martinez, and told the wonderful story of his adventures.

After being cast adrift, the canoe floated down the stream until evening, when it attracted the attention of some Indians, who paddled out from the shore and rescued Martinez from his perilous situation. These were Guianians, who had never before seen a white man, and therefore resolved to take him to their king as a curiosity. He was, however, blindfolded to prevent his seeing the direction they were taking, and led on and on, through forest and over mountain, for fifteen days, until a great city was reached. Arriving here at noon, his bandage was taken off, and Martinez feasted his eyes upon a great plain covered with houses, the roofs of which glittered in the sun as if made of gold. As far as his eye could reach stretched this marvellous assemblage of palaces. In the centre dwelt the great king, but, although the party travelled the whole of that and the next day, they did not reach the palace until evening.

Here Martinez was well treated, and allowed to walk about the city, but not beyond it. He remained for seven months, saw the great lake on the shore of which the city of Manoa stood, and handled its golden sands. However, he was not content to remain, and after repeated petitions to be allowed to depart, was at last furnished with guides and as much gold as they could carry. Arrived at the Orinoco, the cannibals fell upon the party, stole all the treasure save that hidden under some provisions in the two gourds, and left them destitute. After enduring many privations Martinez, however, got a passage in an Indian canoe to Margarita, from whence he expected to go to Spain and report his discovery to the king.

What amount of truth, if any at all, was contained in the story is doubtful. It does not appear to have been told at once, but gradually leaked out, becoming more marvellous as it spread over the West Indies. Adventurers flocked to the Orinoco, and at least a score of expeditions went in search of " El Dorado." Under the command of bold adventurers one party after another entered into the forest, some never to return or to be heard of again. The remnant sometimes came back starving, and broken down with sickness. We read of one Juan Corteso that he marched into the country, but neither he nor any of his company did return again. Gaspar de Sylva and his two brothers sought El Dorado, but fell down to Trinidad, where all three were buried. Jeronimo Ortal, after great travail and spending all his substance, died on a sudden at St. Domingo. Father Iala, a friar, with only one companion and some Indian guides, returned with gold eagles, idols, and other jewels, but when he essayed to pass a second time was slain by Indians. Alonzo de Herera endured great misery, but never entered one league into the country ; he also was at last slain by Indians. Antonio Sedenno got much gold and many Indian prisoners, whom he manacled in irons, and of whom many died on the way. The tigers being fleshed with the dead carcases assaulted the Spaniards, who with much trouble hardly defended themselves from them. Sedenno was buried within the precincts of the empire of the gilded king, and most of his people perished likewise. Augustine Delgado came to an Indian Cacique, who entertained him with kindness and gave him rich jewels, six seemly pages, ten young slaves, and three nymphs very beautiful. To requite these manifold courtesies he took all the gold he could get and all the Indians he could lay hold on, to sell for slaves. He was afterwards shot in the eye by an Indian, of which hurt he died.

And so we might go on to tell of the thousands of people murdered and tens of thousands carried off as slaves. Every gold ornament was stolen, provision grounds destroyed, and the forest tracks strewn with the corpses of those who had been massacred, and marked out by the graves of their murderers. Sometimes treasure and slaves were recaptured and no one left to tell the tale, but more often a few escaped to fight over the booty and perhaps be hanged as mutineers on their return.

The men of that age were undoubtedly great— great warriors, great ruffians, great villains. Only here and there can we distinguish a good man like Las Casas, who did his very best for the Indians against the opposition of the settlers and the lukewarmness of the Spanish Court. He was horrified at the atrocities in the Indies, but the kings wanted their tithes and cared little how they were obtained.

" Get it honestly if you can, but get it," seems to have been their motto, and it was not for many years that anything like humanity was shown, and then only by a few priests.

III.

"SINGEING THE SPANIARD'S BEARD."

ON the discovery of the Indies, Ferdinand and
Isabella at once applied to Pope Alexander the
Sixth to secure the rights of Spain in the new
countries against every other nation, but more
especially against Portugal. Accordingly, the celebrated "Bull of partition" was issued on the 4th
of May, 1493, giving, conceding, and assigning for
ever, to them and their successors, all the islands
and mainlands already found or that might be discovered in future, to the west of a line, stretching
from the north to the south poles, a hundred leagues
from the Azores or Cape de Verde Islands, provided
they were not in the possession of any other Christian
prince. The sovereigns were commanded to appoint
upright, God-fearing, skilful, and learned men to in-
struct the inhabitants in the Catholic faith, and all
unauthorised persons were forbidden to traffic on or
even approach the territories. If they did so they
would incur the indignation of Almighty God and of
the blessed Apostles Peter and Paul.

Such was the gist of the document under which
the enormities mentioned in the preceding chapters

were committed. Portugal, except for some disputes about Brazil, accepted this arrangement, but the other great nations of Europe, especially England, disputed it from the very beginning. Nevertheless, the governments, as long as they were at peace with Spain, took no active part in the matter, but left the work to individuals, even going so far in some instances as to disclaim their responsibility for piracies committed beyond the seas.

English and French seamen, hearing of the treasure continually imported into Spain, soon found their way to the new world, and as early as the year 1526 precautions had to be taken against them. Orders were sent to build castles on the coasts and strong houses, not only for defence against the cannibals, who continued to ravage the larger islands, but to protect the settlements from French corsairs who had already commenced their depredations. The tract of the Spanish fleets led them first to St. Domingo, and thence on to the isthmus of Darien or Panama, where at first the chief port was Nombre de Dios. At these two points it was of great importance that fortifications should be erected, and this was done in the first half of the sixteenth century.

An English merchant named Thomas Tison seems to have been the first of our nation who went to the West Indies, but he got his goods sent from Bristol to Spain. In 1527 King Henry VIII. fitted out the *Dominus Vobiscum* and another vessel for those parts, but little is known of their course. It was, however, reported that they went to Porto

Rico, and got there a cargo of brazil wood, and then proceeded to St. Domingo, where permission was asked to trade. After waiting for the license two days the Spanish batteries fired upon them, driving them off to go back to Porto Rico, where the inhabitants were more friendly.

From this time the corsairs and rovers became more numerous and audacious every year. Some went trading among the Indians of the mainland, others, more bold, forced their goods upon the Spanish settlements under threats of pillage. In 1536 the inhabitants of Havana paid seven hundred ducats to a French corsair to save the city, and because later the pirate was chased by three Spanish vessels, which he captured, he returned and exacted a second ransom.

In 1538 there was a gallant fight in the harbour of Santiago de Cuba, between a Spaniard and a French corsair. The two vessels fought with each other the first day until sunset, when a truce was agreed to, and civilities exchanged between the captains. They sent each other presents of wine and fruit, were very friendly, and mutually agreed to fight only by day with swords and lances. Artillery, they agreed, was an invention of cowards—they would show their valour, and the one who conquered should have the other's vessel. The second day they fought again until evening without either being conquered, and again they exchanged courtesies. That night, however, the Spanish captain, Diego Perez, sent to the people of the city asking if they would compensate him for the loss of his ship if the corsair got the better of him ; if they agreed to do this he would risk his life in their service. Were he not poor and without any other property, he would not have asked them, and as they would be gainers by his victory, he did not think his request at all extravagant. But the authorities refused to pledge themselves to anything, leaving Perez to fight for his own honour, life, and property. The battle continued the whole of the third day, each giving the other time for rest and refreshment, yet neither was conquered, although many had fallen on both sides. After similar courtesies the fight went on next morning, and when evening came the Frenchman promised to continue it next morning. Feeling, however, that the Spaniard was likely to get the better of him, he slipped his cable in the night and made off, leaving Perez to grieve at the drawn battle.

The same year Havana was sacked and burnt, and three years later both English and French did great injury to the Spanish trade. Even Portugal did not escape, but when complaints were sent to the king of France, he said he intended to follow those conquests and navigations which by right belonged to him. In 1545 five French vessels captured the pearl-fishing fleet near the Main, which the owners were compelled to ransom ; at the same time they were forced to buy seventy negroes from the captors. The Frenchmen then took Santa Martha and got a thousand ducats as ransom.

One raid after another took place until the Spaniards were at their wits' ends. Forts were built, *guarda-costas* stationed, and other precautions taken, but the depredations and forced traffic still continued. They cruelly punished all who fell into their hands, and this led to retaliation, not only for their own injuries, but to avenge the slaughter of the innocent natives.

About the year 1530 Master William Hawkins made three long and famous voyages in the ship *Paul*. Hakluyt said he went to Brazil—a thing very rare in those days to our English nation. He became so friendly with the Indians that one of their kings came to England in his vessel, and was exhibited to King Henry, who marvelled to see this savage representative of royalty. Unfortunately the poor fellow died on the return voyage, which made Hawkins fear for the white hostage he had left behind. However, his explanation was accepted, and his man given back unharmed—a result all the more pleasing, as he knew so little of the language, and might easily have been misunderstood.

This is an example of the good feeling of these people towards Englishmen and all who treated them fairly. Even the cannibals became more gentle under good treatment, and would allow the enemies of Spain to land on their shores without opposition. By this time the natives of the Greater Antilles were gone, and with them the thousands of captives from the mainland. Then began the importation of negroes, first from Spain, where the Portuguese had sold a fair number during the previous century, and then from Africa. Spain could not send and fetch the negroes on account of the Papal Bull, which reserved the savage countries east of the line to Portugal. It followed, therefore, that, as Spain claimed the Indies, so her sister country claimed the whole of Africa—a claim as little respected by other nations as that of her neighbour.

Hearing that there was a good market for negroes in the West, Captain (afterwards Sir) John Hawkins,

NEGRO WOMAN RETURNING FROM MARKET.

in 1563, got up an expedition to supply this demand. With three vessels of 120, 100, and 40 tons respectively, he sailed to Sierra Leone, and partly by the sword and partly by other means, got three hundred slaves, whom he carried to Hispaniola. Here he had a reasonable sale, probably forced, for he trusted the

Spaniards no farther than he thought prudent, considering his strength. His returns were so good, however, that he not only loaded his own vessels

NEGRO BARBER.

with hides, ginger, sugar, and some pearls, but also freighted two hulks to send to Spain.

This success induced him to make another venture on a larger scale with the *Jesus* of Lubeck, of 700,

and three other vessels of 140, 50, and 30 tons. He
sailed for Africa in October, 1564, to kidnap slaves,
yet all the time he was very religious in a way. His

NEGRO FAMILY ON HOLIDAY.

orders concluded with the commands to "serve God
daily ; love one another ; preserve your victuals ;
beware of fire ; and keep good company "—*i.e.*, do
not stray from others of the fleet. At several places

he took negroes by force, losing a few of his men in the fights, and with a good number set off for the West Indies. Fortunately, he said, although they

NEGRESSES GOSSIPING.

were in great danger from a gale on this voyage, they arrived without many deaths of either the negroes or themselves. For "the Almighty God, who never suffereth His elect to perish, sent us, on the 16th of February (1565), the ordinary breeze."

The first land they sighted was Dominica, where they watered, and then went on to Margarita, the Governor of which island refused them permission to trade. They then tried several other places, including Hispaniola and Cumana, but also without success. At Barbarota they forced the people to traffic, and here they were joined by Captain Bontemps, a French corsair, with whom they went to Curaçao, and forced a hundred slaves upon the inhabitants. Finally they went to Rio de la Hacha and defeated a body of Spanish troops, after which the remainder of Hawkins' cargo was freely sold.

In his third voyage, on which he started in October, 1567, Hawkins was accompanied by Francis Drake and several other gentlemen adventurers. He took a similar course to that of his former voyages, joined some African chiefs in storming a town, and received, as his share of the booty, five hundred prisoners, with whom he again sailed for the Indies. The alarmed Spaniards dared not refuse to trade, and consequently he soon sold his negroes at a good profit. On his return, however, he was caught in a storm near the coast of Florida and had to take shelter in the harbour of Vera Cruz, where at first his vessels were taken for a Spanish fleet then daily expected. Under this mistake several influential persons came on board, two of whom were retained as hostages.

Next day the Spanish fleet, consisting of thirteen sail, arrived, and on board one of them was the new

Viceroy of Mexico. From this high authority Hawkins got permission to repair his ships, victual, and refit, provided the English kept themselves to a small island in the harbour, for the due performance of which they gave twelve hostages.

But the Spaniards were not prepared to let their enemies off so easily, and made preparations for a surprise. Hawkins, becoming suspicious, sent to inquire about certain shady transactions, and was at once attacked by something like a thousand men. The Spaniards sunk three of his vessels, seriously damaged the fourth, and left him with only one leaky ship in which to find his way home. A great number of his men were killed and others captured, the prisoners to be taken to Mexico and there cruelly used. Two of them—Miles Philips and Job Hortop—managed to escape and return to England, where they gave long accounts of their sufferings, the latter comparing himself to his namesake the patriarch. As for Hawkins, in speaking of his return voyage, he said, that "if all the miserable and troublesome affairs of this sorrowful voyage should be perfectly and thoroughly written, there should need a painful man with his pen, and as great a time as he had that wrote the lives and deaths of the martyrs."

This disaster put an end to Hawkins' slave-trading, but made no impression on the other adventurers to the Indies. Francis Drake now took up the quarrel, and in the year 1572 "singed the Spaniard's beard" to some purpose. Knowing already something of the state of affairs near the isthmus, he resolved to gain his spurs in that direction. He cared not for a forced trade in negroes, but virtually went in for piracy, for although the relations of the mother countries were at that time somewhat strained, war had not yet been declared.

Drake sailed straight for Nombre de Dios, the treasure port, arrived suddenly before the inhabitants had any warning, and landed a hundred and fifty men in the night. Suddenly the town was roused to the fact that the enemy were in possession, and as the people ran off to the forest, they asked each other what was the matter. Unfortunately for Drake, however, through a misunderstanding, the English were alarmed and took to their vessels, so that all the advantage of the surprise was lost. Undaunted by this failure, he determined to attempt something even more audacious—the capture of the Panama train.

We have already seen that African slaves had been imported in considerable numbers; we have now to mention that on the continent they often escaped into the forest. Here they lived like the Indians, and were often in friendship with them, going under the name of Simerons, or afterwards Maroons. Always at enmity with the masters whom they had deserted, they were a terror to the settlers on account of their continual raids on the planta-tions.

Drake determined to get the assistance of these people, which was freely given, and he was enabled to traverse the pathless forest and to lie in wait for the train of mules carrying gold and silver from Panama to Nombre de Dios. This he captured, but, on account of the difficulties of the way, was obliged to leave the silver behind, and content himself with the gold. Then he attacked some merchants, burnt their goods to the value of two hundred thousand ducats, and got safely back to his ships just as the dilatory Spaniards sent out three hundred men for his capture. It was on this excursion that he saw the Great South Sea, and determined to carry English ships into that immense Spanish preserve. How he carried out his resolve, and appeared suddenly off the Peruvian coast five years later, is a story we must leave, as it belongs to another part of the new world.

When Drake returned to Plymouth the news of his adventures, and the more substantial evidence of the gold he had brought, roused others to follow his example. Among them was one John Oxnam, or Oxenham, who has been immortalised by Kingsley in "Westward Ho!" Arriving at the isthmus in 1575, in a vessel of 140 tons, he went to an out-of-the-way river, and hid his bark among the great trees. Landing with his seventy men, he went in search of the Simerons, who took him to a river which flowed into the South Sea, where a pinnace was built. In this the English pulled down to the Pacific, with the intention of capturing one of the treasure ships coming to Panama. They succeeded so far as to get sixty thousand dollars in gold from one bark, and a hundred thousand from another. Not yet satisfied, they went to the Pearl Islands, attacked the negro divers, and took a few pearls, with which they at last returned up the river.

Unfortunately for Oxenham the negroes of the

Pearl Islands carried the news of his presence to Panama, and in two days four boats with a hundred men were sent in pursuit. They found the two barks, which had been released, and from their captains learnt where the Englishmen had gone. Following up the river they were at a loss when they came to three branches, but spying some freshly plucked feathers floating down one of the streams, they followed that until they came upon the pinnace. Six men were on guard, one of whom was killed, but the other five escaped and gave the alarm to their comrades. Pursuing their track through the forest the Spaniards found the store of treasure hidden away under boughs of trees. With this they would have gone back had not Oxenham attacked them with two hundred Simerons before they reached their boats. Being more skilful in bush fighting than the English, the Spaniards repulsed the party, killing eleven and taking seven prisoners, from whom they learnt that the delay was caused by the difficulty of transporting the treasure.

Now the news was sent to Nombre de Dios, and the authorities there found the English vessel and brought her away, thus cutting off the means of escape for those still lurking in the forest. Then an expedition was sent in search of them, and they were found building canoes. Some were sick and could make no resistance, the others fled and took refuge with the negroes, by whom they were ultimately betrayed and taken to Panama. Here Oxenham was interrogated as to his authority for the raid, and was obliged to admit that he had not his Queen's license. All except five boys were executed, the men at once, and the officers a little while afterwards at Lima.

Thus ended one of the most audacious attacks on the Spaniards which only failed through a little want of calculation. Hakluyt, who wrote the account, said the enemy marvelled much to see that although many Frenchmen had come to these countries, yet never one durst put foot upon land ; only Drake and Oxenham performed such exploits. When the news reached Spain the king was so alarmed that he sent out two galleys to guard the coast, which in the first year after their arrival took six or seven French vessels, and put a stop to their piracies for a time.

There was another class of raids in the Indies, of which that of Andrew Barker, of Bristol, was an example. He, and one Captain Roberts, going to trade in the Canary Islands, had their goods confiscated, and were put in prison, from which Roberts escaped and Barker was ultimately discharged. To recoup his losses and revenge himself, Barker fitted out several vessels in 1576, in which he went trading to the Main, and afterwards committed acts of piracy. He took a small vessel off Margarita and a frigate near Carthagena, from which he got five hundred pounds' weight of gold and some emeralds. Now, following the example of Drake, he landed on the isthmus to get help from the Simerons, but could find none. Then, from the unhealthiness of the climate, most of his men fell sick, and eight or nine died, which made him give up this part of his project. Embarking again he took another Spanish vessel with some gold, but after that the party got into difficulties. Barker quarrelled with his ship-master, and one of the vessels became so leaky that they had to let her sink, first removing the cargo into the last Spanish prize. They, however, captured another vessel with a hundred pounds of silver and some provisions, but after that the crews mutinied and put Barker ashore with some others, where they were attacked by Spaniards, and nine, including the captain, killed. The mutineers then went on to Truxillo, which they surprised, but could find no treasure, and were soon driven to flight by a Spanish vessel. On their way home the Spanish vessel sunk, carrying down two thousand pounds' worth of their booty, and on their arrival at Plymouth they were imprisoned as accessories to their captain's death. Although none were executed, yet, says the worthy Hakluyt, "they could not avoid the heavy judgment of God, but shortly after came to miserable ends."

Open war soon came, and culminated in the invasion of England by the "Invincible Armada" of 1588. No longer could there be any question of the Queen's license, and in 1585 Drake, now Sir Francis, fitted out a great fleet to cripple the power of Spain in the Indies. The Spanish authorities were no longer unprepared, but ready to give him a warm reception all along his expected course. The fleet consisted of twenty-five vessels, with two thousand three hundred men, among whom could be found many whose names are famous in the annals of Queen Elizabeth. At the Cape de Verde Islands they burnt the town of Santiago in revenge for the murder of a boy, and after this baptism of fire, proceeded to the island of

St. Christopher's, where they landed the sick, cleaned their vessels, and spent Christmas. Leaving at the end of December, on the 1st of January, 1586, they arrived off Hispaniola with the intention of attacking St. Domingo. The English landed about ten miles distant from that city, marched upon the Spaniards unawares, and took it by surprise, notwithstanding every preparation that had been made, and the careful watch for enemies from the sea.

Drake demanded a large ransom, and because it was not paid at once, commenced to demolish the buildings, which brought the inhabitants to their senses and made them offer the sum of 25,000 ducats (about £7,000), which he accepted. From thence the fleet sailed to Carthagena, where no opposition was made until the troops landed, when a great struggle took place in the streets. The Spaniards had erected barricades, behind which they succeeded in doing some execution, but only delayed the surrender for a short time. After a portion of the town had been burnt, 110,000 ducats were paid as ransom for the remainder, and after a few less brilliant exploits, the fleet went back to England, being thus hurried on account of sickness among the men. Otherwise, Drake had intended to capture Nombre de Dios and Panama, but from this disability had to be content with booty to the amount of £60,000, which would mean something like a quarter of a million at the present value of money. He arrived in time to help in repelling the Armada, and this invasion kept most of the English about their own shores for a year or two.

In 1595, when there were no longer any fears of a Spanish landing, Drake determined on another voyage, and this time with Sir John Hawkins. Getting together six of the Queen's ships and twenty-one other vessels, they arrived safely at the Caribbee Islands, where Hawkins became sick and died. Drake then went on to Porto Rico and attacked the capital, but could do nothing more than capture a few vessels from under the guns of the forts. Going to the Main he captured Rio de la Hacha and a fishing village named Rancheria. These he held for ransom, but was dissatisfied with the number of pearls offered by private persons, the Governor refusing to give anything, and burnt both town and village. Santa Martha was also taken, and then Nombre de Dios, but he found that the treasure had been removed, the inhabitants taking to the forest when they heard his fearful name. Sir Thomas Baskerville took seven hundred and fifty men to go over to Panama, but returned much discouraged by the difficulties of the road. Drake finally burnt Nombre de Dios and every vessel in the harbour down to the smallest boats.

After that, sickness began to tell upon the expedition, and Drake himself was stricken with dysentery. When on the point of death he rose from his bed, put on his full dress of admiral, called his men and gave them a farewell address, then, sinking down exhausted, he died immediately afterwards. Several captains and other important officers also died, and they even lost the chief surgeon ; after that, nothing was left but to return home. Off Cuba they were attacked by a Spanish fleet of twenty vessels, sent out to intercept them, with which they kept up a running fight until the enemy were left behind.   .

On their arrival in England in May, 1596, the sad news of the death of Drake overshadowed all the glory of the expedition. In Spain, however, it was published for general information, and the people congratulated each other that at last their enemy was gone. Henry Savile, in his " Libel of Spanish Lies," said " it did ease the stomachs of the timorous Spaniards greatly to hear of the death of him whose life was a scourge and a continual plague to them." No wonder that the news was so grateful, for none was so daring, and no name like that of Drake ever came to be used as a bogey with which to frighten their children.

Yet there were many gallant adventurers in the Indies at that very time. Sir Robert Dudley and Sir Walter Ralegh were both at Trinidad in 1595, and for several years before and after the English rovers were plentiful in the Gulf of Mexico. In 1591 the *Content* was successfully defended against six Spanish men-of-war, and the galleons were obliged to sail in large squadrons. What with the dangers of storms and the enemy, it was stated that of a hundred and twenty-three vessels expected in Spain during that year, only twenty-five arrived safe.

The number of rovers became at last so great that plunder was difficult to obtain. The Spanish settlers were in continual fear, and naturally took every precaution against their enemies, hiding the treasure on the least alarm, and taking to the forest. The French corsairs were not far behind the English, although as yet they had no proper licenses, and only fought for their own hands. Latterly, also, the Dutch and Flemings had arrived, and although mainly occupied in trading, they did not hesitate to fight on occasion, especially when attempts were made to prevent their traffic. While under the rule of Charles the Fifth they had been free to go to and from the Indies, and no doubt use the knowledge thus gained to further their own interests since their revolt. Like the English, they were at enmity with Spain, but there was also another bond of union—both were Protestant. Queen Elizabeth assisted Holland in gaining her independence, and therefore at this period the relations between English and Dutch were very cordial. But the fellow-feeling of enmity to Spain made even the French corsair unite with the two others, so that pirates, privateers, and traders all combined against the common foe.

IV.

RALEGH AND THE FIRST BRITISH COLONIES.

THE first grant made by Queen Elizabeth for a settlement in America was given to Sir Humphrey Gilbert in 1578, but the father of English colonisation was Sir Walter Ralegh. Although considered a rover, or pirate, by the Spaniards, he was of a different type to Drake, Hawkins, and the other adventurers of the sixteenth century. Not only was he famous as a brave warrior, but at the same time as one of the most learned men of his time ; as enterprising in the arts of peace as on the battle-field.

The " Letters Patent " to Walter Ralegh, Esquire, dated the 25th of March, 1584, may be considered as the first charter of the English colonies. Under them he was empowered to discover, occupy, and possess barbarous countries not actually in the possession of any Christian prince, or inhabited by Christian people, on condition that he reserved to Her Majesty a fifth of all the gold and silver found therein. He was also given all the rights of civil and criminal jurisdiction, and empowered to govern and make laws as long as these laws did not conflict with those of the mother country, or with the true Christian faith of the Church of England. Under this charter the first settlement in Virginia was undertaken, and thus England threw down the gauntlet in the face of Spain.

However, Ralegh did not confine himself to North America—there were other countries not in the actual possession of any Christian prince, the most notable being Guiana. Ralegh had heard the story of "El Dorado" and of the failures of the many German and Spanish knights. He would succeed where they had failed. Englishmen had displayed their mettle in the Indies—if the treasures of Peru and Mexico had raised their enemy to be "mistress of the world" and "sovereign of the seas," why should not he also find other golden countries for the benefit of his virgin queen and country? Because two rich provinces had been discovered, it did not follow that there were no others; on the contrary, the rumours of "El Dorado" were so many that they could not be treated with contempt. And then the natives of the "Great Wild Coast," although cannibals, were friendly to the English, who had always treated them fairly, and there they had the advantage over Spain. The country was open to them, although strictly guarded against their rivals.

The stories had been lately revived by the expeditions of Antonio de Berrio, Governor of Trinidad and Guiana, who had made explorations of the river Orinoco, and possibly exaggerated his reports for the purpose of getting settlers. Captain Popham took some letters from a Spanish vessel in 1594, wherein were found accounts of the "Nueva Dorado," which were spoken of as incredibly rich. Ralegh saw these, and was induced by their reports and his own knowledge of the Indies, which he had gained in working at his colonisation schemes, to go out and look up the matter.

The occupation of Guiana, he said, had other ground and assurance of riches than the voyages to the West Indies. The king of Spain was not so impoverished as the English supposed by their taking two or three ports, neither were the riches of Peru or New Spain to be picked up on the sea-shore. The burning of towns on the coast did not impoverish Spain one ducat, for it was within the country that the land was rich and populous. Therefore England should endeavour to get possession of this yet unspoiled country, instead of wasting her energies on adventures that were of no real benefit, and that hardly touched the real source of her enemy's greatness.

Ralegh arrived at Trinidad in March, 1595, and as a matter of precaution captured the Spanish town of St. Joseph, and the Governor, De Berrio, from whom he heard more stories of El Dorado. Here also he began those conciliatory measures with the natives which characterised all his dealings. He released five chiefs, who had been imprisoned in chains and tortured by dropping melted fat on their bodies, and thus gained their friendship. Unlike other adventurers he thought it necessary to excuse himself for burning St. Joseph, which he did in rather quaint language. Considering that if he entered Guiana by

RALEGH IN TRINIDAD.

(From Gottfried's "Reisen.")

small boats and left a garrison of the enemy at his back, he "should have savoured very much of the ass," he took the place, and at the instance of the natives set it on fire.

Now began a weary voyage up the Orinoco, first through the delta, which is such a maze that they might have wandered for months without getting into the main river had they not secured an Indian pilot. Exposed alternately to burning sun and drenching showers in open boats, they toiled against the powerful stream. Ralegh everywhere tried his best to ingratiate himself with the Indians, succeeding so well that his name became known over the whole of Guiana. He told them that he had been sent by a great queen, the powerful Cacique of the north, and a virgin, whose chieftains were more numerous than the trees of the forest. She was an enemy to the Spaniards, had freed other nations from their oppression, and had now sent to rescue them. To confirm his statement he gave each Cacique a coin so that they could possess the queen's likeness, and these were treasured and even worshipped for a century afterwards.

Everywhere he heard of El Dorado, but it was alway receding farther and farther, until his men became so disheartened that he had to rouse them by saying that they would be shamed before their comrades if they gave up so easily. , However, after reaching the mouth of the Caroni and getting specimens of gold ore, he had to return without doing more than locating the city of Manoa several hundred miles to the east of his farthest point. This was done in so exact a manner that the great lake of Parima, as large as the Caspian Sea, was retained upon the maps of South America down to the beginning of the present century. His ore was probably stream quartz, and in representing it as taken from the rock he probably reported what the Indians had told him. When, therefore, he said that the assay gave its value as £13,000 a ton, there is no reason to suppose a mistake or untruth, for pieces quite as valuable may still be picked up. His " Discoverie of Guiana " is such a mixture of close and accurate observation with the hearsay of the Indians, that it is difficult in some cases to separate truth from fiction. Yet, although historians have charged him with wilful lying, there can be no doubt of his good faith. It has been left to the present century to prove that gold-mines exist on the site of the fabled El Dorado, for it is there that the well-known Caratal diggings are situated.

Ralegh asked the people of England to judge for themselves. He had spent much time and money, with no other object than to serve his queen and country. When they considered that it was the Spaniard's gold which endangered and disturbed all the nations of Europe, that " purchaseth intelligence, creepeth into councils and setteth bound loyalty at liberty," they would see the advantage of these provinces he had discovered. Guiana was a country that had never yet been sacked, turned, or wrought. The face of the earth had not been torn, nor the virtue and salt of the soil spent by manurance ; the graves had not been opened for gold, the mines not touched with sledges, or the images pulled down from the temples.   It was so easily defensible that it could be protected by two forts at the mouth of a river, and thus the whole empire be guarded.   The country was already discovered, many nations won to Her Majesty's love and obedience, and those Spaniards who had laboured on the conquest were beaten, discouraged, and disgraced.   If Her Majesty took up the enterprise, he doubted not that after the first or second year there would be a Contractation House for Guiana in London, with larger receipts than that for the Indies at Seville.

Such was Ralegh's dream.   Another Peru to be conquered, and England to be raised to the highest point of wealth and importance.   But unfortunately he could get no assistance to carry out the grand project.   Yet he was undoubtedly sincere, for did he not send out two expeditions under Captains Keymis and Berrie the following year, to assure the Indians that he had not forgotten them?   Keymis found one tribe keeping a festival in honour of the great princess of the north, and anxiously waiting for the return of Gualtero, which name, by the by, was similar to their word for friend.   They made fires, and, sitting in their hammocks, each man with his companion, they recounted the worthy deeds and deaths of their ancestors, execrating their enemies most spitefully, and magnifying their friends with all the titles of honour they could devise.   Thus they sat talking and smoking tobacco until their cigars (their measure of time) went out, during which they were not to be disturbed, " for this is their religion and prayers which they now celebrated, keeping a precise fast one whole day in honour of the great princess of the north, their patron and defender."

The explorations of Ralegh and his captains were published all over Europe, with the result that attention was generally drawn to Guiana. Already some Dutchmen had been trading on the coast for many years, and it was even reported that they had established a post in the river Pomeroon, the centre of the province of Caribana. As early as 1542 Flemings had settled at Araya on the coast of Venezuela, where they collected salt and were left undisturbed as long as the Netherlands belonged to Spain. Ralegh seems to have purposely ignored the presence of these people in Guiana, probably to prevent any question of prior rights on the part of a friendly nation. But, after all, the Dutchmen could only have been there on their own responsibility, and their temporary occupation had no meaning from a national point of view.

Now that Guiana was made known, vessels of other nationalities went trading along the coast, everywhere meeting with a hearty welcome from the Indians as long as the visitors were not Spanish. They were only so many additions to their friends—their enemies were confined to Trinidad and the Orinoco, leaving the whole coast of Guiana to its rightful owners. In fact, the Spaniards could no more subdue the Caribs of the Main than they could those of the islands. Only in Trinidad, where the Arawak was employed against the cannibal, was a settlement made possible.

Ralegh was unable to carry out his great project, but others were not backward in attempting to settle in the country. First came Charles Leigh, who in 1604 founded a colony in the river Oyapok, which failed partly from the lack of assistance from England and partly from too great a dependence on the promises of the Indians to supply food. Sickness followed on starvation, Leigh died, and a mutiny took place, after which the survivors got back to Europe in a Dutch trader, which fortunately arrived when all hope of succour had been abandoned. Robert Harcourt followed to the same river in 1609, like Leigh, getting promises of assistance from the Indians by using the name of Ralegh. With their consent he took possession of the country, " by twig and turf," in the name of King James. This ceremony was performed by first cutting a branch from a tree, and then turning up a sod with the sword, thus claiming everything in and on the earth.

Harcourt's colony lasted several years, and in 1613 he received from James the First a grant of all that part of Guiana lying between the rivers Amazons and Essequebo, on the usual condition of the fifth of all gold and silver being handed over to the king. In the same year the Dutch trading factory at Kyk-over-al on the river Essequebo was established, and this was probably the reason why the English grant made that river the boundary of their possessions, leaving the Hollander to establish himself between the Essequebo and the Orinoco.

Meanwhile, in 1603, poor Ralegh had been tried on a charge of aiding and abetting the plot to raise Arabella Stuart to the throne of England, on the death of Queen Elizabeth. Any one who reads the account of his trial will perceive at once the absurdity of the charge, yet Ralegh was convicted and sentenced to be hanged, drawn, and quartered. However, even with all his hatred for the knight, King James dared not carry out the sentence, but instead, kept him imprisoned in the Tower.

Here Ralegh still hankered after the treasures of Guiana, and in 1611 he made a proposition to the Government to send Captain Keymis to find the rich gold mine which had been pointed out to him by an Indian. If Keymis should live to arrive at the place and fail to bring half a ton or more of that rich ore of which he had shown a sample, Ralegh himself would bear all the expense of the journey. "Though," said he, "it be a difficult matter of exceeding difficulty for any man to find the same acre of ground again, in a country desolate and overgrown, which he hath seen but once, and that sixteen years since—which were hard enough to do upon Salisbury Plain—yet that your lordships may be satisfied of the truth, I am contented to adventure all I have (but my reputation) upon Keymis's memory."

This proposition was rejected, and the poor knight lingered on in the Tower, attended during part of the time by two Guiana Indians, Harry and Leonard Regapo. In 1616, however, he at last recovered his liberty on condition that he went to Guiana and brought back gold, but at the same time the king refused to pardon him. Nevertheless he took up the matter with an amount of enthusiasm which showed his entire confidence in its ultimate success. All his own money and as much of his wife's as could be spared was spent in fitting out the expedition, and he also got contributions from many of his friends. The king even went so far as to give him a commission to undertake a voyage to the south parts of America, or elsewhere in America, inhabited by heathen and savage people, with all the necessary rights of government and jurisdiction ; yet with all this the old sentence hung over his head.

The expedition of fourteen vessels started in March, 1617, but even from the commencement the voyage was disastrous. First a gale was encountered, which drove the fleet to take refuge in Cork Harbour, where it lay until August. This seems to have put a damper on the commander, who now began to realise how much depended on his success. He was twenty-two years older than when he went on his first voyage to Guiana, and most of those years he had spent in captivity. Is it any wonder that when the excitement attendant on his release had gone off he became sick and utterly prostrated ? Such was his condition when the fleet arrived at Cayenne, where he went to look for his Indian boy Harry, who had gone back to his people and was now wanted as interpreter.

So low was Ralegh's condition that he had to be carried ashore, and although he soon became a little better under a course of fresh meat and fruits, he never wholly recovered. So great was his weakness, both of mind and body, that he deputed Keymis to lead the party up the Orinoco, while he rested at Cayenne ; in a few days he would go on to Trinidad and wait there until they returned. Keymis accordingly went on, accompanied by young Walter Ralegh, a number of other gentlemen, and four hundred soldiers. They arrived at the site of the supposed gold mine without accident, but found that since the first expedition some Spaniards had built "a town of sticks, covered with leaves," and this stood in the way of their approach to the mine. Possibly Keymis now thought of his master's expression in regard to St. Joseph, and did not care to "savour of an ass" by leaving the enemy to interfere with his work. He therefore attacked this town of St. Thome, and set it on fire. Unfortunately young Ralegh was killed in the fight, and the thought of how he could tell this bad news preyed upon the mind of Keymis until all relish for gold-seeking was lost. The Spaniards took to the bush, from whence they sallied forth on any small party of the English, and ultimately put them into a state of confusion. The mine could not be found, the adventurers began to complain that they had been fooled, and Keymis was so troubled that he seemed neither to know nor care anything about treasure-seeking.

Ralegh had meanwhile arrived in the Gulf of Paria, where he received the news of the burning of St. Thome and the death of his son from some Indians. Presently Keymis arrived, utterly dejected, to find his master broken down and more woe-begone than himself. Ralegh said he was undone, and that Keymis was entirely to blame. Not even a sample of ore—the king would believe him a liar and a cheat. Then, this attack on a Spanish town! Did not Keymis remember that these were not the days of the virgin queen, when to "singe the Spaniard's

GOLD HUNTING.

beard " was worthy of praise? Did he not know that James was friendly with the king of Spain and wanted to get from him a princess for his son Henry?

Keymis had been the intimate friend of Ralegh through all his troubles. He had remained faithful even when threatened with the rack at the time of the trial. As a kind of steward he had administered the prisoner's estate, and was a trusted friend and confidant of the family. He had seen young Walter grow up to manhood, and now through his fault the youth had been killed. For the first time the bereaved father was angry with his captain; perhaps if Keymis died the whole blame would be laid upon his shoulders, and Ralegh be exonerated. He went to the cabin allotted to him, loaded a pistol, shot himself, and then, as he feared the wound was not mortal, finished the suicide by driving a long knife into his heart.

Thus died poor Keymis, but unfortunately this did not make any difference to his master. If Ralegh had been prepared to throw all the responsibility on his lieutenant, the king could only be satisfied with treasure. Even if James had been inclined to overlook the affair, the Spanish ambassador would not condone such an offence. He is said to have rushed into the royal presence with the cry of " Piracy! piracy! piracy!" at the same time demanding the immediate capture and punishment of the raiders. It followed, therefore, that Ralegh was arrested immediately on his return, and finally executed under the old sentence, but by decapitation instead of hanging.

His last days were passed with resignation and fortitude. His old spirit was entirely broken, and although he petitioned the king for grace and pardon, he did so in a hopeless way. He had many sympathisers, and to satisfy them the king's printers issued a little book entitled " A Declaration of the Demeanour and Carriage of Sir Walter Raleigh," obviously inspired by the king himself. Here was a thing unheard of before or since ; a sovereign excusing himself for his actions ! If anything were required to prove the prisoner's innocence, this was sufficient. Did James want to salve his own conscience, or was it intended to satisfy those who clamoured on account of the injustice of the execution? No doubt many of the old sea dogs who had served under Drake and Hawkins were still living, and remembered when Plymouth bells rang at the news of fresh arrivals from the Indies. " But now, forsooth, you must not burn down a thatched hovel without a great to-do being made." If Spain wanted peace, why did her people murder a ship's company in cold blood a little while before? Out upon it ! The good old days had passed and England was going to ruin.

However, even King James's sneaking friendship for Spain could not keep back colonisation altogether. Something like moderation was introduced, and only pirates pure and simple kept up the old traditions. As for the king he hardly knew how to steer, what with the petitions for reprisals from English seamen on the one hand, and complaints of the Spanish ambassadors on the other The result of this want of policy is well shown in the case of Roger North one of the adventurers in the last expedition of Ralegh, who, in 1619, wished to re-establish the colony in the Oyapok, which had virtually sunk to nothing. An association called the Amazon Company was formed, and, notwithstanding Spanish protests, the king granted " Letters Patent," under which North got up an expedition in four vessels. Then the Spanish ambassador began to storm, and the weak king revoked the patent, calling upon the members of the Company to renounce their rights. North, who had been warned that something was going on, hurried up his preparations, and was off so quickly that he sailed on the 30th of April, 1620, fifteen days before the proclamation revoking his license was published.

On his return in January following he was arrested and sent to the Tower, where he remained until July. Meanwhile his cargo from Guiana was seized on the ground that it had been obtained from Spanish possessions, but with all his willingness to oblige Spain the king could not get the case proven. It followed, therefore, that North was released, and his goods restored, but as the cargo was mainly tobacco it had become much damaged by neglect.

This detention of North, and the consequent delay in sending out supplies to the Oyapok, led to the downfall of the infant colony. Hearing nothing from England the settlers became disheartened, and if it had not happened that Dutch traders arrived there occasionally they would have been starved. Even as it was one left after another until few remained, and when, six years later, " the Company of Noblemen and Gentlemen of England for the Plantation of Guiana" was formed, the settlement had to be commenced anew. However, some of those who left carried the English flag to the island of St. Christopher's, where a settlement was commenced in 1624 by Thomas Warner. Thus, as Ralegh was the father of English colonisation, so his beloved Guiana became the parent of the British West Indies.

James the First died in March, 1625, and with him went the English subservience to Spain, never to be restored. During his reign British enterprise had been kept back ; now it broke down all obstructions. True, New England and Bermuda were settled during his reign, but they owed little to him or his government. As soon as the Royal obstructionist was dead, colonisation schemes came to the front. Before even a month had passed, on the 14th of April, John Coke came forward with a proposition to incorporate a company for the defence and protection of the West Indies, for establishing a trade there, and for fitting out a fleet to attack the Spanish settlements. About the same time, also, the Attorney-General made some "notes" on the advantages derived by the Spaniards and Dutch from their West Indian trade, showing that it was neither safe nor profitable to England for them to remain absolute lords of those parts, and suggesting that the new king should entertain the matter and openly interpose, or else permit it to be done underhand ; then if it prospered he could make it his own at pleasure.

What was done in these particular cases does not appear, but that a new policy was introduced is certain. In September following the case of St. Christopher's was brought before the Privy Council, which apparently confirmed what had been done, in taking possession of the island. In the " information " laid over it was stated that Thomas Warner had discovered that island, as well as Nevis, Barbados, and Montserrat, and had begun the planting and colonising of these islands, until then only inhabited by savages. King Charles was asked to take them under his royal protection and grant Thomas Warner their custody as his lieutenant, with the usual powers of jurisdiction.

The result was not altogether to the liking of the petitioners, Ralph Merrifield and Thomas Warner, for in July, 1627, a grant of all the Caribbees was made to the Earl of Carlisle. This was sweeping enough, however, to suit those who wanted English colonies, however it ignored the rights of the first settlers in St. Kitt's and Barbados, which latter island had been settled a few months after the first.

Now, also, Roger North came forward with his story and got the revoked patent renewed, so that he could go on with the settlement in the Oyapok. For a time it did very well, but the tide had turned in favour of the islands, and Guiana was soon abandoned to the Dutch and French.

The most important of the two islands first colonised was Barbados, which, fortunately for her comfort, never suffered from such calamities as befel the sister island of St. Christopher's. As far as the English were concerned Barbados was discovered by a vessel going out to Leigh's settlement, in Guiana, in

1605. A pillar was erected with the inscription, " James, King of England and this island," but nothing was done in the way of a settlement until immediately after Warner commenced planting in St. Kitt's. The most intimate connection existed between Barbados and Guiana from the earliest times, as in fact it does to the present day, for Captain Powell, the commander of the little company of pioneers, sent to his Dutch friend, Groenwegel, in Essequebo, for a party of Arawak Indians to teach the new-comers how to plant provisions, cotton, and tobacco.

In 1630 another group of islands was added by the granting of a patent to the "Governor and Company of Adventurers for the Plantation of the Islands of Providence, Henrietta, and the adjacent islands." Under this charter possession was taken of the Bahamas, but little was done in the way of settling them for about a century. Thus West Indian colonisation was commenced, and claims made to all the smaller islands on behalf of England.

But it is not to be supposed that France and Holland were going to let everything go by default —on the contrary, they soon began to settle in some of the very islands which had been granted to the Earl of Carlisle. The Dutch, as we have seen, were traders from the beginning, preferring the so-called contraband traffic with the natives and Spanish colonists to anything like the raids of English or French. Yet, in their plodding way they went on steadily, and as early as the year 1600 took possession of the island of St. Eustatius. When the

Spaniards awoke to the fact that the Dutch were injuring their trade, they began to enforce all the old prohibitions and seized the smugglers. But the Hollander commenced to feel his power, and gave his enemy several lessons, which made him feel that the United Provinces with their symbol of a bundle of darts were not to be despised.

In 1615 the Dutch took the capital of Porto Rico, and in 1621 their West India Company was formed with territorial and trading rights over all the unoccupied countries of Africa and America. Suddenly as it were the despised Hollander became a power in the West Indies, and the Company was soon strong enough to conquer Brazil, which it must be remembered was, with Portugal and all her colonies, then in the hands of Spain. About the year 1627 Piet Heyn destroyed a Spanish fleet in Mataça Bay, Cuba, the booty from which was something enormous. Altogether, the West India Company was said to have captured 547 vessels, mainly off the coast of America, the prize money from which amounted to thirty million guilders (£2,500,000), while the damage to Spain was at least six times as much.

Now also the French began to claim their share. In 1625 Mons. d'Enambuc went on a piratical expedition to the Caribbean Sea, but without any intention of founding a colony. However, off the Cayman's islands he was attacked by a Spanish galleon of much superior force, and although he succeeded at last in driving her off, his vessel was so crippled that he had to put into St. Christopher's for repairs. Here he found Warner already established, and with him a few Frenchmen.   On account of his condition and the beauty of the island, he became inclined to settle, and as the English and French were then on good terms, Warner saw no objection.   The consequence was that St. Kitt's became divided between the two nationalities, with results in the future most disastrous to both.

At first, however, the assistance of the French was very welcome.   The Caribs were still a power in the smaller islands and gave a great deal of trouble to the young colony.   At first they were friendly, but when the settlers wished to oppress them by taking away their lands and compelling them to supply provisions, open war began.   Hearing from an Indian woman that a conspiracy was forming to destroy all the white men, Warner determined to be beforehand with them. He massacred a hundred and twenty of the men, took the women as slaves, and drove the remainder off the island.   But these powerful savages were by no means conquered, for those who escaped soon came back with three or four thousand of their friends from neighbouring islands, and at first it appeared as if the whites would have been utterly exterminated.   By a supreme effort of both French and English, however, this great invasion was repelled, the defenders killing about two thousand, and capturing fifteen large peri-aguas, with a loss to themselves of about a hundred, most of whom died from poisoned arrows.   This was a bond of union between French and English, and Warner and d'Enambuc amicably divided the island between them.

CARIB ATTACK ON A SETTLEMENT.
(From Gottfried's " Reisen.")

V.

BUCCANEERS, FILIBUSTERS, AND PIRATES.

Now that settlements were commenced the old system of piracy was somewhat discountenanced by the home governments, and many of the adventurers began to become a little more civilised. But there was still a large number of them who became known as buccaneers, filibusters, freebooters, marooners, and brethren of the coast, who continued to worry the Spaniards, and even to attack other nationalities on occasion. They had taken to the trade, and, when no longer able to carry it on in a quasi-legitimate manner, did so on their own lines.

The claim of Spain to the whole of America was the great cause of offence. Had she been content with what her people could occupy, there would have been little trouble, but the "dog in the manger" policy could hardly be recognised by other nations. It followed, therefore, that when complaints were made to France and England of the ravages on the Spanish coasts, the sovereigns told the king of Spain to protect his own shores, disclaiming on their own parts any responsibility whatever.

The earliest accounts of the buccaneers are confused with those of the French corsairs, of which mention has been already made. They sailed along the coast from one island to another, trading a little, capturing Spanish vessels, fighting the guarda-costas, and now and again repairing to some out-of-the-way place to put their ships in order or even to assist the Caribs in their raids. The advantages of combination were soon felt, and with these also the necessity for places of rendezvous. Even the English adventurers became accustomed to obtain wood and water from Dominica, but this island was not conveniently situated for the French corsairs. They wanted an uninhabited place near enough to Hispaniola and the track of the Spanish vessels for them to be quickly pounced upon and for the corsairs to as quickly escape. Then there must be a food supply, and on the great island of Hispaniola were countless herds of wild cattle which ranged over a wilderness utterly depopulated.

The palmy days of the Hispaniola planter were over, and although he imported negro slaves to some extent, he was virtually ruined. One after another left for the newly discovered countries on the Main, and for Peru and Mexico, leaving the island to a few merchants and wealthy planters, who found it to their interest to remain. Hispaniola was little more than a house of call on the road to the treasure countries, which meant that although the port of St. Domingo was fortified, the greater portion of the island was open to any one who chose to occupy it.

Salt was a scarce commodity in those times, but it could be obtained in some of the smaller islands, notably Tortuga, which for that reason became the resort of the buccaneers. But the Indians had learnt how to preserve meat without this useful substance, by smoking it over a fire of green branches and leaves. Even Europeans knew something of this process, although we believe they never preserved their beef and bacon entirely without salt as did the Indians their game. The process was very simple. Four sticks with forked ends were pushed into the ground, and on these uprights a sort of rack of other sticks was laid to make an open platform, where the pieces of meat were laid above a fire until well dried and impregnated with smoke. This stage was called a boucan, or barbecue, and from their using it to prepare supplies for their voyages the corsairs became known as buccaneers.

There were no tinned provisions in those days, nor had the proper means of keeping food on long voyages been yet perfected. It followed, therefore, that a food supply in the Indies had to be provided, and the Spaniards unintentionally did good service to their enemies by placing hogs on most of the islands to breed and be available in emergencies.

It is obvious that the hunting of semi-wild animals and curing their meat required time, and for that reason a division of labour was initiated. While one party went cruising in search of Spanish vessels, another ranged the country to capture and prepare the supplies against their return. Thus a rendezvous became necessary, and in time plantations were established in this neighbourhood to gradually develop into a settlement. Now and again the

Spaniards discovered these places, but as they were generally of little value, their loss was of no importance ; if destroyed the buccaneers could easily escape to another locality. When the enemy burnt their vessels, they easily built canoes with which they soon captured others and became as strong as before. The hunters grew to like their hardy life with its perfect liberty, and became so inured to the climate and open air as to be utterly unlike the effeminate planters. They were even little subject to the diseases of the country, and could live for months at a time on nothing but meat. As for clothes, they made these from the skins of animals, and all they really required from outside was powder and lead for their firearms.

They became known as the brethren of the coast from their custom of each choosing one comrade as a bosom friend and brother. Everything gained by either was common to both, and the company were very strict in enforcing their law against unfaithfulness in a companion, or unfair dealing in any way among themselves. Sometimes they marooned a culprit by leaving him alone on some small island to die of hunger, or perhaps to become a " Crusoe " for many years. The wounded received compensation according to a fixed tariff, from the common stock or from contributions ; thus the loss of an arm was valued at five hundred crowns, and other mutilations at corresponding rates.

As the attacks of the Spaniards became more common, the small bands united, and division of labour became more exact. Some were hunters of wild boars, others of cattle, a few became planters, but the main body were always sea rovers. At first the hunters were on good terms with the Spanish planters and entered into engagements to supply them with meat. A party would go off into the interior and stay away for months at a time, eventually returning with large supplies borne on the backs of their horses. During all this time they lived in rough shelters which could be erected in an afternoon, and were much exposed to the vicissitudes of the weather. Now they made up for their long term of privation by carousing to their hearts' content, and when drunk, often fought and killed each other. In the settlements there were generally a few women, and these often became the cause of contentions ; there were also bond-servants who were treated most cruelly.

Sometimes they made incursions on the Spanish settlements, which led to stronger efforts for their extermination that at last considerably reduced their numbers. In fact, had it not been for the continual accessions they would soon have died out, or have given up their trade and settled down as planters. Hispaniola became at last almost untenable, for the Spaniards, unable to find any other way of putting them down, organised several hunting parties with the view to utterly destroy the wild cattle and thus deprive them of their means of living. Not that this was easily done, for it took many years, during which the hunting parties from both sides fought and killed each other, committing enormities which made the quarrel all the more bitter.

About the year 1632 a party of buccaneers captured the island of Tortuga from the Spaniards, the garrison of twenty-five men surrendering without a blow. Here was now the grand rendezvous of the French, for which it was perfectly suitable from its proximity to the food supply and the track of the Spanish vessels. It was situated on the north of the western portion of Hispaniola, and not very well suited for plantations, although good tobacco was grown there. There were, however, plenty of sea fowl and turtle to be had, as well as their eggs, which formed a large portion of the diet of the inhabitants.

This island became a veritable pandemonium—the sink of the West Indies. It was the place of call for rovers of all nations, the market for their booty, and the storehouse for everything in the way of supplies. The merchants pandered to the tastes of their customers, and drinking and gambling went on continually. But in 1638 it was surprised by the Spaniards, who began to be alarmed at this nest of pirates at their very doors. They chose a time when most of the rovers were away on a cruise, and the buccaneers gone hunting in Hispaniola. All they captured were killed—even those who surrendered being hanged as pirates. Only a few escaped by hiding among the rocks and bushes to come forth after the enemy had left, which they did without leaving a garrison.

A grand attempt to expel the hunters from the main island was now organised, in which a corps of five hundred lancers ranged the island in bands of fifties. Many of the buccaneers were killed, but the remainder combined together under an Englishman named Willis and again took possession of Tortuga.

From this rendezvous near Hispaniola the main passages between the islands were under observation, but a similar station was required near the Isthmus, and this was established about 1630 in the Bay of Campeachy. Like that at Tortuga its beginnings are lost in obscurity. At first one or more of the small islands or keys was used on occasion—later fortifications were erected, and a watch always kept for the enemy. The excuse for the settlement was the logwood trade, but this did not become of much importance until after the English conquest of Jamaica.

Like the true buccaneers these pirates were fond of hunting, but their game was principally Indians, whom they attacked and carried off from the Main, the men to sell to the plantations and the women to keep for themselves. When they arrived after a cruise and sold their booty, they would have a jolly time with drinking, gambling, and firing of guns, until the island would seem to be the habitation of devils rather than human beings.

There were also other pirate resorts, notably the Virgin Islands and the Bahamas, but these were generally used only by one company, and never rose to the position of general resorts. It is to these that most of the romances refer, but the stories of Pirate and Treasure islands rarely have much foundation in fact.

How privateers became pirates is well shown by a case that occurred in the latter half of the seventeenth century. A vessel went cruising from the

Carolinas, and after being out for eighteen months had gained so few prizes that the crew began to complain. After discussing the situation, they resolved to try the South Sea, where they hoped to find the Spaniards less prepared. Meeting with very bad weather at the entrance of the Strait of Magellan, they were, however, obliged to turn back, and then the majority decided to become pirates. Eight men who refused to agree were marooned on the island of Fernando Po, their late comrades leaving them a small boat in which they expected to be able to get to some English colony.

The vessel left, and commenced her piratical work at once by capturing a Portuguese ship larger than herself, the crew being brought and landed on the same island. In the night the Portuguese made off, taking with them the Englishmen's boat as well as their own, leaving the eight privateers to do the best they could. However, they were not easily daunted, and at once began to cut down trees and build a sloop of four tons, which they finished in six weeks, meanwhile living on sea fowl and their eggs, which were plentiful. Finally they sailed for Tobago, but missing that island got to Tortuga, where they arrived almost perishing with hunger and thirst, having had nothing to eat or drink for six days. Even then they were not discouraged, but after resting awhile, set sail in the same boat for New England, passing along the Spanish islands, often unable to land for water on account of the enemy, and lying under cover of the mangroves, to be almost devoured by mosquitoes. Even with all this care they were taken at last, stripped, thrust down in the hold of a Spanish *guarda-costa*, and finally kept as slaves in the island of Cuba.

In the early years of the seventeenth century few of the adventurers had any commissions, but as the mother countries began to establish settlements, letters of marque were granted when there was a war. The corsairs and pirates then became privateers, only to go back to their old trade when peace was nominally restored. Some played fast and loose with these commissions, sometimes having both French and English at the same time, either to be used according to circumstances. The French Governors went so far as to sell these documents signed and sealed, but without names, so that they passed from hand to hand ready to be filled up when the pirate wished to escape the yard-arm. The young colonies were too weak to incur their displeasure—in fact they were glad to encourage their visits, as the settlers could always pick up good bargains when they sold their booty. Yet, with all that, there was a dread of them, even among their own countrymen, which prevented that feeling of safety which best consists with the progress of a colony.

We can say little of individuals, as there were so many, but we may mention a few of the most striking characters and their daring exploits. They inspired such dread among the Spaniards that at last the latter hardly dared to defend themselves against them, but on their approach immediately surrendered. If the cargo was rich quarter, was granted, but if otherwise, or anything was found secreted, the whole company, officers, crew, and passengers, were forced to leap overboard. Pierre Legrand with his twenty-eight men once attacked a great Spanish galleon, and before going alongside scuttled his own vessel so that it sunk as the pirates leapt on to the enemy's deck. With no possibility of retreat the men fought like devils and quickly got possession of the galleon, with the usual result.

When other nations had compelled respect from Spain their vessels were sometimes chartered to carry rich cargoes, which thus sailed under the protection of another flag. But the pirates were not to be cheated so easily, for they had their spies on the look-out, and often managed to glean information. On one occasion Captains Michael de Basco and Brouage heard of two Dutch vessels leaving Cartha-gena with treasure and at once followed, attacked and captured them. Exasperated at being beaten by a force much smaller than their own, the Dutch captains told Michael that he could not have over-come them if he had been alone. "Very well," said the audacious Frenchman, "let us begin the fight again, and Captain Brouage shall look on. But if I conquer I will not only have the Spanish silver you carry, but your own ships as well." The Dutch were not inclined to accept this challenge, but made off as soon as they could after the treasure had been taken into the pirate vessels, fearing they might otherwise lose their opportunity.

Captain Lawrence was once unexpectedly over-taken by two Spanish sixty-gun ships, the crews of which numbered fifteen hundred. Addressing his men, he said—" You have experience enough to be aware of your danger, and too much courage to fear. On this occasion we must avail ourselves of every circumstance, hazard everything, and attack and defend at the same time. Valour, artifice, rashness, and even despair itself must now be employed. Let us fear the disgrace of a defeat; let us dread the cruelty of our enemy; and let us fight that we may escape him." After he was applauded with loud cheers, Lawrence took aside one of the bravest of his men, and in the presence of all, gave him strict orders to fire the gunpowder at a given signal, thus telling them plainly they must fight or be blown up. Meanwhile the enemy had approached very close, and Lawrence, ranging his men on both sides of the vessel, steered between the two great monsters, firing a broadside on either hand as he passed, which they could not return for fear of damaging each other. He did not succeed in capturing them, but they were so demoralised by his determined attitude, and the number of killed and wounded, that they were glad to make off.

Montbar was a Frenchman who had heard of the atrocities of the Spaniards and the exploits of the buccaneers, and determined to go out to the West Indies to join in the fray. On his voyage from France he met a Spanish vessel which he attacked and boarded with a sabre in his hand. Passing twice from bow to stern, he carved his way through the enemy, entirely reckless of danger, and by his example animated his comrades until the vessel was taken. Then standing apart while the spoil was being divided, he gloated with savage pleasure over the corpses that lay on the deck.

Arrived at Hispaniola he heard from the buccaneers that they could do little in the way of planting because of the continual attacks on their settlements. "Why then," said Montbar, roughly, "do you tamely submit to such insults?" "We do not!" they answered; "the Spaniards have experienced what kind of men we are, and therefore take advantage of the time when we go hunting. But we are going to join with some of our companions, who have been even worse treated than ourselves, and then we shall have hot work." "If such be the case let me lead you," said Montbar, "not as a commander, but first in the post of danger."

They were quite willing to have him as leader, and the very same day he went at the head of a party to find the enemy. Meeting a small body of Spaniards he rushed upon them with such fury that hardly one escaped, and this at once justified them in their choice. He afterwards became such a terror all over the West Indies as to be known as "the Exterminator."

Lolonois was another ruffian, who commenced his career by taking a Spanish frigate with only two canoes and twenty-two men. This vessel had sailed from Havana especially to put down the buccaneers, and had on board a negro executioner who was engaged to hang the prisoners. Hearing this from the negro, Lolonois ordered all the Spaniards to be brought before him, and going down the line, he struck off one head after another, licking his sword after each blow. He afterwards went to Port au

Prince, where four vessels were fitting out for his capture. These he took and threw all their crews into the sea, except one man, whom he sent to the Governor of Havana with the news, and a warning that he would treat the Governor himself in the same way if he had the opportunity.

After this he ran the best prizes aground and sailed for Tortuga in the frigate, where he joined Michael de Basco. With four hundred and forty men this worthy pair sailed for the Main, where they plundered the coast of Venezuela, set fire to Gibraltar, and held Maracaybo for ransom. They carried off all the crosses, pictures, plate, ornaments, and even bells from the churches, with the intention of using them in a great cathedral to be erected on Tortuga.

Although the buccaneers were mostly French they were not confined to that nationality. The famous or notorious Captain Morgan was a Welshman, who began his career in the West Indies as a bond-servant. One of his greatest exploits was the capture of Porto Bello, which had taken the place of Nombre de Dios after that town had been burnt by Drake. He even out-did Drake and every other adventurer before him by storming Panama, from whence he obtained a very rich booty. Here he fell in love with a Spanish lady, who, however, threatened to stab herself rather than yield to his embraces. Even when he tried the gentlest measures which such a ruffian could think of, she still refused to yield, so that he had ultimately to comply with the wishes of his companions and leave her. Panama was burnt, the retreat across the isthmus safely performed without any serious misadventure, and Morgan sailed away to Jamaica with the lion's share of the plunder.

In this great expedition the buccaneers of all nations united to form a combination hitherto unknown. But, as this was the first time that such a thing had occurred, so also was it the last. As for Morgan his career was ended; his comrades charged him with treachery and made it unsafe for him to come within their reach. He therefore settled down in Jamaica, made himself right with the authorities there and in England, was knighted by King Charles the Second, and professed now to have a great dislike to piracy. On two occasions Sir Henry Morgan became acting Governor of Jamaica, and in that capacity did his best to discountenance buccaneering.

In 1683 a great expedition was organised at Tortuga by Van Horn, a Fleming, noted for his courage and ferocity. In the heat of an engagement he would pace the deck, and urge his men to fight by shooting any one who even flinched from a ball. He thus made himself a terror to cowards and the admiration of the brave; like Montbar, gaining the respect and confidence of his followers. Like the French leader also, he was careless about his own share of the booty, leaving everything to his men, which naturally increased his popularity. With twelve hundred men in six vessels he sailed for Vera Cruz, and surprised the town at night. Most of the inhabitants took refuge in the churches, and the buccaneers posted sentries with barrels of gunpowder in front of each, giving orders to blow up the buildings on the least sign of an attempt to escape. After plundering the houses they demanded about half a million pounds from the prisoners as ransom for their lives and liberties. This was not obtained, however, for while waiting the collection a large body of troops was seen approaching from the interior, and a fleet of seventeen vessels came into the harbour from Spain. Yet the buccaneers were determined to get something towards the ransom, and to this end seized fifteen hundred slaves, with which they quietly sailed away in defiance of the enemy, promising to call again for the balance of the ransom. The Spanish fleet let them pass without firing a single gun, and they went back to Tortuga, there to spend a year in rioting and carousing.

When their money was all spent they resolved to try the most arduous of adventures, a raid on the ports of the Great South Sea. And it happened curiously that at that very time the English pirates were getting ready for a similar venture, without either having knowledge of that of the other party. About four thousand men were engaged, some going by way of the Straits of Magellan and others across the isthmus. The English and French met, and at first agreed to work together, but for want of one leader who could command and be respected by both parties, the expedition proved almost a failure. Possibly also the French had not forgotten Morgan's treachery, and this caused distrust and prevented any cordial feeling.

Those who travelled across the isthmus stole boats on the other side, and with them captured larger vessels, until this little frequented sea became almost as dangerous to Spanish ships as the Caribbean. Most of the smaller ports were surprised, and even Guayaquil was captured, mainly because they were not provided with forts and other defences. In fact, the people were so unacquainted with war and so wrapped up by the supposed security of their position, that even when the alarm was given little could be done. Silver became so common that nothing but gold, pearls, and precious stones would satisfy the spoilers, yet with all their easy conquests they got little real benefit. Some died of sickness, and many from the results of drunkenness and debauchery. The storms of Cape Horn and the Straits wrecked several vessels, and drowned both spoil and spoilers, while those who attempted to return by land were equally unfortunate. They died in the bush of fever and dysentery, or were cut off by ambuscades of the enemy, often losing their booty if they escaped with their lives.

What a journey across the isthmus really meant at that time is well exemplified in the case of Lionel Wafer. In 1681 he was a surgeon on board an English vessel under Captain Sharp, one of those privateers who went cruising in the South Sea. After spending some time there the party divided, one portion deciding to cross overland, and the other to continue the cruise.

Wafer went with those who intended crossing the isthmus, the whole numbering forty-four white men and three Indians. They marched from the Pacific shore one afternoon, and towards night arrived at the foot of a hill, where they put up several rough sheds. Rain had already begun to fall—such rain as is only known in the tropics—and they had to crouch under these imperfect shelters until midnight, with streams of water running down their backs and rivulets flowing about their feet. By morning they felt less discomfort and were glad to warm their chilled limbs by walking up the hill. Here they came upon an Indian path which led to a village, where they were gratified with food and a drink made of Indian corn. After resting awhile they agreed with one of the Indians to guide them on the next day's journey, and that night rested in the village.

Next morning they went on again, and at mid-day arrived at an Indian hut, the owner of which was so morose and surly that at first he refused to have anything to do with them. After they had spoken kindly and asked him to guide them on their journey, he roughly answered that he was prepared to lead them to the Spanish settlements. This of course would never do, and they offered him beads, money, axes, and knives to gain his good-will, but all without effect, until a sky-blue petticoat was dangled before the eyes of his wife. This turned the scale, for her persuasions being added to theirs, he at last consented to procure a guide, excusing himself from the task on the plea that he was lame from a cut. He wished to detain them with him for the day, as it still rained, but they were in so great a dread of being discovered by the enemy that, having obtained the guide, they marched three miles farther before stopping for the night.

On the fourth morning the weather was fairer, and they travelled for twelve miles over hills and through slushy morasses, crossing one river after another to the number of about thirty. Rain poured down again in the afternoon and during the greater part of the night, so that they had much ado to keep their fires from going out. What with the discomforts of their situation, the want of proper food, and the chilliness preceding intermittent fever, they even forgot for the time their fears of the Spaniards. However, as the sun rose they went on again until, after travelling seven miles through the forest, they reached the hut of a Spanish Indian, who supplied them with yams, sweet potatoes, and plantains, but no meat except the flesh of two monkeys, which they gave to the weak and sickly.

While resting here Wafer met with an accident. One of the company, in drying some gunpowder on a silver plate, carelessly placed it near the fire where he was sitting, with the result that it exploded and tore the skin and flesh from one of his thighs, rendering him almost helpless. He had a few medicines in his knapsack and dressed the wound as well as he could under the circumstances, but rest and proper food were needed, and these he could not have. The consequence was that, after struggling along with the others until he sank down exhausted and suffering from excruciating torture, he was left behind with two sick men at an Indian village, where they were presently joined by two others who had broken down.

Observing the condition of Wafer's wound, the Indians treated it with a poultice of chewed herbs on a plantain leaf, and in twenty days it was healed.

Nevertheless, although they did him this kindness, they were not over civil, but on the contrary treated the five white men with contempt, throwing them their refuse provisions as if they were dogs. One young Indian proved kinder, and got them some ripe bananas now and then, but the others were annoyed because the main body had compelled some inhabitants of the village to go with them as guides against their will. The weather was then so bad that even the Indians considered travelling almost impossible, and this annoyed them all the more, especially when the guides did not return.

Day after day passed, and the Indians becoming more incensed at the non-arrival of their people, began to think of avenging themselves on Wafer and his comrades. Thinking that the guides had been murdered, they determined to burn them to death, and even went so far as to erect a great pile of wood for the purpose. But almost at the last moment their chief interposed, and offered to send away the Englishmen in charge of two guides.

Accordingly they set out, their only food supply a little dry Indian corn, and their only resting-place at night the wet ground, still exposed to drenching rains which fell every day. The third night they went to sleep on a low mound, and in the morning woke to find it a little island with water extending as far as their eyes could reach. To add to their trouble, the Indian guides had disappeared, leaving them to remain here without shelter and almost starved for three days. Then the waters fell and they commenced the weary work of steering to the north by means of a pocket compass—a task the difficulty of which can only be appreciated by one who has attempted it.

However, they soon reached the bank of a deep river, the stream of which was rushing along like a mill race. Here a lately-felled tree lying across showed them where their comrades had passed, and they commenced to climb over astride as the trunk was so slippery. One of the party was so weak and so overburdened by four hundred pieces of eight (silver dollars) that he fell, and was immediately carried down the stream out of sight.

Giving him up as lost, the four survivors went wandering about, looking for the footprints of their comrades, but could find no trace of them, probably on account of the floods. Fearing a mistake, they again crossed the river and recommenced the search on the other side, where they were surprised to come upon their lost companion sitting on the bank, which he had managed to gain by grasping the bough of a tree as he was borne swiftly past. Finding no signs of a trail, they again went on working with the compass as before. On the fifth day they had nothing to eat but a few wild berries, and the day following arrived at another great river where not even a tree lay across to give them a passage. They had only their long knives, but with them they set to work and cut down bamboos, with which rafts were made by binding the sticks with bush-ropes. They had just finished and were resting awhile, when a terrible storm came on. The rain fell as if from a cascade, thunder rolled and lightning flashed, accompanied by a sulphurous odour which almost choked them. There was no shelter but the trees of the forest, and the fire was put out at once, leaving these half-starved wretches to shiver and shake with ague all through the afternoon and up to midnight.

Then the waters began to rise, and in the darkness—that total absence of light under the canopy of foliage, where two men sitting together only know of each other's presence by feeling, for the din of the elements is absolutely deafening—Wafer began to appreciate the fact that the swirl of the flood had reached his feet. With no possibility of communicating with the others, he felt his way to a hollow silk-cotton tree, into which he crawled, and climbed upon a heap of debris that stood in the centre. Here he fell asleep from sheer exhaustion, or more probably, perhaps, fainted. When he awoke he said it was impossible for words to paint the terrors that overwhelmed his mind. The water reached to his knees, notwithstanding that the mound was five feet above the ground level, and he was afraid it would reach still higher. However, as the sun rose the flood went down, and presently he was glad to crawl out and stretch his chilled limbs. But he was all alone, and at first thought his comrades had been drowned. He shouted, but no answer came back, except the echo of his own voice. Giving way to despair, he threw himself on the buttress of a tree, from which condition he was roused by the appearance of first one and then another, until the little company was again complete. They also had found similar refuges and now came to look after their rafts.

But the bundles of canes had become water-logged and useless, so they resolved to retrace their steps if possible to the Indian village. On their way they unfortunately missed shooting a deer which lay beside the path, and had nothing to eat but macaw berries and the pith of a tree. Seeing the track of a wild hog they followed that, and ultimately came upon two provision fields. But even with this prospect of food they were so much depressed that, although perishing with hunger, they were afraid to venture near the Indian huts, and lingered about for some time. However, at last Wafer summoned enough courage to go into one of them, when almost immediately he was so affected by the close atmosphere and the odour of some meat cooking over the fire, that he fainted. ·

The kindly Indians assisted in his recovery, and gave him something to eat, when he was pleasantly surprised to find there the very same guides on whose account he and his comrades had been nearly roasted to death. On telling them where the others were, the Indians went out and brought back three, but had to carry food to the fourth before he could gain enough strength to walk the short distance. Here they were treated with the greatest humanity and tenderness, and after resting a week they again started with four guides, to reach the same river that had before checked their progress, in one day. Here, finding a canoe, they proceeded up stream until, arriving at the dwelling of the chief who had saved them from torture, they were told it was impossible to go on in such weather.

Wafer and his companions stopped here for several months—in fact the chief wished to retain them altogether. As a physician, Wafer was respected and loved; but at last, wishing to depart, by repeated importunities and the promise to come back with some good hunting-dogs, and then to marry the chief's daughter, he was at last furnished with guides. Over high mountains, along the edges of precipices, and through dense forests they toiled until they came to a river flowing north, on which they embarked, and reached the shores of the Gulf of Darien two days later. Here they were overjoyed to find an English vessel, the crew of which gave them a hearty welcome, making up to some extent for their long and perilous journey.

VI.

WAR IN THE YOUNG COLONIES.

AT the beginning of the seventeenth century Spain was nominally at peace with the other great powers, except the Netherlands, which had not yet come to the front. By the treaty of 1604 Queen Elizabeth made up the English quarrel, and in 1609 even Holland was conceded a truce for nine years.

Thus amity was supposed to exist, and the raids of licensed privateers came to an end. Yet there was "no peace beyond the line." Not to mention corsairs and pirates, the English were as determined on their part to get a share of America as were the Spaniards to keep them out if possible. The founders of Virginia were resolute to lose their lives rather than abandon so noble a colony. Even King James dared not give it up, although in 1612 and the following year there was a hot contention with the Spanish Secretary of State on the matter. Spain was discontented that the colony should have the royal sanction, and at the same time demanded its removal, accompanying this with a threat to drive out the settlers, as well as those in the Bermudas. But James could not admit the Papal Bull, and as the

9

English were firm, the claimants of the whole of America contented themselves with protests.

In the West Indies, however, Spain went farther. Here she had undoubtedly the right by discovery, although not by actual possession, save in the Greater Antilles. The weak English king who succeeded the strong-minded Tudor princess was not prepared to contest the Spanish supremacy here, but simply answered the complaints against English adventurers by disclaiming all responsibility. Neither England nor France had officially taken the ground that only actual possession created territorial rights, but many Englishmen were clamouring loudly to that effect. We have already noticed in another chapter James's policy, or want of policy, and the change which took place a few weeks after his death—we have now to deal with the results of that alteration.

In 1621 hostilities were renewed between Spain and the Netherlands, but even during the nominal truce the Dutch invaded Margarita, and demolished the fort, but without, however, taking actual possession. When the truce was over hostilities were recommenced with a vigour that rather astonished Spain, for in the interval the Netherlands had progressed wonderfully. In 1625, the year of his accession, Charles the First entered into a treaty, offensive and defensive, with the United Provinces, which of course brought England into collision with Spain, and open war began again in the West Indies. In 1629 a fleet of thirty-five vessels under Don Frederic de Toledo conquered the island of St. Christopher's and removed most of the English settlers, only a few of whom managed to escape to the mountains, while the French got off in two of their vessels. The French refugees suffered a great deal from the want of preparation for their hurried flight, and arrived at the island of St. Martin's perishing with hunger and thirst. Here they dug holes in the sand and obtained a supply of brackish water, which was so unwholesome that some died from drinking it in excessive quantities. After the Spaniards left they returned to St. Christopher's to find a few English, who, annoyed at their desertion, wanted to keep the island to themselves, but the French were too numerous and soon took possession of their old quarters.

In 1632 the Dutch took possession of Tobago, and two years later of Curaçao, which latter island soon became their great stronghold in the West Indies, and the principal depôt for the contraband traffic with Venezuela. At that time no Spanish vessels went to this part of the Main, but finding that the trade was of some importance to the .Dutch, the authorities now granted licenses to drive their rivals out of the market. But the Spanish traders could not compete with the Hollanders, and this so annoyed the authorities that they determined to extinguish smuggling at any cost. This they were unable to do by catching the delinquents, but they could punish those who dealt with them. The result was the infliction of heavy fines and confiscation, with disgraceful punishments, from which many were ruined. Yet with all that the trade was so lucrative to both parties that neither was inclined to give it up—the

Dutch took care of themselves, while cheap commodities could generally command a market, whatever the risk. The fact was the mother country imposed so many restrictions, and exacted such heavy fees for licenses, that the cost of an article was doubled or trebled as compared with that of the Hollander.

In 1627 a French Association was incorporated under the title of "The Company of the Islands of America." They appointed the Sieurs d'Enambuc and du Rossy to settle the islands of St. Christopher and Barbados as well as others situated at the "entrance of Peru." Nothing was done at Barbados, as the English were already in possession, but in 1634 examinations of Dominica, Martinique, and Guadaloupe were made, which ended in the two latter islands becoming French colonies in 1635.

Meanwhile, in November, 1630, a treaty was signed at Madrid between England and Spain, after which peace was supposed to again prevail. Nothing was said about the West Indies, probably because Spain knew that further protests were useless. Hardly had this been settled before, in 1635, France declared war against the common foe, and her corsairs could now legally carry on their work of pillage and destruction. In 1638 the island of St. Martin's, which had been partly occupied by French and Dutch, was captured by Spaniards, who expelled the inhabitants and replaced them by a strong garrison. In the same year Colonel Jackson, with a force from the English islands, captured Santiago de la Vega in Jamaica, and plundered it of everything valuable, after which,

in retaliation, the island of New Providence, one of
the Bahamas, was captured by Spain. Neither place
was, however, occupied by the captors, who only did
as much damage as they could and then left.

Almost from the commencement of their settlements the French had quarrelled among themselves,
but until the struggle which ended in the execution of
Charles the First, there had been few difficulties in
the English islands. The Barbadians, it is true,
protested against the claim of the Earl of Carlisle, in
which they were joined by the people of St. Kitt's,
but this was settled without disturbance. Now, however, the effects of "the great rebellion" began to be
felt across the seas, and disaffection towards the Parliament, and loyalty to the king, were promoted by
a number of Royalists who had fled from the disturbance in the mother country.

In 1650 the West Indies were virtually in revolt
against the Parliament, and on the 10th of September
an embargo was declared in England against vessels
bound for the Caribbee Islands, Bermuda, and
Virginia. This was followed on the 27th by an Act
prohibiting all commerce with these colonies because
of their rebellion against the Commonwealth. Virginia and the Bermudas had declared for King Charles
the Second after the execution of his father, and sent
emissaries to Barbados for the purpose of inciting
them to join in the revolt.

At the commencement of that year Barbados
was in a state of ferment, waiting only for the spark
which would plunge the island into civil war. Even
at this early period the inhabitants of Little England,

ST. KITT'S.
(From Andrews' "West Indies.")

as it is called, were very loyal, and had something of
the conceit which has characterised them ever since.
True, there were "Roundheads" on the island, but
hitherto party differences had been put in the background—now they were brought into prominence.
When the agent of the Bermudians asked that
Barbados should declare for the king, the majority
were in favour of the project, but, as a matter of
course, the others, who were of considerable importance, refused.   At first the Royalists went so far as
to advocate the banishment of their opponents, but
were unable to find any reasonable excuse for such a
high-handed proceeding.   However they brought in
an Act to imprison all who went to a conventicle, or
who seduced others from repairing to the Public
Congregation or from receiving the Holy Sacrament.
For a second offence the penalty was forfeiture of all
lands, goods, chattels, and debts by those whom they
called "the enemy to the peace of the island."

This was to have been published on April 15, 1650,
and kept secret until proclaimed, to prevent trouble.
But it appears that Colonel Codrington, a member of
the Assembly, divulged it in his cups, for which he
was fined twenty thousand pounds of sugar, and
banished from the island.   A deputation of Parlia-
mentarians then waited upon the Governor, to enter
their protest against the new law, and were asked
to leave the matter in his hands, as he had to deal
with "violent spirits."   Finally, the proclamation was
delayed, on the ground that there were many errors
in the copy, and the two parties stood at bay.

On the 23rd of April the Roundheads petitioned

the Governor to issue his writ for a new Assembly, on the ground that the present body had sat for its full term. This he agreed to do, and thus alienated the Cavaliers, who said he was a most emphatic Roundhead and enemy to the king. Handbills and posters now began to be circulated calling attention to the "damnable designe" of the Independents, of which, they said, Colonel Drax, "that devout zealot (of the deeds of the Devil, and the cause of that seven-headed Dragon at Westminster), is the Agent." One of the writers declared that he should think his best rest but disquiet until he had sheathed his sword in the bowels of the same obnoxious personage.

The Cavaliers were still adding to their numbers by the arrival of more refugees, while Colonel Drax and his friends fell into the background. The new-comers had mostly been ruined by the civil war, and were naturally desirous of doing something to retrieve their fortunes ; it followed, therefore, that anything that led to the confiscation of the estates of the obnoxious party would be to their advantage. The Cavaliers set to work to rouse the island by going about on horseback, fully armed, everywhere challenging those they met to drink the health of Charles the Second and confusion to the Independent dogs. This, with the rumours of a Roundhead plot and the various manifestoes, induced the Governor to issue a proclamation declaring that in future if any persons spread such scandalous papers they would be proceeded against as enemies of the public peace, at the same time forbidding any one to take up arms in a hostile manner.

This produced little effect, for the leader of one of the roving bands, Colonel Shelley, refused to disband. On this the Governor issued commissions to raise a militia for the preservation of order, but by the time that a hundred men had been collected an alarm went forth that the Cavaliers were advancing on Bridgetown. This was the 1st of May, and by that time the Cavaliers were prepared to act. Their leader was Colonel Walrond, who, on being sent for by the Governor, and saying they had no evil intention, was allowed to depart. However, they took possession of the town, and then came forward with the demand that all Independents and other disturbers of the peace should be at once disarmed. To this the Governor agreed, provided the well-affected should vouch for their safety. They also stipulated that the magazine on the bridge should be put under their protection, that those who obstructed the peace and laboured to ruin the loyal colonists should be punished, that twenty persons whose names they gave should be forthwith arrested, and that the Governor should speedily call together the Assembly to try them; meanwhile they refused to disperse until these things were done. The Governor could do nothing but accede to these demands, but even then there was something more which they considered the climax—"that our lawful soveraigne Charles the Second be instantly in a solemn manner proclaimed king."

This staggered the Governor, who said it was a matter for the General Assembly, in which opinion he got them at last to agree. However, they were

not yet content, but insisted that at the dissolution
of the present Assembly only such men as were
known to be well-affected to His Majesty and con-
formers to the Church of England should be chosen
and admitted. After that they must be promised an
" Act of oblivion " for the lawful taking up of arms,
safe-conduct for all officers on legislative business,
and, finally, that the Governor must come to them
without the companionship of any disaffected person
and put himself under their care.

All this was perforce agreed to, and on the 3rd of
May Charles the Second was declared king of
England, &c., as well as of Barbados, and at the
same time the Book of Common Prayer was proclaimed to be the only pattern of true worship.

Behind all this was a fact which no one mentioned,
but which probably everybody knew—on the 29th of
April Lord Willoughby had arrived in the harbour,
bearing a commission as Governor of the Caribbee
Islands, from the fugitive King Charles and the Earl
of Carlisle. No doubt the whole demonstration was
got up on his account, the Cavaliers wanting to have
the king proclaimed first, so that there should be no
difficulty about the commission. Everything was
ready now, and nothing was heard but uproarious
drinking of His Majesty's health, the Cavaliers going
from house to house and compelling others to follow
their example. As for Lord Willoughby, he left the
Governor to carry out the stipulated measures, while
he went to look after the other islands under his
jurisdiction.

Now the Royalists of Barbados began to persecute

the leaders of the obnoxious party, beginning with the twenty they had named to the Governor. Some, seeing their danger, had got off to England, but those who remained were sentenced to pay a million pounds of sugar and to be banished. Then nearly a hundred others were indicted and ordered to leave before the 2nd of July, while all their commissions of the peace or in the militia were cancelled. Wives were banished with their husbands, and unless the estate-owners humbly submitted, paid their fines, and appointed well-affected persons as attorneys, their properties were confiscated. Yet with all that, when an attempt was made to get to the bottom of the rumoured plot, no trace of it could be found. Some of the more moderate of the Royalists even began to doubt whether they were not going too far, but they salved their consciences by saying that everything was done in the interest of the king.

When the news arrived in England it created a great stir. In November some merchants and planters interested in the island asked for permission to make reprisals on their own account. They wanted licenses to trade there with five or six able ships, and letters of marque to use in case of obstruction, or a refusal to comply with certain demands. These demands were to repeal all Acts dishonourable to the Commonwealth, to renounce obedience to Charles Stuart, to acknowledge the supreme authority of the Parliament, to banish certain "active incendiaries in the late troubles," and, finally, to recall those who had suffered, so that they might enjoy the same rights as the other inhabitants. A further petition asked for the removal of

Lord Willoughby in favour of Edward Winslow, a man of approved fidelity to the Commonwealth.

The Parliamentary Government did not adopt these proposals, as they intended to reduce the island in a regular manner. In January, 1651, a fleet was made ready for this purpose, but being employed in the reduction of the Scilly Islands, it could not be got ready for the West Indies until June following.

Meanwhile Lord Willoughby had returned, and was doing his best to conciliate the Barbadians of both parties. He did not altogether approve of what had been done, but repealed the Acts of sequestration, thus putting the inhabitants in good spirits for the expected invasion. It was rumoured that Prince Rupert was coming out from Marseilles, and this made things appear brighter, encouraging them to put their forts in order.

The English fleet did not actually leave Plymouth until the 5th of August. It was under the command of Sir George Ayscue, who took six or seven merchant vessels under convoy, probably those referred to in the petition. He reached Barbados on the 15th of October, when as yet no news had been heard of Prince Rupert; in fact, that great seaman had been dissuaded from crossing the Atlantic. Fourteen Dutch vessels were captured in Carlisle Bay, the sudden arrival of the fleet preventing their escape.

Willoughby had some six thousand foot and four hundred horse stationed at different parts of the island, and was determined to hold it for the king, looking forward daily to see Prince Rupert arrive.

He had heard from a Dutch vessel that the king was marching on London with an army of Scots: this also tended to make his resistance all the more stubborn. From a few Roundheads, who managed to come off in the night, Ayscue learnt this, but he was as equally determined to subdue the island as Willoughby was to defend it.

On being called upon to surrender the island for the use of the Parliament of England, the Governor replied that he acknowledged no supremacy over Englishmen save the king and those having commissions from him, directing the letter to the admiral on board His Majesty's ship the *Rainbow*. He also said that he had expected some overtures of reparation for the hostile acts upon the ships in the bay. After this defiance nothing was left but to prepare first for a strict blockade, and then to effect a landing. The strength on shore was too great for any open attack, and Ayscue managed to send a proclamation addressed to the freeholders and inhabitants, urging them to accept in time his offers of peace and mercy. In answer to this the Assembly met and passed a declaration to "sticke to" Lord Willoughby and defend the island to the utmost.

In England a great deal of interest was felt in the struggle, and the demand for news of the expedition created a supply giving circumstantial accounts of what had *not* taken place. One of them was headed, "Bloody news from the Barbados, being a true relation of a great and terrible fight between the Parliament's Navie, commanded by Sir George Ayscue, and the King of Scots' Forces under the command of the

Lord Willoughby; with the particulars of the fight, the storming of the Island, the manner how the Parliament's Forces were repulsed and beaten off from Carlisle Bay and the Block House, and the number killed and wounded." And all this before any attempt had been made beyond the blockade !

On the receipt of the news of the battle of Worcester, Ayscue sent another flag of truce to give Willoughby the information, saying that he did so as a friend rather than as an enemy. He was acting in that quality, by stating the true condition of England, and leaving him and his friends to judge of the necessity for due obedience to the State of England ; otherwise they would be swallowed up in the destruction so shortly and inevitably coming upon them.

In reply, Willoughby said he had never served his king so much in expectation of prosperity as in consideration of duty, and that he would not be the means of increasing the sad affliction of His Majesty by giving up that island. To this Ayscue rejoined, that if there were such a person as the king, Willoughby's retention of that place signified nothing to his advantage, and therefore the surrender could be small grief to him. He well knew the impossibility of the island subsisting without the patronage of England, and the admiral's great desire was to save it from ruin and destruction.

As Willoughby refused to surrender, Ayscue determined to attack the Hole or James's Town, which he did on the 2nd of November, beating off its defenders, taking thirty prisoners, and spiking the four guns of the fort. On the 1st of December the fleet which had been sent to reduce Virginia arrived, and on the temporary addition of this force, Ayscue again sent to Willoughby, as he stated, for the last time. In reply he was told that the Assembly would consider the matter in two or three days, but this reply did not please the admiral, so he tried to hurry up the decision by landing at Speight's Town. Against the stubborn opposition of twelve hundred men he stormed and took the fort, which he held for two days, ultimately retiring, however, after burning the houses, demolishing the fortifications, and throwing the guns into the sea.

After that the correspondence was continued, Ayscue entreating Willoughby to spare the good people of the island the horrors of war. To this the Governor replied, that they only took up arms in their own defence ; the guilt of the blood and ruin would be at the doors of those who brought force to bear. Then the Virginia fleet sailed for its destination, and Ayscue recommenced hostilities by again occupying Speight's Town.

By this time, however, there was a party on the island in favour of peace, and they began to bestir themselves, thus making the Royalists more determined. They put forth a proclamation inviting the inhabitants to endure the troubles of war for a season, rather than by base submission to let the deceitful enemy make them slaves for ever. But the Roundheads now began to assemble under Colonel Modiford at his house, to the number of six hundred men, who declared for the Parliament, and threatened to bring Willoughby to reason, the admiral going so far as to visit them surreptitiously to read his commission. Hearing of this, Willoughby got two thousand four hundred men together and appeared near the house, but did not venture to attack it, as by this time he had become somewhat disheartened.

This brought things to a crisis, and on the 10th of January arrangements were made for a commission from both sides to make arrangements for terms. After a great deal of hesitation on the part of the admiral, the capitulation was at last signed, the articles being exceedingly favourable both to the inhabitants and Lord Willoughby. So lenient were they that Ayscue had to excuse himself to the home authorities for fear that he might have been misunderstood. They were, in short, liberty of conscience, continuation of the old government, and of the old Courts of Justice, no taxation without consent of the Assembly, no confiscations, all suits to be decided on the island, no acts of indemnity, no oaths against their consciences, a temporary cessation of all civil suits, and finally that Lord Willoughby should retain all his private property in the islands as well as in Surinam, with full liberty to go to England. These articles were signed on the 11th of January, 1652, and the "storm in a teapot" came to an end, the Barbadians proudly boasting that they had been able to defy the mighty power of the Commonwealth. Most of the leaders were banished from the island, some going to Surinam, where a colony had been established by Lord Willoughby soon after his arrival in Barbados. Among them was Major Byam, who became Governor, and virtually held the settlement for the king until he came to his own again. This is all the more curious because Cromwell knew the circumstances, yet made no effort to bring the people under submission. At first the settlers established a little Commonwealth of their own, with Major Byam as president, but when his term had expired, instead of giving place to another he declared he had a commission as Governor from the king, although he refused to show the document to any one. With enough Royalists to back him, he thus held office until the Restoration, notwithstanding the complaints of the Parliamentary faction and their requests to the home authorities for redress.

Meanwhile, early in 1652 England went to war with the Dutch, and this seriously interfered with the trade of that nationality in the West Indies. The Navigation Act was another blow to them, although it could not yet be enforced altogether. Cromwell made himself respected in such a manner that peace with Holland was restored in April, 1654, thus leaving him free to carry out his designs against the old enemy—Spain.

Since Queen Elizabeth's time the English Governments had done little in the way of worrying the Spaniards, although pirates had been busy almost without intermission. Now, however, Cromwell was at liberty, and he began to see that they wanted a little correction to prevent their having too much of their own way in America. The Spanish ambassador was cringing enough when he saw what a powerful leader had arisen, and did his best to avert the impending storm. It is even stated that he assured the Protector of his master's friendship, and declared that if he took the Crown of England Spain would be first in her approval. Cromwell was not to be mollified by soft speeches; he had got peace at home, and was determined to have it across the seas as well. He was quite willing to arrange for a treaty, but it must be on his own terms, not at the dictation of Spain. A commission was appointed to meet the ambassador and discuss the grounds of the agreement, and they began at once with the West Indies. A long list of depredations was produced for which the English demanded satisfaction before going farther. The English had been treated as enemies wherever the Spaniards met them in the West Indies, even when going to and from their own plantations, notwithstanding the former treaty, and the Commission insisted on a proper indemnity. The English must be free to trade everywhere—in fact the old claim of Spain to the whole of America must be finally abandoned.

The Spanish ambassador replied that the inquisition and trade to the West Indies were his master's two eyes, and that nothing different from the practice of former times could be permitted. On hearing this Cromwell, seeing that neither indemnity for the past nor promises of amendment in the future could be obtained, prepared for war, and commenced by fitting out an expedition to conquer Hispaniola.

In December, 1654, we find the first mention of a special service under the command of Generals Penn and Venables, and early in the following year the fleet sailed for Barbados. With five thousand men from England, and as many from the West Indies,

the expedition arrived near St. Domingo on the 13th
of April, 1655, frightening the inhabitants so much
that they fled to the woods on its approach. However, the affair was so badly managed that no benefit
accrued from following the example of Drake, which
appears to have been the object of the leaders. Like
the great Elizabethan hero, they landed at a distance
from the town with the intention of marching along
the shore, but instead of landing ten miles off they
went as far as thirty. For four days the troops
wandered through the mangrove bushes, without
guides, and even without provisions, thus giving the
runaway Spaniards time to rally from their fright and
come out after them. Weary, entangled in the
swamps, and utterly unfit to cope with an enemy,
the English became an easy prey ; the slaughter was
considerable, and it was even stated that those killed
were mostly shot in the back while trying to escape.

Unwilling to attempt anything further in Hispaniola,
Penn and Venables took off the dispirited remnant
and sailed for Jamaica, hoping to do something there
to prevent failure altogether. Not that there were
any laurels to be gained in that direction, for the
inhabitants only numbered three thousand, and half
of these were negro slaves. A few shots were fired,
and then the inhabitants took to flight, leaving the
English in possession of the island. A capitulation
was agreed upon with the old Spanish Governor, who
was brought in a hammock to sign it, but many of
the people took to the woods with their slaves, and
refused to be bound by the articles. A body of two
thousand men was then sent to scour the interior

and bring them back, but they could find nothing
save great herds of wild cattle. Afterwards, in pure
wantonness, the churches and religious buildings were
demolished, the cattle killed or driven far away, and
the provision grounds devastated, with the result that
the invaders were soon starving. In less than a
month two thousand were sick, many had died, and
the remainder had become mutinous. Altogether
the whole affair was so badly managed that Cromwell
became almost mad at the news, and sent both commanders to the Tower on their return.

However, Jamaica was captured, and for the first
time in the history of the West Indies a Spanish
possession went into the hands of another nation.
Some thought the island of no importance as compared with Hispaniola—it was certainly of little value
to the Spaniards. However, a few English people
foresaw something of its future importance, and did
their best to develop the island. In October Cromwell issued a proclamation offering certain advantages
to settlers from the other islands, or from England, so
that it might be occupied as soon as possible. It
stated that by the providence of God Jamaica had
come into the possession of the State, and that they
were satisfied of its fertility and commodiousness for
trade ; it had therefore been resolved to plant it. To
this end it was made known to the people of the
English islands and colonies the encouragements
offered to those who removed their habitations there
within two years from the 29th of September, 1656.
Twenty acres of land would be granted to every adult,
and ten for each child, they would have freedom to

hunt wild cattle and horses, be given the privilege of mining except for gold and silver, and freedom from taxes for three years.

It resulted from this that many planters from Barbados and St. Kitt's went over, and in a very few years Jamaica was more prosperous than it had ever been while in the possession of Spain. In November, 1656, Cromwell ordered the Scotch Government to apprehend all known idle masterless robbers and vagabonds, male or female, and to transport them there, and at the same time the Council of State ordered that a thousand girls and as many young men should be enlisted in Ireland for the same purpose. As for the adventurers who went with the expedition, they were reported as being so lazy "that it could not enter into the heart of any Englishman that such blood should run in the veins of his countrymen"—they were so unworthy, slothful, and basely secure, out of a strange kind of spirit desiring rather to die than live. As for planting, little was done by them, although every possible inducement and encouragement was given.

Meanwhile letters of marque were issued to privateers for the West Indies, which drove the Spaniards to send their treasure from Peru to Buenos Ayres, a route that had been abandoned since the time of Queen Elizabeth. Now also they began to make efforts for the recovery of Jamaica, and in May, 1658, thirty companies of infantry, under the command of the late Governor, landed on the north side of the island. Here in a small harbour they entrenched themselves, and built a little fort before their presence became known to the English. However, Governor D'Oyley at last heard of the invasion, but it was nearly two months after their arrival before he could proceed to approach them by sea. When he arrived, however, with seven hundred and fifty men, he at once stormed their fortress and drove them to their vessels, in which they fled to Cuba. This put an end to the matter; but the old Governor returned, and lived with the remnant of the Spaniards and their slaves in the mountains.

Now at last even the Pope had to acknowledge other sovereignty than that of Spain, and this he did in a letter to Father Fontaine, of the Dominican Mission, on the 25th of July, 1658. Therein he acknowledged the king of France as ruler of the conquests and colonies his subjects had made in the American islands. Thus was the Bull of partition at last cancelled by the successor of its original promulgator, and the ground for the exclusive claim to America cut away. At this time France was also at war with Spain, but the following year a treaty was signed, and in 1660, on the restoration of Charles the Second, peace was restored with England.

At the first private audience of the Spanish ambassador with the king, he delivered a memorial demanding the restoration of Jamaica to his master, on the ground that it had been taken by his rebel subjects, contrary to the treaty between the two Crowns. Instead of doing this, however, Charles despatched a vessel with letters to the Governors of the Caribbee islands, asking them to encourage all persons willing to transplant themselves to the larger islands. At the same time the Royal African Company, the great slave-trading corporation of that time, was asked to make Jamaica its headquarters for the sale of negroes. Then it was arranged to send women from England to be wives for the planters, Newgate and Bridewell to be spared as much as possible, so that poor maids might have a chance, with whom it was stated that few English parishes were unburdened.

On the 1st of December, 1660, King Charles the Second made a move which must be considered as of the greatest importance to the development of the British Colonial Empire—he founded the " Council for foreign plantations," which later developed into the Colonial Office. This Council were to inform themselves of the state of the plantations and of how they were governed, keeping copies of all grants in a book. They were to write to every Governor asking for exact accounts of their proceedings, the nature of their laws and government, as well as statistics. They must establish a correspondence with the colonies, so that the king might be informed of all complaints, their wants, what they cultivated, their commodities, and their trade, so that all might be regulated upon common grounds and principles. They must adopt means for rendering them and England mutually helpful, and bring them into a more uniform government, with a better distribution of justice. Especial care was to be taken for the execution of the Navigation Act, and consideration given to the best means of providing servants, to which end care was to be taken that no persons were forced or enticed away by unlawful means. Those willing to be transported were, however, to be encouraged, and a legal course was to be settled for sending over vagrants and others who were noxious and unprofitable in England. Learned and orthodox ministers were also to be sent, and instructions given for regulating and repressing the debaucheries of planters and servants. The Council were also to consider how the natives and slaves might be invited to, and made capable of, baptism in the Christian faith, and finally to dispose of all matters relating to the good government, improvement, and management of the plantations.

Thus England commenced her great career of colonisation, the results of which we see to-day. While taking all due account of Virginia and New England, we cannot but note that it was in the West Indies where the "prentice hand" was first tried. Jamaica was the main object of these provisions—to that island the king's attention had been specially directed, and it was here that many difficulties had to be encountered before it could be made a worthy appendage of the Crown. Most of the other islands were in the hands of private persons or companies, while this was under the control of the State. No matter that the island had been annexed by rebels, Charles the Second was determined to hold it fast for England, in spite of all the protests of Spain.

VII.

THE PLANTERS AND THEIR SLAVES.

WHEN the first European adventurers went to the West Indies, serfdom was still common in Spain. The peasantry were, as a rule, bound to the soil, and could neither be taken away by their lords nor remove at their own will. The consequence was that only soldiers, mariners, and free men from the towns took part in the first expeditions. The townsmen had mostly been brought up to the trades of their fathers, and were hardly fit to cultivate the land even in Spain, much less, therefore, were they suited to the tropics. They could not demean themselves by performing anything so servile, but must get their land cultivated by others. As the serfs were not available, first Indians and then negro slaves and white bond-servants were employed.

We have seen how the Indians were exterminated, and how the first planters in Hispaniola were ruined by the want of labour. Even the Spanish priests could see that the poor Arawak's nature was quite distinct from that of the European peasant. The serf had been kept under subjection for centuries; his father and grandfather had worked in the fields, and he must do the same. The armourer, the mason, and

A SURINAM PLANTER.
(From Stedman's "Surinam.")

the weaver carried on their trades, because they had been born into the respective guilds as it were. The Indians, on the contrary, were free, and had always been so; yes, more free than any people in the old world. They died, and the planter had to look elsewhere for his labour supply. Then commenced the cry which has been continually rising from the plantations ever since—More servants! More slaves! More coolies!

For many years the Portuguese had been kidnapping negroes on the west coast of Africa. By their connection with Morocco they had learnt that the natives of the interior were brought to and openly sold in the Moorish towns—possibly they themselves had purchased some of them. To bring home a number after every voyage to the coast was therefore nothing strange, nor was it anything novel to sell them in Portugal to help pay the expense of the voyage. From Portugal to Spain this negro slavery spread, until it became fairly common in both countries.

When the cry for labourers came over the Atlantic—even before the extermination of the natives—a few negroes were sent out. Finding them more docile and better able to endure hard labour than the Indians, more were called for, the benevolent priests also urging the matter to save the remnant of the Arawaks. The demand created a supply, and soon the Portuguese found themselves embarked in a lucrative trade, of which they commanded the monopoly. Thus began a traffic which has been unreservedly condemned by the most enlightened of humanity,

A NEGRO FESTIVAL.
(*From Edwards' "West Indies."*)

and praised alone by those whose very livelihood depended upon it.

On his second voyage Columbus carried the sugar cane, which was destined to have such an influence for good and evil on the West Indies. Its produce was at first known as a kind of honey, and recognised as an expectorant and comforting medicine. Now it had made its way into the kitchens of the great, where it was considered as one of the spices, and with them became more and more used every year. In early times the cane was cultivated on the warmer shores of the Mediterranean, and, after their discovery, in the Canary and Cape de Verde islands. At the period of the discovery of America sugar was sold at about eightpence a pound, equivalent to something like three shillings nowadays. As the demand continued to increase large plantations were laid out in Hispaniola, until it became the staple product of the colony.

Cotton was known in the old world, but as yet had hardly come into use in Europe. In the West Indies it was generally cultivated in a small way by every native, and on being forwarded to Spain, the "tree wool," as it was called, soon came into use. Then came another product, tobacco, which was quite new at that time, although probably known in the far East. It seemed strange to the new-comers that people should carry firebrands in their mouths, and at first they took tobacco-smokers for juggling fire-eaters, until they also learnt the sustaining power of the "weed." This soon took place, and by the year 1550 tobacco was well known in Spain and Italy.

VOYAGE OF THE SABLE VENUS.
(*From Edwards' "West Indies."*)

Probably also the Dutch knew it quite as early, for it was in the Netherlands that it became more quickly appreciated than in any other country, probably on account of its particularly comforting properties in marshy districts. Soon afterwards Jean Nicot introduced it into France, and probably Master Hawkins brought samples into England from Brazil, although Ralegh is stated to have been the first English smoker. Towards the end of the sixteenth century its use became so common all over Europe that Popes and Churchmen thundered their curses against the "filthy habit," and later poor King James wrote his " Counterblast to Tobacco," which only had the effect of making it better known.

Here at the beginning were two commercial products which grew well in the West Indies, with a doubtful third to come to the front as soon as it became known. As yet coffee had not been introduced—this followed in the next century. Notwithstanding the large profit on sugar the Spaniard would not labour in the field, and in the end the plantations became fewer and fewer until only one or two were left. This falling off tended to keep up the price, and although the Dutch bought much cotton and tobacco from the Indians of the Main, and the Portuguese began to grow sugar in Brazil, the supply was always limited.

There was room for more plantations, and the first people to take advantage of this opening were the English. Their many different colonies in Guiana all commenced planting with tobacco : Virginia and the Bermudas did the same. All through the reign

SLAVES·LANDING·FROM·THE·SHIP.
(From Stedman's "Surinam.")

of James the First, however, the trade was obstructed in so many ways that a great deal of their produce was sent to the Netherlands and thus escaped the English duties. Probably also the smuggling of tobacco, so notorious at a later period, began at this time, as the Dutch were always noted free-traders, not only on the Spanish Main, but in Europe as well.

Like the Spaniards, the English adventurers were soldiers and sailors, and therefore did not work in the field. Subject to the raids of the European claimants of the territory as well as the incursions of ferocious cannibals, they went about literally with pistols in their belts and swords at their thighs. Now they had to show a good face to some buccaneer company, and anon to fight the French or Dutch when war broke out. Later, when there was no fear of enemies from without, they had a continual dread of slave insurrections. It followed, therefore, that the planter was always on the alert, and, even if he felt inclined, could do little in the way of cultivation.

In England serfdom had virtually come to an end, and the agricultural labourer might go where he pleased. But the love of country, the unknown but magnified perils of a sea voyage, and stories of cruel Spaniards and man-eating Caribs, prevented many from going to the Indies, notwithstanding the great inducements offered. The English planters found it difficult to get negroes, as their enemy controlled the trade. As for the Indians, they had to deal with cannibals whose women cultivated small clearings, but resented anything like coercion, while no labour whatever could be got from the men. Something had to be done. If the English labourer would not come willingly, he might be kidnapped, and the carrying out of this work led to the organisation of bands of ruffians, who went sailing along the coasts, especially of Scotland and Ireland, to pick up likely fellows wherever they found opportunity. However, this caused such an outcry that extraordinary efforts were made on the part of the Government to put down " spiriting," as it was called.

In June, 1661, the Council for foreign plantations considered the best means of encouraging and furnishing people for the colonies, and they thought that felons condemned for small offences, and sturdy beggars, might be sent. They had several complaints of men, women, and children being spirited away from their masters and parents, and later the Mayor of Bristol and the Lord Mayor of London petitioned the king for authority to examine ships, with the view of finding out whether the passengers went of their own free will. It was stated that husbands forsook their wives, wives fled from their husbands, children and apprentices ran away, while unwary and credulous persons were often tempted on board by men-stealers. Many who had been pursued by hue and cry for robberies, burglaries, and breaking prison, also escaped to the plantations. Certain persons, called spirits, inveigled, and by lewd subtleties enticed, away young persons, whereby great tumults and uproars were raised in London, to the breach of the peace and the hazard of men's lives.

These abuses led to an Order in Council, published

in September, 1664, for registering persons going
oluntarily, and commissions were given to the Lord
High Admiral and the officers of the ports to establish registration offices and give certificates. Yet
the spiriting still went on, for in April, 1668, Sir
Anthony Ashley Cooper was asked to move the
House of Commons to make the offence capital.
His petitioner, said he, had found one lost child, and
after much expense and trouble, freed him, but there
were several others in the same ship, and other ships
in the river at the same work. Even if the parents
found their children, they could not recover them
without money, and he was sure that if such a law
were passed the mercy to these innocents would
ground a blessing on those concerned in introducing
it. This Act was finally passed on the 1st of March,
1670, punishing the spirits with death without benefit
of clergy.

There were, however, other means of procuring
servants. In 1649, when Cromwell took Drogheda
by storm, about thirty prisoners were saved from the
massacre to be shipped to Barbados, and in 1651
seven or eight thousand Scots, taken at the battle
of Worcester, were reserved for a similar fate. After
the Restoration, however, there was an intermission
in such supplies, and the planters began to look to
Newgate and Bridewell for their labour supply.

The supply was by no means equal to the demand,
for the agents in London of the planters of Virginia,
Barbados, St. Christopher's, and other islands were
equally clamorous for their share. As for King
Charles the Second, he granted the prisoners as a

privilege to his favourites, and even mistresses, who generally sold it to the highest bidder. The agent must have had influence to get into the presence of the holder, say of a hundred prisoners sentenced to transportation, and this was only obtainable by largess to door-keepers and servants. Then came the trouble of obtaining delivery from the prison authorities, and here again fees were demanded. In one case that is recorded the amount paid to the gaoler of Newgate was fifty-five shillings a head. But even now the trouble was only beginning. The prisoners were supposed to be delivered at the door of the gaol, and the planter was under a heavy bond not to allow one to escape. He must account for each by a certificate of death on the voyage or of landing in Barbados, on penalty of five hundred pounds for every one missing. It followed, therefore, that a sufficiently strong guard had to be provided, and provision made for attempts at rescue by the prisoners' friends. Even this was not all, for the concession simply granted a certain number, and it rested with the gaoler to palm off the old, weak, and infirm on those who were at all wanting in liberality. Then, at the best the prisoners were hatters, tailors, and haberdashers, rather than agricultural labourers, many of whom ultimately proved valueless. If a large number was available, and there were several applicants, the competition became quite spirited—every one wanted his pick before the others, and the gaoler made the best of the occasion, leaving those to whom he allotted the refuse to curse their evil fortune.

Up to the passing of the Navigation Act the Dutch had been free to trade with English colonies, and had brought a fair number of negroes : and afterwards the king established the Royal African Company to prevent the supply being cut off. The average price of the African was then about £16 or 2,400 pounds of sugar, but the Dutch sold their slaves for a little less, which led the planters to evade the Navigation Act when they had opportunities.

The white bond-servant was valued at about 2,200 pounds of sugar, very little less than the slave for life, although he had generally but five years to serve. The cost of transport was about £5 per head ; it followed, therefore, that if the London agent got his prisoners cheap he made a good profit. There was also another way of making money in this business. Some of the gaol-birds had friends who were willing to pay good sums on consideration that the convict should be virtually freed on his arrival. Many a sum of fifty pounds was obtained in this way, sometimes without helping the bond-servant in the least. How were the relations to prove that the promise had not been fulfilled, and if they did so what redress could be obtained ? They certainly could not go to law, as the whole transaction was illegal.

We have seen how Charles the Second tried to people Jamaica with free settlers, but this did not prevent the transportation of criminals. In 1665 four young men, who had been convicted of interrupting and abusing a preacher, were whipped through the streets of Edinburgh and afterwards sent to Barbados, and in 1684 some of the Rye

House plotters were reprieved on condition that they
served ten years in the·West Indies.   When these
plotters arrived in Jamaica, the Governor, "by His
Majesty's command," directed the Assembly to pass
an Act "to prevent all clandestine releasements or
buying out of their time," so that their punishment
should not be evaded.   But it was after the Monmouth rebellion, in 1685, that the greatest deportation
took place.   The miserable followers of the duke
were executed by Judge Jeffreys until even his thirst
for blood was somewhat slackened, when the remainder were sent to the plantations.   The story
of one of these unfortunates gives such a graphic
picture of the life of a bond-servant that we cannot
do better than give an outline of the " Relation of
the great sufferings and strange adventures of Henry
Pitman, surgeon to the late Duke of Monmouth."

Having been taken prisoner after the battle of
Sedgemoor, he was committed to Ilchester Gaol, had
his pockets rifled, his clothes torn off his back, and
was remanded until the Wells assizes. While in
gaol he was inveigled into telling all he knew, by
promises of pardon, and then his acknowledgments
were treated as a confession.   Those who pleaded
not guilty on the first day of the trial were convicted
and executed the same afternoon ; others who con-
fessed were equally condemned.   After two hundred
and thirty had been hanged the remainder were ordered
to be transported to the Caribbee islands, of whom Pitman was one.   With some others, including his brother,
he was disposed of to an agent who took £60 from
his friends to set him free on his arrival at Barbados.

The Legislative Assembly of that island, however, in consequence of the " most horrid, wicked, and execrable rebellion," lately raised, and because many of the rebels had been transported for ten years, passed a special Act, under which they were bound to serve, notwithstanding any bargain to the contrary. If they attempted to escape they were to be flogged, and burnt in the forehead with the letters " F. T.," meaning " Fugitive Traitor."

By this law Pitman's hopes were frustrated, and, utterly disheartened, he was not inclined to work at his profession for the master to whom he had been sold. Although the status of a surgeon was not then as high as it is now, it was yet a great downfall to practise the profession on rations of five pounds of salt beef or fish per week, with nothing else but corn meal. As for the fees, which were large, the master pocketed them, leaving Pitman to endure the discomforts of a tropical residence and semi-starvation as best he could. On one occasion he refused to go on with his work, and for this he was beaten by his master until the cane used was broken in pieces. Then the master became bankrupt, and, with his brother, Pitman was sent back to the merchant to whom they had been first consigned.

Here his brother died of the hardships he had experienced, and Pitman resolved to escape, notwithstanding the risk of attempting such a thing. Having made the acquaintance of a poor man who was willing to help, he got a consignment of goods from his friends in England, with which to raise the means. A boat was purchased for twelve pounds ;

but this led to inquiries, as the buyer was known to be poor, and his creditors began to come down upon him. However, Pitman contributed enough to satisfy them, meanwhile postponing his departure until suspicion had been lulled.

On the evening of the 9th of May, 1687—this being a holiday, when most of the people were revelling—he and seven other bond-servants got safely off in their open boat, with a small supply of provisions and water, a few tools, a compass, and a chart. They intended to make for the Dutch island of Curaçao, six hundred miles distant; but even before they were out of Carlisle Bay their frail craft began to leak, and they had to tear up their clothes to stop the gaping seams. At sunrise they were out of sight from the land, but so enervated by sea-sickness that some would willingly have gone back. However, they went on as best they could, with nothing but their hats to bale out the water, which still continued to trickle into the boat. They were a little more comfortable as the sun rose, but when night came a gale arose which kept them employed baling for their lives. To add to their difficulties the rudder broke, and they had to steer with an oar.

Five days passed in this manner, the refugees hardly able to get an hour's rest for the baling and continual fear that the boat would sink if left alone. On the sixth morning they saw Margarita, but could not land on account of the rocky shore, which nearly wrecked them on their making the attempt. Sheering off, they next day sighted Saltatudos island, one of the Dry Tortugas, where they met a boat manned with privateers, who treated them very kindly, and wanted them to join their company. To this, however, Pitman and his companions would not agree, and this annoyed the privateers, who burnt their boat and virtually kept them as prisoners. When they went on a cruise the refugees were left in charge of four men, and had much ado to find enough turtle to keep them from starving. After remaining here for three months an English privateer arrived, and, at their request, took them on to New Providence, to which the inhabitants had just returned after being driven off by Spaniards. Pitman at last got to Amsterdam, and from thence to. England, where the revolution had just taken place, and his friends had succeeded in obtaining a free pardon.

The white bond-servant, being under a short engagement, was generally worked to his utmost capacity No matter if he died before the end of his term as long as he paid for the expense incurred. But Englishmen were no more inclined to be slaves then than they are now, and the planters of St. Kitt's found them so troublesome to manage that they soon became afraid of buying, and showed a preference for negroes. Some of the English servants committed suicide, and it is recorded that a pious master told one of them, who had expressed his intention of destroying himself, that he trusted that God would give him more grace, than, for a short term of trouble in this life, to precipitate himself into hell.

Even in the earliest times some of the planters were absentees, living in England. The system was always more or less fortune-hunting, the whole end and aim being to get rich and return to the old country. There were, as we have seen, many difficulties and dangers to encounter, and not the least of the drawbacks was the want of good society. We who live in an age when there is daily communication with the whole world, can hardly conceive how entirely these pioneers were cut off from their friends. The long voyage was full of discomfort, and at the best uncertain as to its termination. The words still found on bills of lading, " the act of God or the queen's enemies," had a meaning then hardly appreciable by the present generation. Barbary pirates and French corsairs ranged the Channel ; in the broad Atlantic storms shook the crazy vessels to pieces ; and when they escaped these dangers, it was often to fall into the hands of the buccaneers when in sight of their destination. Then there were hurricanes on both sea and land, and earthquakes on some of the islands. Vessels were sunk in harbour, houses blown away, and sugar buildings torn down. As for the negro huts, they were carried off altogether, and the crops injured so as to become useless. Then, perhaps, when the planter had strained himself to the utmost to put things straight, another tornado would put him in a worse plight than before.

Yet with all this the planter struggled on, generally doing his best to carry the traditions and fashions of the mother country into his new home. We have already noticed Barbados, and how it was affected by the "great rebellion." Many other examples might be noted had we sufficient space. The planter was nearly always a gentleman, even if he had begun his career as a transported rebel. Some were gallants, and dressed in the extreme of London fashion, often living beyond their means. Others were merchants, trading with their own vessels, and selling their surplus goods for produce to make up cargoes. With their own sugar, and as much as they could procure from others, they filled their ships for the homeward voyage, and in return got enough merchandise for trading. These were the fortune-hunters, who were always looking forward to that happy time when, with money in their pouches, they could once more settle down in Merry England. The old country was always "home," as it is still for the West Indian, although perhaps neither himself nor his parents ever saw it—then it was the will-o'-the-wisp that drove him to endure all the discomforts of a life in the tropics, often to die of fever before his work was hardly begun.

While Jamaica was under the dominion of Spain little was done to develop the island. The Indians were exterminated, as in Hispaniola, to be replaced by wild cattle and horses, and fifteen hundred negroes were introduced to cultivate provision grounds. From these, passing vessels, which called in on their way to Mexico, got their supplies. As yet it was not a rendezvous for buccaneers, and taken altogether it was quite insignificant. Thousands of white men and tens of thousands of negroes were required before it became the important island which ultimately rivalled Hispaniola. However, although the Spaniard was driven out he left his sting behind in the shape of his slaves, who took to the mountains, to be afterwards known as Maroons, and to worry the English colonists for over a century.

And here, as we are dealing with the planter and his labour supply, we must say something of the negro slaves, to whom the West Indies were indebted for their very existence as European colonies. Unlike the American, the African had known slavery for ages. Prisoners taken in war were kept in servitude as a matter of course; debtors were slaves to their creditors, and even children were sold by their parents. Yet there were great differences between the tribes—the Coromantees, for example, were particularly troublesome, and the Foulahs often dangerous. The first slave-traders took their cargoes from the more northern coasts, and from this cause, perhaps, as well as the want of proper supervision in the Indies, runaways, or Simerons, were mentioned at very early periods. Later, the trade was carried on in a particularly judicious manner, and the more docile tribes selected, to be sold in the colonies as "Prime Gold Coast Negroes."

In their native countries these people were all virtually slaves to their chiefs, and as such were liable to be sold at any time. The authority was unlimited; the slightest offence meant slavery; death was the only alternative. Often when, for some reason or other, the negro was rejected by the trader, he was executed at once. Adultery was punished by the sale of both offenders, and debtors could be sold by their creditors. Bryan Edwards, author of a history of the West Indies, took much pains to procure information from the slaves themselves, through an interpreter; and as they had no reason to misrepresent their cases, we can safely give the outlines of one.

The most interesting story is, perhaps, that of the boy Adam, a Congo, about fourteen years of age when he was brought to Jamaica. His country was named **Sarri,** and was situated a long distance from the coast. While walking one morning through a path, about three miles from his native village, the boy was captured by one of his countrymen. With his prisoner the man hid himself in the woods during the whole of the day, and at night stole away from the neighbourhood, going on like this for a whole month. Then he came to the country of another tribe, where he sold the boy for a gun, some powder and shot, and a little salt. His new owner afterwards sold Adam for a keg of brandy to another black man who was going about collecting slaves, and when twenty had been collected they were taken to the coast and sold to a Jamaica captain.

Of the five-and-twenty interrogated by Bryan Edwards, fifteen frankly declared that they had been born in slavery, and were sold to pay the debts, or bartered to supply the wants, of their owners. Five were secretly kidnapped in the interior, and sold to black merchants; the other five fell into the hands of the enemy in some of those petty wars which were continually going on, when, if there had been no market for their sale, they would almost certainly have been killed.

It is hardly necessary to state that in giving these

statements we are not attempting the impossible task of vindicating slavery either of the black or white man. It would be well, however, if, in mitigation of the offence against the negro, his former condition were taken into consideration, and the undoubted fact that he was better treated by the West India planter than by his own countrymen. His lot was by no means so hard as slavery had been to the Indian and white bond-servant. He did not sink under the hardships of a life of toil in the burning sun, but was happy in his way, and in most cases better off than his descendant, the West Indian peasant of to-day. He was certainly treated as a domestic animal, but his value was always high enough to prevent anything like ill-usage. There were certainly people who could be cruel to their negroes, as there are yet men so low as to brutally flog valuable horses, but that such were common is a statement utterly without foundation. As a well-kept animal, the planter took a pride in him, fed and doctored him, patted him on the back, and proudly showed him to his friends. All this appears very degrading to humanity, but after all the negro did not see it in that light. On the contrary, he took a pride in exhibiting his strong muscles and in showing the "buccras" what a fine nigger massa had got.

The slave of the rich planter, like the horse of the English gentleman, was undoubtedly very comfortable. First, he was a picked lot—the healthiest, strongest, and most suitable for his work—one of those "pieces d'India," as the best negroes were called by the traders. Then, as an expensive chattel, everything was done to make him still more valuable, and to prevent his deteriorating. But unfortunately there was another class—the miserable, broken-down creatures sold cheap as refuse lots to poor white men or even to slaves. Yes, the slaves bought their diseased fellow-countrymen, to work on their own allotments, treating them as the costermonger sometimes does his donkey. Half-starved, hard-worked, and covered with sores, they lingered in misery until death came to make them free. Some were so disfigured with yaws, or leprosy, that none but a negro could bear the sight of them ; these were kept out of the way and treated worse than mangy dogs.

VIII.

THE STRUGGLE FOR SUPREMACY.

BY the time of the Dutch war of 1665 the pretensions of Spain to the exclusive possession of the Indies had been entirely ignored. Now began the great struggle of other nations for supremacy, and the position of " sovereign of the seas," the islands and Guiana becoming scenes of contention between English, French, and Dutch. To these struggles is greatly due the positions the naval powers of the world hold to-day, and especially that of Britain.

As it was mainly a demand for free trade which led to so many attacks on the Spanish possessions, so it was now the same question which led to the struggle between the two great mercantile nations which succeeded Spain and Portugal, as these had followed Venice and Genoa. In the West Indies there was no line of demarcation between these new powers, and consequently their interests often clashed, but on the whole the colonists were favourable to the Dutch, and did all they could to evade the Navigation Act.

Early in 1665 preparations were made in Barbados to repel an expected invasion by the Dutch. Vessels were ordered to keep together and protect each other, and men-of-war were sent out to afford convoy. Already the English buccaneers had been somewhat discountenanced by the home government, although they were generally encouraged by the colonies, especially Jamaica, which derived considerable advantage from their sales of booty. Now that there was a demand for all the forces that could be gathered together, the Governor of that island gave the rovers letters of marque, under which they were empowered to ravage the Dutch colonies. At St. Eustatius they succeeded in carrying off everything portable, including nine hundred slaves, and even such heavy articles as sugar coppers and stills. De Ruyter made an attempt on Barbados on the 20th of April, but the people there made such a stand that he had to retire. He commenced the attack at ten o'clock in the morning with his fourteen vessels, but by three in the afternoon the fleet was so much damaged that he was forced to move away his own ship, with a hole in her side "as big as a barn-door." He then went on to Montserrat and Nevis, where he captured sixteen ships, but did not take either of the islands.

In Guiana, the English from Barbados captured the Dutch trading factory in the river Essequebo, as well as the young sugar colony in the Pomeroon, and in retaliation the Dutch took Surinam. In January, 1666, France joined the Netherlands, and an English fleet was sent out to protect Barbados, which now began to feel alarmed at the possible result of such a powerful combination.

Then came the critical period for the island of St. Kitt's, which, as we have before stated, had been divided between English and French, the former holding the middle portion with the enemy on either side. As soon as the news of the declaration of war arrived, the relations between the two nationalities, which had often before been much strained, became ruptured. The English Governor, Watts, gave his rival three days' notice, and prepared to attack him, with the assistance of five hundred men from Nevis, and two hundred buccaneers. General de la Salle, on the French side, asked and obtained forty-eight hours' longer grace, and took advantage of this to steal into the English territory with a large body of horse and foot, as well as a mob of negroes armed with bills and hoes. The slaves also carried fire-brands, and were said to have been promised, in return for their assistance, freedom, English women as wives, and the liberty to plunder and burn. At the town of St. Nicholas a gentlewoman with three or four children, on trying to escape, was forced back into her blazing house and kept there until the whole family were burnt to death. A party of English, who advanced to check their progress, was over-whelmed by the number of the enemy and driven back, thus leaving them to advance over the island with fire and sword.

Governor Watts took things so coolly, that Colonel Morgan (not the famous Sir Henry), who led the buccaneers, went to rouse him, and found he was lounging about in dressing-gown and slippers. Presenting a pistol to his breast, Morgan called the

Governor a coward and a traitor, at the same time swearing he would shoot him dead if he did not at once take his place at the head of the forces. The contingent from Nevis had already gone over to the French quarter near Sandy Point, and, after a hard struggle, had taken the post, when the Governor at last followed behind. Coming up late his men fired on the mingled French and English, indiscriminately slaughtering both. After that everything was confused, neither party distinguishing friend from foe, with the result that the Governor, Colonel Morgan, several other officers, and most of the English, were killed. After that the main body of the French arrived, driving before them a confused mob of women and children, who ran shrieking to their friends for help. Nothing remained for the English now but to fly or sue for quarter, and the French became masters of the whole island, with a body of prisoners twice as numerous as themselves.

In 1667 a petition was forwarded to Charles the Second on behalf of several thousand distressed people, lately inhabitants of St. Christopher's. In this it was stated that the island had been one of the most flourishing colonies—the first and best earth that ever was inhabited by Englishmen among the heathen cannibals of America. They prayed that a colony so ancient and loyal, the mother island of all those parts, the fountain from whence all the other islands had been watered with planters, might not remain in the hands of another nation. Since the surrender they had been continually oppressed, until thousands had left for other parts. Many had sold their estates for almost nothing, and had been stripped and plundered at sea of the little they had saved. If the inhumanities of the French nation were examined, their bloody and barbarous usage of the Indians, their miserable cruelties to prisoners of war, all nations would abhor their name. They would make Christians grind their mills instead of cattle, leave thousands to starve for want, and send other thousands to uninhabited lands.

In 1666 Lord Willoughby, who had gone back to Barbados on the restoration of Charles the Second, fitted out an expedition to recapture St. Kitt's, but his fleet encountered a hurricane, and neither his vessel nor one of his company was ever heard of again. The following year his nephew, Henry Willoughby, made an unsuccessful attempt for the same object. On the 10th of May of the same year a fight took place between the English and French fleets off Nevis. On the English side were ten men-of-war and one fire-ship, while the enemy had more than double that number. One of the English vessels was blown up, but, undaunted by this disaster, they drove the enemy before them to the very shores of St. Kitt's, where they took shelter under the guns of Basse-terre.

Peace was signed at Breda in July, 1667. The gains of territory by any one of the three nations were not considerable, and the result went to prove that England could hold her own against the only two powers who were able to dispute her supremacy. During the war she had captured New Amsterdam (now New York) from the Dutch, and they in turn had taken Surinam. As it was agreed with Holland that both parties should retain what was then in their possession, Surinam was virtually exchanged for what is now the capital of the United States. Antigua and Montserrat, which had been taken by the French, were now restored to England, and St. Christopher's returned to its former condition, but without the least prospect of the two nationalities ever being again on friendly terms.

Now that the war was over the trade of the privateers came to an end, and further efforts were made to make them settle down. Having received orders to discountenance them, the Governor of Jamaica deputed Colonel Cary to report on the matter. Cary thought they should not be discouraged, as already harm had been done to Jamaica by such attempts, and in the future the want of their help might be prejudicial. On the news that the commissions against the Spaniards were called in, several English privateers resolved never to return to Jamaica, unless there was a war, but in future to carry on their operations from Tortuga. To divert them from injuring the Spaniards, the Governor had, during the late war, appointed Cary to treat with them for the reduction of Curaçao, to which they at first consented, but afterwards disagreed. If, said Cary, they had two of His Majesty's nimble fifth-rate frigates, they would be able to keep the privateers to their obedience, observe the enemy's movements, and guard their own coasts from rovers. There was no profitable employment for the privateers against the French and Dutch; these fellows,

being people that would not be brought to plant,
must prey upon the Spaniard, whether they were
countenanced at Jamaica or not. There was such
an inveterate hatred of the English in those parts
by the Spaniard, that he would not hear of trade
or reconciliation, but, on the contrary, inhumanly
butchered any of the islanders he could cowardly
surprise. The French interest daily increased in
the Caribbees, Hispaniola, and Tortuga, and if this
was suffered to grow it would in a short time prove
of dangerous consequence.

Here we have plain speaking. It was not to the
interest of England for the pirates to become too
closely connected with the French, as they would
then be helping to build up the prosperity of a nation
that might any day become our enemy. As for the
rovers themselves, they cared little or nothing for
the interests of their country ; they were willing to
plunder the Spanish possessions because they got
something worth having ; with those of the French
and Dutch it was another thing. It is evident that
Cary troubled himself but little as to how a cargo
was obtained as long as Jamaica profited by the
transaction.

We may here also call attention to the differences
between the characters of the nations which now
commenced a great struggle for mastery in these
parts. The Dutch were, above everything else, an
association of traders, and although they could
fight on occasion, they hardly ever went out of their
way to pick a quarrel. Their wars with England
were brought about by mercantile disputes, the first

two, as we have already seen, mainly on account of the Navigation Acts. The English, "the nation of shopkeepers," were naturally rival traders, but they did not altogether confine themselves to traffic, being rather inclined to alternate or mix it up with something like piracy. Such transactions as those of Hawkins were not carried on by any other nation, the Hollander being more inclined to take advantage of the swiftness of his fly boat than the metal of his guns. The French were rarely traders, for even their plantations were largely supported by buccaneering. When, after a peace, some of the rovers settled down for a time, they were always ready to abandon their fields at the first rumour of a war. England thus stood between the two others as a stumbling-block; she interfered with the trade of the one and offended the dignity of the other; thus coming in for many blows, which only made her all the more able to resist and conquer.

The character of the Dutchman is well shown in the curious difficulty which hastened a third breach of the peace with England in 1672. In 1667 a fleet from the Netherlands captured Surinam, and forced the authorities of the colony to capitulate on favourable terms. By these articles the inhabitants were at liberty to sell or transport, when or where they pleased, all or any part of their possessions. After the peace, a few went to Barbados, but the majority found it difficult to dispose of their plantations, and therefore remained in hopes of a better market on the arrival of new Dutch settlers. At that time the Dutchmen were few and mostly poor; they had been ruined by the war, and in many cases driven from their settlements by the English. It followed, therefore, that there were no buyers, and the plantation owners, trusting to the capitulation, decided to wait rather than abandon their flourishing properties.

In June, 1669, the Dutch Governor issued a proclamation calling upon all the English who intended to leave to give notice within six months, after which a like term was given them to dispose of their goods, when they might leave for English colonies under free passes from the authorities of both nations. In case they were unable to sell their slaves, the Governor would take them over at the market price, but only those negroes who had been in their possession at the rendition of the colony could come under this arrangement.

At first sight this looked very fair, but the English saw at once that something was wrong. In the first place they understood that under the capitulation they were free to take away all their property, including slaves, and at the then market prices they saw that a forced sale would be a serious loss. Although not expressly intimated, they also understood that the Governor meant they were not to carry them away, and this at once caused much dissatisfaction. Things were, however, in such a critical state that little notice was taken of the proclamation ; in fact, the people had not as yet made up their minds what to do. Such a sacrifice as was required from those who had flourishing properties, naturally made them hesitate ; and when the English Government inquired about the matter, they were told by the Dutch authorities that the people were so well satisfied that they intended to remain.

Such was, however, not the case, and when the year of grace had expired, and they were virtually prevented from leaving with or without their negroes, they sent memorials to King Charles the Second asking for his interference. It was another case of Egyptian bondage; the Dutch would not let the people go—except a few of the poorest. It can easily be understood that it was not very pleasant to lose the best colonists and have nothing left but a lot of abandoned plantations. This would have been a poor exchange for New York, and it is evident that the Dutch knew very well what they were doing, and had the welfare of Surinam at heart. But, in face of the capitulation, they were undoubtedly wrong, and when they began to oppress the English for claiming their rights, they went a great deal too far.

When Major Bannister, who had been acting Governor under the English, protested against this, he was arrested and transported to Holland, where he obtained his release only by the intervention of the English ambassador. Then complaints were made to the Dutch Government, but it was two years before permission was granted for commissioners from England to go out and transport those who wanted to leave. Even then secret orders were sent to put every possible obstruction in their way, which was done by bringing suits for debt, and otherwise putting the English in positions which made it impossible for them to wind up their affairs. It followed, therefore, that only a few more went away, carrying with them the prayers of the more important to be delivered from such bondage.

Matters now came to a crisis. Other questions had arisen between the two powers, notably some in connection with the Eastern trade, and the refusal of Holland to honour the English flag. War broke out in 1672, and this time the French joined England against the Dutch, who had to stand alone. French and English buccaneers were let loose to plunder the colonies, and they made the seas so dangerous that hardly one of the enemy's vessels could show herself in the West Indies. The Dutch colonies were thus cut off, and even the settlements of Essequebo and Berbice had to go without their usual supplies. This deprivation caused much dissatisfaction among the garrison of the latter colony, and led to a mutiny, which resulted in the incarceration of the Governor, who was not released until next year, when the belated supplies arrived.

Spain was also involved in the war the following year, and thus all the nations interested in the West Indies were fighting at once—Holland and Spain against France and England. The French buccaneers had already gained a footing on Hispaniola ; now they attempted to get possession of the whole island, but could not succeed. However, they went on to Trinidad, which had always been a Spanish island, and plundered it of a hundred thousand dollars.

The Spanish and Dutch colonies suffered greatly, but Englishmen by no means escaped altogether.

As an example of their treatment by the enemy, the case of John Darbey is interesting. In April, 1674, he and six others were taken by a Dutchman from a small English vessel, while sailing from St. Thomas to Antigua, and carried to Havana. There they were kept in irons for five weeks, and then set to work as slaves on the fortifications. After enduring great misery for three months, they were removed to work on board a ship, which was captured by the French off St. Domingo, when they were of course released, and finally carried to Jamaica. Here they told of the sufferings they had endured and witnessed —the story of which more and more embittered the English feeling against Spain. On one occasion Darbey had seen eight men brought in from a New England bark, who afterwards attempted to escape. They marched along the shore hoping to attract the notice of some friendly vessel, but the Governor sent a party of soldiers in pursuit, and they were all murdered at once save the master, who was brought back, executed, and his head stuck on a pole. He also saw the commander of a man-of-war bring in a New England vessel and hang five men at the yard-arm, where the corpses were used as targets by him and his officers. The same captain wanted himself and several other Englishmen to sail with them, but because they indignantly refused, he deliberately stabbed one of them with his sword, killing him at once.

In February, 1674, a treaty was signed at Westminster in which there was a special clause bearing on the English in Surinam. To the intent that there might be no more mistakes, the States General agreed that the articles of capitulation should not only be executed without any more prevarication, but also that His Majesty of Great Britain should be free to depute commissioners to examine into the condition of his subjects and agree with them as to the time of their departure. Also that no special laws should be made to hamper them in any way in the sale of their lands, payments of their debts, or barter of their goods, and that vessels should be as free to go to Surinam, as they and their servants should also be free to depart.

Accordingly, in March, 1675, three commissioners were instructed to proceed there, and were enjoined to see that the provisions of the treaty were properly carried out, to press for debts owing to the English, and to endeavour to get over the difficulty of their obligations to the Dutch. Vessels were provided to carry the settlers wherever they wished, and provision made for victualling them on the voyage, as well as for a short time after their landing in their new homes.

Now at last it might be presumed that the exodus could be freely managed ; yet even then the Dutch authorities tried to put obstructions in the way. Among the servants of the English were many Indians, some of whom were nominally free, and these the Dutch Governor demanded should be put ashore, to prevent the mischiefs and cruelties of the heathen, their friends, who might avenge themselves for the deportation on those who remained in the colony. The English claimed that these people went of their own free will, and that some of them were much attached to their white masters, which was probably true. Besides these, most of whom were got off against the Governor's protests, there were ten Jews with 322 slaves, in preventing the departure of whom he was more successful. They were not, strictly speaking, British subjects, although they had lived under the flag for many years, and the commissioners did not insist on their admission.

Finally, three vessels sailed away for Jamaica in September, 1675, carrying 1,231 people, including thirty-one Indians, and more negroes than whites. On arriving at that island-they were granted lands in St. Elizabeth, afterwards known as Surinam quarters, and thus Guiana again became a factor in the development of the English islands. As for the Jews, even they were afterwards allowed to depart when they memorialised the king and got him to press the matter.

Even yet, however, the last had not been heard of this detention, for it cropped up again in the case of Jeronomy Clifford, one of those who actually left with the others for Jamaica. He was then a lad, and went off with his father, returning again to the colony as the second husband of an Englishwoman who had property there. It appears that, as surgeon of a Dutch vessel, he was so kind to a dying planter named Charles Maasman, that his widow went to London and married him in August, 1683.

Not getting on very well in Surinam, Clifford and his wife resolved to sell out and take their slaves with them to Jamaica, but in this they were frustrated.

The Dutch felt very sore about the former migration, especially when Jamaica plumed herself on her great acquisition, and taunted them with the fact that they got little by the transfer of the colony. When, therefore, Clifford made known his intention, the Governor told him he could not remove his wife's property because she had inherited it from a Dutch subject. Clifford had some of that doggedness which has been observed so often in Englishmen, and was determined to obtain what he considered his rights. Under the capitulation he might leave at any time, and he did not consider that this right had been in any way forfeited.

However, the Dutch Governor said otherwise, and, to prevent the alienation or removal of his property, put it in trust, and then endeavoured to set his wife against him so that she might refuse to leave. By some tittle-tattle about a female cousin of Clifford, her jealousy was aroused, and she petitioned for a divorce on the grounds of cruelty and adultery. However, when she found out the object of the traducers of her husband, she asked that her petition be annulled and made void, because she had been misled and drawn away by the ill advices of others— now she was sorry, and well satisfied and content with him. This having been read before the Court of Justice, a council of Dutch planters, they showed their animus by deciding that Mrs. Clifford was a weak and silly woman, and that it appeared to them that her husband, to the prejudice of his wife and that land, had endeavoured to remove his goods, which they would willingly prevent. They therefore

ordered the plantation to be appraised and put in
commission, forbidding either Clifford or his wife
from diminishing, removing, or making away with
the estate, but only to enjoy the interest and produce as long as they lived and corresponded well
with each other. They also wished the wife much
joy of her reconciliation, and condemned her to pay
the costs both present and future. Finally, considering her frowardness and ill-nature, and for an
example to all other like-natured women, they condemned her to pay a fine of five thousand pounds of
sugar.

Clifford, who yet stood by what he considered his
right, was now subjected to a number of petty perse-
cutions. His wife went to England, leaving him her
attorney, and he began to pester the Governor to
remove the illegal arrest on his estate. At last this
importunity led to his arrest, and he was sentenced
by this same Court of Justice to be hanged, as a
mutineer and disturber of the public peace. But,
being " more inclined to clemency than to carry things
to the utmost rigour of justice," they commuted this
sentence to imprisonment for seven years, with a fine
of a hundred and fifty thousand pounds of sugar.

As may be supposed, this arbitrary judgment only
made Clifford more exasperated. He still went on
petitioning and protesting that he was not a Dutch
subject, as he had refused to take the oath of allegiance, and that therefore he was only standing up for
his rights. However, he was imprisoned in the fort,
where every effort was made to prevent his communicating with England or the English colonies. Not-

withstanding these precautions he managed to send several letters, meanwhile threatening the Court that if they kept him any longer he would be forced to use such means of relief as he should be advised. After some delay his communications reached Barbados, Jamaica, and New York, from whence they at last reached King William, who soon got him released. But even then Clifford could not get back his estate, and although he went to London and petitioned the king, who directed inquiry of the ambassador at the Hague, he could never get any redress. For seventy years he, and his heirs after his death, kept up a stream of petitions and memorials, without result, in the end claiming for illegal detention, damages, and interest, over half a million pounds.

During the short peace which followed the treaty of Westminster attention was again directed to the buccaneers, who were now called pirates, and treated as such even in Jamaica, with the result that many of them settled down. It has been stated that Charles the Second shared in their gains even after he had issued proclamations against them, but this sort of thing now came to an end. The French continued their depredations up to the year 1680, when the king issued a proclamation, forbidding the further granting of commissions, and recalling those which had been issued, at the same time ordering that those who persisted in the trade should be hanged as pirates. This tended to bring the less-audacious to settle down, but even to the beginning of the present century piracy was still known in the West Indies.

While Sir Henry Morgan was Acting Governor of Jamaica, in 1781, Everson, the Dutch pirate, came to Cow Bay on that island, but Morgan captured him and his crew and sent them off to Carthagena, to be punished by the authorities there for the ravages they had committed on the Spanish coasts and shipping. During the ex-buccaneer's administration he also got an Act passed to restrain privateers, and keep inviolable all treaties with foreign states. Any British subject who treated a foreign prince or State in a hostile manner should be punished with death as a felon.

Peace did not last long, however, for in 1688 the French began to move against Holland, and the year following King William was also bound to declare war. Almost immediately the English were again driven out of St. Kitt's, the French, as on the former occasion, committing outrages quite unjustifiable among civilised nations even in war. They also took St. Eustatius from the Dutch.

As if there were not enough pirates in the West Indies, the French brought some more from their own coast—the celebrated corsairs, who had held a position in Europe during the wars similar to that of the buccaneers in America. Some rovers, who had lately settled in Cayenne, were agreeably surprised at the beginning of the year 1689 by the arrival of Du Casse, who soon enrolled them under his banner and started to pillage the Dutch and English colonies.

The first attack was made upon Surinam with nine vessels, but after three days' fighting the Dutch obliged the corsairs to retire, leaving one ship aground to be captured. Two of the squadron were, however, more successful in Berbice, which, after the enemy had destroyed one or two plantations, was obliged to pay a ransom of twenty thousand guilders (£1,666), which was settled by a draft on the proprietors in Amsterdam, and which curiously enough appears to have been afterwards paid. Another privateer destroyed the small settlement in the Pomeroon river, and obliged the few inhabitants to fly to Essequebo, and to afterwards abandon the place altogether. Du Casse then went on to the islands, where he did much damage to both Dutch and English, finally, in 1697, Spain being also on the other side, joining De Pointis to attack and capture Carthagena.

The corsairs were privateers with proper commissions, authorised by the French Government to pillage and destroy and divide the plunder among themselves after setting aside the king's share. Up to the present France could hardly be said to have a navy, and these private adventurers to some extent filled its place. True, there were a few king's ships, but the treasury was often so bare that they could not be properly armed or manned without assistance from outside. Then, perhaps, one or more would be put at the disposal of a renowned corsair, on condition that the State should be put to no expense. Courtiers, ministers, and merchants would come forward and form a joint stock company, equip the ship or fleet as the case might be, and share the plunder.

Du Casse settled down as Governor of the French part of Hispaniola, which by this time had been

taken over, and he appears to have encouraged the
buccaneers on account of their assistance to the
colony. When that great corsair, Jacques Cassard
came out, he was therefore enabled to supply him
with as much help as he required.

Cassard, in 1712, was supplied by the merchants of
Marseilles with a large fleet, with which he sailed to
the West Indies, beginning, as Du Casse had done,
with Surinam, where he arrived on the 8th of October,
with eight large and thirty small vessels. The Dutch
were not so fortunate this time, for he sailed up and
down the river for three weeks, burning, pillaging,
and carrying off slaves, until most of the inhabitants
took to the bush. Among other exploits he is said
to have broken open the Jewish synagogue, killed a
pig within the sacred precincts, and sprinkled its
blood over the walls and ornaments. He was ultimately bought off for over £50,000, which, in the
absence of enough coin, was paid in sugar, negro and
Indian slaves, cattle, merchandise, provisions, stores,
jewellery, and a very little cash.

While remaining in Surinam Cassard sent three
vessels to Berbice, which was easily captured, and for
which a ransom of three hundred thousand guilders
(£25,000) was demanded. But this settlement was
far worse off than Surinam, and had neither goods
nor money to pay such a large amount, which was
out of all proportion to that of her neighbour. After
raising 118,000 guilders in various ways, the balance
was accepted in a bill of exchange on the proprietors,
two of the leading planters of the colony being taken
as hostages and security. Not satisfied with this, the

corsairs insisted on a further sum of ten thousand guilders in cash, as ransom for the private estates, on the ground that they had been paid only for the fort and properties of the Government. There was not so much money in the whole river, and after collecting every bit of plate and jewellery they possessed, to the value of six thousand guilders, the enemy had to take the balance in sugar and stores.

Now came the most curious part of this transaction. The two hostages died, and the proprietors refused to pay the draft—in fact, they said Berbice was not worth so much. Nevertheless the colony could not be taken over as a French possession, and even when the peace of Utrecht was signed in 1713, nothing could be done. Here was an anomaly—a Dutch settlement in the hands of French merchants as security for a debt. On account of trade restrictions its produce might not be brought to France, and the owners of the draft neither knew what to do with the document nor its security. The Dutch proprietors were equally at a loss, for they knew very well that, if they ignored the claim of the corsairs, revenge would be taken on the first opportunity—during the next war, if not before. At last one of the Marseilles merchants was deputed to go to Amsterdam, and after a great deal of haggling he sold the draft to a third party at a reduction of about forty per cent.

Meanwhile Cassard had captured St. Eustatius, and exacted a large ransom. From thence he resolved to proceed to Curaçao, the great stronghold of the Dutch, and the depôt for goods used in the contraband traffic with the Spanish colonies. Here there were many Jews, who had large stocks of merchandise, and as the booty would be certainly great, Cassard resolved to risk everything on such an exploit. On his arrival he sent a boat ashore with a demand for the surrender of the island, to which the Governor sent a jeering reply, as he considered the place impregnable. However, the corsair fleet stood in for the harbour, but were greeted with such a heavy fire that Cassard was forced to retire and call a council. The balance of opinion was against going any farther. The officers said the Dutch guns were of heavier metal than theirs, the currents round the island rendered a landing almost impossible, and the entrance to the harbour was so narrow that it could easily be commanded by the two forts. However, Cassard himself and a few others were in favour of the attempt, and it was ultimately resolved to carry it out on the morrow.

To deceive the Dutch, Cassard sent part of his fleet on a cruise round the island, while he with the remainder commenced to bombard the forts, keeping this up during the day as if that were his line of attack. The following night, however, he embarked most of his men in small craft, and keeping the lights on his ships burning, managed to land under cover of the darkness. Fortunately for him, this manœuvre was not perceived by the Dutch, for he had quite enough to do in contending with a strong current and in avoiding sunken rocks, which made the landing so perilous that it is doubtful if even these hardy fellows would have attempted it during the day, when the dangers would be conspicuous. However, they got ashore without serious accident, and at once erected a breastwork for the light guns they had brought.

Morning broke, and Cassard expected to see the second half of the squadron returned from its cruise, and ready to support him, instead of which it was visible several miles to leeward. To add to his difficulties, the Dutch had discovered the landing, had erected a powerful battery a mile away, and were preparing to attack him before his reinforcements could come up. Yet in face of all this he was undaunted. He must, however, attack at once, and this was done, with the result that the forts were taken. Cassard was wounded by a musket ball in the foot, yet he did not relinquish the command, but followed this first success by turning the guns of the forts on the town. At the same time he sent a flag of truce to the Governor, declaring, that if the place were not at once surrendered at discretion he would bombard it. In reply, the Dutch attacked the forts, but were repulsed with great loss, and at last terms were discussed, with the result that the ransom was fixed at 600,000 louis d'ors. This amount was considered so reasonable that the merchants hastened to pay it over and get rid of him, which they did in three days.

On his arrival in Martinique, Cassard found he had been superseded in the command, and that the fleet was ordered home. Giving the buccaneers their share of the booty, he sailed for Brest, and on the way met an English squadron. The French admiral signalled his vessels not to fight, but Cassard, turning to his second in command of the vessel, said his duty to his king was above that to his admiral—he would fight His Majesty's foes wherever he met them. On that he bore down upon the English and captured two small craft before nightfall, afterwards making his voyage to Brest alone.

This want of subordination so incensed the admiral that he preferred several charges against him, one being that he had retained more than his share of the booty. Whether this charge was true or not, the "Hero of Nantes," as he was called, fell into disgrace, followed by great poverty. Almost a beggar, he was at last sent to prison for importuning a cardinal and king's minister too much, by claiming what he considered his rights. There he ultimately died, and, like some others who have been as badly treated in life, has now a statue erected to his memory in his native town.

IX.

THE STRUGGLE FOR THE DARIEN TRADE.

CARTHAGENA and Porto Bello were the great trading stations for the Spaniards in the Indies. The latter had taken the place of Nombre de Dios, since that town had been destroyed by Drake, and was now the port to which the treasures of Peru were brought overland from Panama. The galleons from Spain, after calling at St. Domingo, went on to Carthagena, where the first great fair of the year was held. Here the traders from the inland provinces of New Granada came to get their supplies from Europe, which they paid for in gold, silver, emeralds, and produce. For the short time the vessels remained, the people of the town woke up from their year's inactivity, and made the most of the occasion. Stores were in demand, and lodging-houses required for the visitors, so that the cost of living went up by leaps and bounds. Those who had slaves got enormous profits by their hire, and even the negroes themselves made large sums beyond the amounts they had to pay their masters. The whole place lost its air of desertion and became the scene of such bustle and confusion as would hardly be conceivable to those who saw it as a " sleepy hollow " during the *tiempo muerto*, the dead time, as it was called.

Having done with Carthagena, the galleons went on to Porto Bello, the beautiful haven, said to have been the most unhealthy place on the Main. By reason of its noxious air and barren soil there was a scarcity of provisions, which led to its desertion at ordinary times. In anticipation of the fleet, however, it woke up and became even more lively than Carthagena. The only reason for its existence was the trade across the isthmus, otherwise it would have been deservedly abandoned. Here was held the great fair, that at the other port being petty in comparison. The concourse of people was so great that a single chamber for a lodging during the busy time sometimes cost a thousand crowns, while a house would be worth five or six times as much. As the galleons came in sight, the people began to erect a great tent in the *Plaza* to receive their cargoes, where they were assorted and delivered to the various consignees or their representatives. The crowd of men and animals soon became so great that movement was difficult. Droves of mules came over the isthmus loaded with cases of gold and silver, which were dumped down in the open streets or in the square, for want of storehouses. Yet, with all the confusion, it is said that theft was unknown, and losses through mistakes very rare. But not only were there thousands of mules and their drivers, but small vessels continually arrived from different parts of the coast, bringing goods and people, to increase the hubbub. Here was a cargo of cinchona bark, there another of cacao, and further on, by no means the least important, were boat-loads of fresh vegetables and fruits to supply the great assembly. This went on for forty days, after which the port was deserted and the town resumed its poverty-stricken air. Then two persons in the streets formed a crowd and half a dozen a mob. Solitude and silence reigned, where so lately the bustle and noise had been rampant, and the *tiempo muerto* ruled until the following year.

It can be easily understood that the influence of the Porto Bello fair was not only felt on the Gulf side, but on the shores of the Pacific as well. Panama was largely dependent on the transport business, which employed a great number of mules and slaves. Even in the absence of buccaneers and pirates the road was always difficult, and sometimes even dangerous. Heavy rains caused great floods, which delayed the traffic for days, and left the tracks on the hills so slippery that even that sure-footed animal the mule was often carried over a precipice. Then there were cannibal Indians and Simarons always lurking in the forest, ready to cut off stragglers. On the rumour of a buccaneer landing on the coast—it might be a hundred miles away— the traffic was at once stopped and the merchants began to "fear and sweat with a cold sweat," as Thomas Gage very quaintly puts it.

The Spanish merchants no doubt deplored this state of things, and would have been thankful for a good road instead of such an unutterably worthless bridle track. There was, however, a side to the question which probably influenced them—a way that would be easy for them would also be more accessible to their enemies. Then, again, a good road should have been the work of the Spanish Government rather than of the settlers, but it was useless to expect anything from that direction. Nevertheless, a good road and even a canal were mooted before the end of the sixteenth century, thus anticipating the Panama railroad and canal of our own time. But, although the advantages were patent, the difficulties were so many as to be practically insurmountable, and nothing whatever was done.

Towards the end of the seventeenth century came a sudden craze for carrying out gigantic schemes of various kinds, practicable or impracticable, useful or worthless, utopian or utterly absurd. Among them was the Mississippi scheme in France and the South Sea Bubble in England, of which the latter was intimately connected with the Indies. The time had arrived when people began to think of trading on credit or pledges, and of combining together for carrying on banks and other commercial operations. Private banks had existed for several centuries, and more or less public establishments in the great commercial centres, such as Venice, Amsterdam, and Hamburg, but up to the present there was no Bank of England. In fact the great principle that allows an enormous trade to be carried on without the actual interchange of specie or commodities had just been discovered, and the people of France and England went mad over it.

The pioneer of the system in England was William Paterson, who seems to have been acquainted with Dampier and Wafer, both of whom knew the isthmus of Darien very well.   He is also said to have travelled in the West Indies himself, and even to have visited the Porto Bello fair, but this is not quite certain.

Paterson first came into prominence by bringing forward a scheme which ultimately led to the establishment of the Bank of England on the 27th of July, 1694.   From this he appears to have derived no actual benefit, however, although he was one of the first directors, upon a qualification of £2,000 stock, which he sold out after the first year, and thus withdrew.   Probably he wanted his money to carry out the new project for a settlement on the isthmus of Darien.

In the course of this history we have advisedly used the word " English " instead of " British," in speaking of our nation, because as yet Scotchmen were little concerned in colonisation schemes.   In fact, except as transported rebels or convicts, they had hardly any interest in the plantations.   This was the result of Navigation Acts, which debarred Scotch merchants and vessels from trading, by ordering that all traffic with the colonies should be carried on in English vessels and from English ports.

Paterson's idea was to take possession of the isthmus of Darien, establish a Scotch colony at a convenient harbour on the Gulf side, and then open up a proper road by which the trade would be so much facilitated that it would become the great highway. Seated between the two vast oceans of the universe, he said, the isthmus is provided with excellent harbours on both sides, between the principal of which lie the more easy and convenient passes. If these ports and passes were fortified, the road could easily be secured and defended, thus affording the readiest and nearest means of gaining and keeping the command of the South Sea—the greatest and by far the richest side of the world. With the passes open, through them would flow at least two-thirds of the produce of both Indies. The time and expense of the voyage to China and Japan would be lessened more than half, and the consumption of European commodities soon doubled, and annually increased.

He contended that Darien possessed great tracts of country up to that time unclaimed by any European, and that the Indians, the original proprietors, would welcome the honest and honourable settler to their fertile shore. The soil was rich to a fault, producing spontaneously the most delicious fruits, and required the hand of labour to chasten rather than stimulate its capabilities. There crystal rivers sparkled over sands of gold—there the traveller might wander for days under a canopy of fruit-laden branches, the trees bearing them being of inestimable value as timber. The waters also abounded in wealth. Innumerable shoals of fish disported themselves among the rocks, and the bottom was strewn with pearls. From the dawn of creation this enchanted country had lain secluded from mortals—now it was revealed and opened to Scottish enterprise. Let them enter and take possession of this promised land, and build a new city—a new Edinburgh, like Alexandria of old, which grew to prodigious wealth and power from its position on another isthmus—to soon become famous as the new emporium of a new world.

The reader who has seen our account of Lionel Wafer's miserable journey will be able to discount these florid statements, but the Scotch people seem to have taken everything for gospel. Now, at last, they would have a colony—a plantation of more value than any of those that the English had begun to boast of. They were enthusiastic, and although poor, did their very best to contribute, actually promising the large sum of £400,000. England also subscribed to the extent of £300,000, and Holland and Hamburg £200,000. Everything looked bright, and at last a concession was obtained for the "Company of Scotland, trading to Africa and the Indies."

Strange to say, Paterson entirely ignored the claims of Spain, although he must have known that she would strenuously object to such a settlement. It was all very well to say the place belonged to the Indians, but the very fact of its vicinity to the great trading centre and channel of communication with the Pacific coast should have made him anticipate trouble. Even if he argued that the buccaneers were practically unmolested along the Mosquito shore, he must also have known that their position was by no means secure, and even had this been the case, that it would have afforded to argument in favour of his project.

To be successful he must also have had the support of the English Government, but unfortunately this was denied. Jealousy and envy between the two countries led to representations adverse to the scheme being made to King William, with the result that the Company was discountenanced, and that most of the promised subscriptions outside of Scotland were withdrawn. Then came dissensions among the leaders themselves, and this lost them half the amount from their own county. Yet with all that Paterson was undaunted, and, notwithstanding the diminished funds at command, he still resolved to go on.

On the 26th of July, 1698, twelve hundred men in five ships sailed for a place near the entrance of the Gulf of Darien, a hundred miles to the east of Porto Bello. It was afterwards stated that the vessels were rotten and ill-found, although gaily decked with flags on the day of departure, which hid some of their deficiencies. The provision supply was bad, and, to crown all, the captains were coarse, brutal, and ignorant, continually quarrelling with each other. Through envy, Paterson had been prevented from having any voice in the arrangements, and although he went with the expedition, he entered the ship as ignorant of her equipment as any other passenger. But he evidently had his doubts, for he asked for an inspection of the stores, only to have his request treated with contempt.

On the 27th of October the fleet came to anchor in a fair sandy bay three leagues west of the Gulf of Darien, now known as the Port D'Escocés. It was an excellent harbour surrounded by high mountains, and capable of holding a thousand sail in security from wind and tempest. The settlers named the district Caledonia, and considered it to be fertile and even healthy. They commenced at once to erect a fort, to which they gave the name of St. Andrews, and a cluster of houses for the town of New Edinburgh. These labours gave them little time for planting, and it naturally followed that they had to live on the provisions brought from Scotland, which, bad at the beginning, were now almost worthless. Paterson sent emissaries to the neighbouring Spanish settlements to ask for their friendship, and went himself into the interior to arrange treaties with the Indians, so that the Scotch might have a good title to the land. In this latter object he was successful, and it was agreed that peace should be kept between the natives and the colonists, "as long as rivers ran and gold was found in Darien."

After six days' absence he returned to find a great change in the settlement. A spirit of mutiny and discontent had broken out, those who worked hard being naturally dissatisfied with others who did nothing. Then the provisions became rotten, and even then were so reduced in quantity that the people suffered from want and its consequent sickness. Four months passed, and nothing but daily discouragements were encountered ; not even a little gold to enliven their spirits. Hard work under a tropical sun began to tell upon them, and although the friendly natives brought a little game, it was almost useless among so many. Every day, however, the number was reduced by death, fevers, and dysentery playing sad havoc, until those who remained were utterly dispirited.

To add to their troubles they were refused supplies from Jamaica, King William having sent instructions to the Colonial Governors to discountenance the colony in every way. Paterson sent to Jamaica to get food for the starving people, and instead, his empty vessel brought copies of the Proclamation that had been issued in that island. This stated that as His Majesty knew nothing of the intentions and designs of the Scots at Darien, and as their settling on the isthmus was contrary to the peace of Spain, every one was commanded not to hold any communication with them, and not to supply arms, ammunition, provisions, or anything whatsoever, on their peril.

In this desperate condition they awaited supplies from Scotland, but these did not arrive, for the ship had foundered on her way, and even Paterson began to be discouraged when day after day passed without relief. Even the reduced number could no longer exist, and with heavy hearts they prepared to leave. They had a ship, but no provisions for the voyage, and on account of the prohibition were prevented from victualling at one of the islands. At last, however, they got together as much barbecued fish and game as the Indians could procure, with a few fruits, and sailed away. But even now fate was against them. Hardly had they got out of the harbour before they were becalmed off this deadly shore for many days, their scanty supply of food diminishing when it was so much wanted for the long voyage. However, the remnant of about thirty, survivors of the twelve hundred, at last arrived at Charlestown, Carolina, in a most miserable condition. Paterson was himself so worn out that he lost his senses for a time, becoming quite childish, yet he recovered, to go back to Scotland and ask the Company for another expedition.

This he urged on the ground that the first had failed simply through the want of supplies and the action of the English Government. Some were in favour of still carrying out the project, and these drew up a petition to the king, giving it for presentation to Lord Hamilton. William the Third, however, refused not only to receive the petition, but even to grant an audience to its bearer. Lord Hamilton would not be put off, however, but watched for his opportunity, and found it one day as the king was mounting his horse. He laid the petition on the saddle, which made His Majesty cry out, "Now, by heaven, this young man is too bold," adding in a softer tone, "if a man can be too bold in the service of his country." With that he threw the document from him and rode off, afterwards, when memorial after memorial came from Scotland, issuing a Proclamation against the worry of such petitions.

Notwithstanding this refusal, another expedition was sent out, the management of which was as bad as that of the first. But this time the Spaniards were on the alert, and hardly had the settlers begun to put things in order before the enemy was upon them in force. Famine and sickness again fell upon New Edinburgh, added to the horrors of a siege, which ultimately led to a capitulation on fair terms. But so weak were they as the Spaniards allowed them to embark, that their late enemies out of pity helped to heave their anchors and set their sails.

It was long before the Scotch people forgot or forgave their sister kingdom for her action in thus frustrating their darling project. Besides impeding the Union, it is said to have strengthened the Jacobite feelings in the rebellions of 1715 and 1745. Even as late as the year 1788, when it was proposed to erect a monument in Edinburgh to King William the Third and the "glorious revolution," the affair was remembered, and some one suggested that the pedestal should have on the one side a view of Glencoe, and on the other the Darien colony. Queen Anne, in 1702, tried to pacify her Scotch subjects by an autograph letter, stating that she regretted the Company's losses and disappointments, but this did not kill the ill-feeling. As for Paterson, in 1715 the English House of Commons voted him the sum of £18,241 as some indemnity for his losses, but as the bill was thrown out by the House of Lords, he got nothing.

Thus ended one of the most disastrous of British attempts to colonise the Indies. From beginning to end it was an example of the Dutch caution of William of Orange, as contrasted with the recklessness of Queen Elizabeth's time or the sturdy defiance of Cromwell. The king was not prepared to risk war for an idea, yet at the same time he would not prohibit the expeditions.

From 1702 to 1713 there was war between England and Holland on the one side, and France and Spain on the other. By the treaty of Utrecht, which again brought peace, the English received the concession for the exclusive supply of negro slaves to the Spanish colonies for thirty years. This *Assiento* contract was given to the Great South Sea Company, which resulted from one of those joint-stock manias, now epidemic in France, England, and even Holland.

The Company was projected by the Earl of Oxford in 1711, and, like the Mississippi scheme in France, was intended to assist the Government, which was virtually bankrupt. As yet there was no funded national debt, but large sums were owing to the army and navy, which had been provisionally settled by debentures, that could be discounted only at a serious loss' to the owners. Down to the establishment of the Bank of England in 1693 no public loan existed, but this was commenced by borrowing the capital of that institution. At the peace of Ryswick, in 1697, the public debt amounted to twenty millions, but by the time the South Sea Company was started the arrears of pay made it half as much again. Part of the great scheme was to advance this amount on security of English customs duties amounting to £600,000 per annum, and a monopoly of the Spanish trade in the Indies as far as the *Assiento* contract would permit.

Whether the whole affair was a fraud from the commencement is doubtful ; there were certainly misrepresentations in the prospectus, either wilful or possibly in good faith. Spain was to allow free trade to England in four ports on the Pacific, and three vessels besides slavers were to go to the isthmus

MAP OF TERRA FIRMA.

(From Gottfried's "Reisen.")

every year—concessions never promised nor intended by Philip the Fifth. The slave trade was a fact, and according to the statements it would give fabulous profits.

Visions of boundless wealth now floated before the eyes of the English people, and they at once began to rival the French in their madness, as they had in their colonisation. The English Government was ready to make every possible concession because it wanted to be rid of the incubus of thirty millions, and therefore did nothing to check the Company. As the stock was issued it was at once bought up, and then sold again at a considerable advance. Everybody expected to make fortunes, therefore they must get shares at any price. Rumours of peace with Spain, and great concessions that would bring all the riches of Peru and Mexico into their coffers, roused them still more. Gold would soon be as plentiful as copper, and silver as iron. The shareholders would be the richest people the world ever saw, and every share would give dividends of hundreds per cent. per annum. The bill making the Government concessions was passed in April, 1720, when the stock was quoted at £310 for a hundred pound share. Strange to say, it then began to fall, but the projectors put forth a rumour that England was about to exchange Gibraltar for a port in Peru, and confidence was restored at once. So great was the increased demand that another million was issued at £300 per £100 share, and these were so much run after that the fortunate owners were at once offered double what they had paid. Then another million was offered at £400, and in a few hours applications were received for a million and a half.

People were so eager to invest their money that they swallowed almost any bait thrown to them. Hundreds of bubble companies hovered on the outskirts of the parent, among them one for settling the barren islands of Blanco and Sal Tortugas, another to colonise Santa Cruz, and a third to fit out vessels for the suppression of piracy. But perhaps the most absurd was "a company for carrying on an undertaking of great advantage, but nobody to know what it is."

Near their highest point the South Sea Shares were sold at £890, but so many wanted to sell at that price that they soon fell to £640. This put the directors again upon their mettle, and they set to work with fresh rumours and pushed them up to £1,000, from which they suddenly went down, with a few fluctuations, until utterly worthless. The treasurer of the Company ran away to France when the blow fell, but the directors were arrested and their estates ultimately confiscated. Thousands of people were ruined, and the public credit received a blow from which it took many years to recover.

Meanwhile the South Sea Company had not been altogether idle. Besides the slave vessels they were entitled to send *one* ship annually to the Carthagena and Porto Bello fairs, this being called the *Navio de permisso.* It was not to be larger than five hundred tons, yet the Company picked out the biggest they could find and filled it with goods, to the exclusion of food and water, which were carried in small store vessels that waited outside the harbour. This caused a great deal of dissatisfaction, as the English brought so much that they could under-sell the Spanish merchants in their own market. In 1715 the *Bedford*, nominally of six hundred tons, was seized at Carthagena on the ground that her burden was excessive. By the Spanish measurements the cargo was said to have amounted to 2,117½ tons, and the excess was confiscated and ordered to be sold. However, the English protested, at the same time passing over some valuable presents to the authorities, with the result that a remeasurement was ordered, which made the amount only 460 tons.

In 1716 the Spaniards took Campeachy and sixty English logwood vessels, which occasioned another war. The English claimed that they had an undoubted right to cut logwood at that place, and that former kings had always maintained them in this. For a long time they had quietly possessed a part of Yucatan, uninhabited by Spaniards, and they claimed not only the privilege of wood-cutting, but of settlement as well. Probably the little notice taken of their attack on the Darien colony made the Spanish authorities think England ready to bear any insult, but they soon found out their mistake. War was declared in 1718, and all the property of the South Sea Company, including debts, was confiscated, the whole amounting to £850,000. This would have been a great blow to the Company had it been genuine, but as we have seen, its mercantile transactions were secondary considerations.

Peace was restored by the Treaty of Madrid in June,

1721, when the *Assiento* contract was renewed in favour of the Royal Company instead of that of the South Sea. So much dissatisfaction had been created by the concession for a trading ship, however, that the English did not insist upon its continuance, and therefore only slave vessels were to be permitted to visit the Indies in future. Everything that had been seized from the South Sea Company was to be restored, or its equivalent value paid, but the amount actually received only came to £200,000, which did not go far to help the unfortunate shareholders.

Thus, this small measure of free trade with the Spanish Indies came to an end, and things went on much the same as before. English, Dutch, and French vessels still carried on the contraband traffic, doing all they could to evade the law, often with the assistance of the local authorities. The Spanish settlers got their supplies so much cheaper in this way than through the usual channels, that they were not likely to give up buying as long as the smugglers ran the risk. At last, however, the authorities received very strict orders to enforce the law, with the result that vessels were often captured, their cargoes confiscated, and crews imprisoned. Then the Spanish *guarda-costas* claimed the right to search vessels of other nationalities, and to confiscate them if they found produce from their colonies on board, or other evidence that they were carrying on illicit trade.

This led to another dispute with England, which claimed compensation for such seizures and the abolition of the right of search. English vessels had always resented this overhauling, and latterly several had fought the *guarda-costas* rather than submit, with the result that, when captured, their crews were treated with a severity often amounting to cruelty. In 1739 several petitions were presented to the British Parliament, complaining of such outrages, and asking the Government to obtain redress. Among them was one from Captain Jenkins, the master of a Scottish vessel, who was examined by the House. His story was that he had been boarded by a *guarda-costa*, the Spaniards from which searched his vessel without finding anything contraband. Apparently enraged at their discomfiture, and possibly annoyed by the jeers of the English, they cut off one of Jenkins' ears and told him to carry it to his king with the message that they would do the same to him if he came near the Main. Finally, according to Jenkins' statement, he was further tortured and threatened with death. "What did you think when you found yourself in the hands of those barbarians?" asked a Member of the House; to which the captain replied, "I recommended my soul to God and my cause to my country." The severed ear he exhibited in Parliament as he had done elsewhere whenever he told the story.

It was then stated that the losses from Spanish depredations by plundering and the taking of fifty-two vessels, since 1728, amounted to £340,000. In every case the masters and crews were brutally treated, and in some cases murdered. The English demand for compensation was met by the reply that the king had ordered inquiries to be made, and that if any of his subjects were found guilty they would be punished according to their deserts; also that orders would be given to conform exactly to the treaties. It was, however, claimed that the treaty of 1667 did not contain any clause bearing on the navigation and commerce of the Indies, and that the English had been wrong in supposing they had a right to sail and trade there; they were only permitted to sail to their own islands and plantations, and were therefore subject to confiscation if they changed their course to make for the Spanish possessions without necessity. There were then in Havana fifteen British vessels which had been detained on one pretext or another, and about the same time the *Success* from London to Virginia was captured off Montserrat, and her captain and crew set adrift in an open boat to find their way ashore as best they could.

In January, 1739, a convention between Great Britain and Spain was arranged, under which the latter agreed to pay £95,000 on account of these demands, less the value of certain vessels which they agreed to restore. This did not satisfy the West India merchants, and they petitioned against it. The indemnity was to be paid on the 10th of July, but that date having passed without a settlement, Great Britain issued letters of marque and ordered all Spanish vessels in her waters to be seized. Spain commenced reprisals the following month, and war was actually declared by Great Britain on the 19th of October. The declaration stated that for several years past unjust seizures and depredations had been carried on, and great **cruelties** exercised.   **The** British **colours** had been ignominiously insulted, against the **laws of** nations and solemn **treaties, and** Spain had lately **ordered** British subjects **from** her dominions within **a shorter period** than had been covenanted by express stipulation in those treaties.

In July previous **a** fleet under Admiral **Vernon had** sailed from Spithead, and **after** a short **cruise off** the Spanish coast, **went** over to the West Indies, arriving at Antigua **the 27th** of September. Going **on to Jamaica, Vernon prepared for** a grand raid on the Spanish settlements, leaving **for** Porto Bello on the **5th of November with six** vessels and 2,500 **men.** They arrived on **the 21st,** and bombarded **the** forts, which **made a stout** resistance ; but while this **was** going **on, the** British landed and took the town, thus compelling the **forts** to capitulate.   Two warships and **several** other vessels were **captured, as well as** specie **to** the amount **of** ten thousand dollars, but **the town was not** pillaged, although **the** guns **were either** taken away **or** rendered useless, and t**he forts as** far as possible demolished. **This was** virtually the **end** of **that** stronghold, **as it** was afterwards allowed to fall into **decay,** to be ultimately replaced by Chagres, **Grey Town,** and **Colon.   Later,** also, **the** treasure **from Peru** had much diminished, and the isthmus sunk in importance, especially **after the way round** Cape Horn and through the Straits **of** Magellan was adopted **more and** more.

As the dispute with **Spain** had arisen **from her** action in the **Indies, so** retaliation **on the part of Great Britain** was greatest **on the Main. In** February,

1740, Vernon again sailed from Jamaica, and on the 6th of March bombarded Santa Martha, but did not capture it. After repairing damages at Porto Bello he went on to Chagres, took a Spanish man-of-war from under the guns of the fort, captured the place, and demolished it. In January, 1741, Sir Chaloner Ogle came out from England with a fleet, and joined him, making a force of 12,000 men in twenty-nine sail-of-the-line besides smaller vessels.

This great fleet sailed for Hispaniola in hopes of encountering that of Spain and France, but not finding it went on to Carthagena. This, the other great stronghold on the Main, was guarded by two powerful batteries, a boom across the entrance to the port, and four Spanish men-of-war just inside. After a long cannonading the batteries were silenced, a landing accomplished at night, and a passage made by which the fleet entered the harbour. Here, however, further progress was checked by sickness and disagreements among the commanders, with the result that the siege was raised and partial success ended in miserable failure. This was followed by another check at Santiago de Cuba, which virtually terminated all hopes of further great exploits, although attempts were made on La Guayra and Puerto Cabello.

Yet with all this the Spaniards undoubtedly received a great lesson. Their men-of-war were captured from under their fortresses, and small English or colonial vessels performed such deeds of daring as had hardly been equalled since the Elizabethan age. The old spirit still existed, although it might lie dormant for a time—the men were there when the hour came. In 1740 Captain Hall in a New England privateer came to an anchor under the fort of Puerto de la Plata, pretending to be a Caracas trader. He wanted to land in the night and surprise the town, but found that the inhabitants kept such a good watch that he had to give up that idea. However, the Governor was sick and sent to ask the loan of Hall's surgeon, and here was the opportunity he wanted. The surgeon, quartermaster, and an interpreter visited the Governor, and at the same time seven of Hall's crew landed and surprised the fort, dismounted the guns, marched into the town and plundered it, finally escaping with the loss of only one man.

Peace was at last concluded on the 7th of October, 1748, but nothing was said in the treaty of the right of search. The *Assiento* contract was confirmed, and one English trading ship allowed as formerly ; free trade with the Indies, however, was still one of those things which could never be conceded.

X.

SLAVE INSURRECTIONS AND BUSH NEGROES.

WITH war almost continuously raging at their very doors the West Indian planters not only risked their fortunes but their lives. During the seventeenth century England spent something like thirty-five years in fighting her enemies, and in the eighteenth, forty-six. As long as the quarrel was with Spain alone the colonists cared but little, but when France turned against them the struggle was much fiercer. The French were always most audacious in their assaults, and the consequences were all the more disastrous because they were such near neighbours. We have already spoken of St. Kitt's and the difficulties produced on that island by its division between the two nationalities. These were only terminated by its entire cession to England, which did not take place until the peace of Utrecht in 1713. Meanwhile, besides the two defeats of the English already mentioned, they were driven out in 1689, to return the following year and expel the enemy, retaining entire control until the peace of Ryswick gave France again her share. Then in

1702 England once more held full possession until the island was assured to her entirely.

Barbados, alone among the British West Indian islands, stands in the proud position of a colony that has never fallen into the hands of another nation. It has never even been seriously attacked beyond the attempt of De Ruyter. And yet the island was poorly fortified, as compared with the great strongholds of the West Indies such as Carthagena and Curaçao. Possibly "the game was not worth the candle," for on the one hand there was little plunder to be had, and on the other a strong force of hardy Englishmen to be encountered. We have seen already how the Parliamentary fleet was kept at bay, and what an amount of trouble the islanders gave before they capitulated. Even then they were not actually conquered, although there could be no question as to the ultimate result.

But not only had the colonists to stand up against the enemy from outside, but there was another danger which lay within their plantations and dwellings from which even Barbados was not free. The slaves had to be kept under subjection, and the planters must always be on the alert to anticipate riots and insurrections. For although the negro in most cases was submissive, at times he recovered that savage nature which had only been suppressed by force and discipline.

When we read of flogging to death and other horrible cruelties of the planters and authorities, we are inclined to sympathise with the African and look upon his masters as worse than brutes.

A REBEL NEGRO.
(From Stedman's "Surinam.")

15

But to appreciate the full significance of these punishments we must judge them by the codes in existence at the time, remembering that nothing was ever done to the blacks that had not also been endured by whites for similar crimes. True, these punishments were retained for slaves after they had become obsolete for Europeans, but then the negro was undoubtedly stubborn and less amenable to persuasion than any other race. Like a mule he had to be broken in and trained, and like that stubborn animal he often gave great trouble in the process. There were differences of opinion as to various ways of teaching the negro, and it was only a long experience that ultimately led to gentle conciliation instead of flogging.

The slaves often ran away, and had to be hunted for and brought back. In the larger islands and on the Main they hid in the forest and swamp, where they formed communities, to which other runaways flocked until they became strong enough to hold their own. From these recesses they often came forth to pillage the plantations, murder the whites, and get the slaves to go off with them in a body. If the buccaneer was ferocious he had at least some method in his madness; the poor ignorant African, on the contrary, let his passions dominate him entirely. In revenge for fancied tyrannies he would commit the most atrocious crimes, torturing his prisoners by cutting them to pieces or even flaying while they still lived.

Is it any wonder that when caught the bush negro or maroon was severely punished, and that the utmost rigour of the law was exercised? As for flogging, every one knows how common that was at the beginning of the present century. Some of us can even look back to a time when the use of the rod and whip on delicate children was a matter of course. Even fine ladies took their little ones to see executions that now horrify us to think of; in a similar way the planter's wife stood at her window to see the punishment of her house-servant.

We could tell of negroes burnt to death, where a downpour of rain put out the fires and left them to linger in torment for hours, of taking pieces of flesh from the unhappy criminals with red-hot pincers, and, most horrible of all, breaking on the wheel. These punishments often took place in the middle of a town, but only on one occasion have we seen any mention of the horror of the scene, and this referred to the smell of burning flesh. Yet the criminals—for it must be remembered that they had been legally convicted and sentenced—showed a stoical indifference to pain almost incredible. As savages they gloried in showing their ability to endure torture, only craving sometimes for a pipe of tobacco to hold between their teeth until it fell.

The maroons or bush negroes began to form communities on the Main and in the larger islands from very early times. In Jamaica they were the remnant of the Spanish slaves who ran away on the arrival of the English, with accessions from deserters at later periods; in Surinam some of those who had been sent into the forest to prevent their capture by French corsairs. In both places they maintained

THE EXECUTION OF BREAKING ON THE RACK.
(From Stedman's "Surinam.")

their independence, and ultimately made treaties with the colonial authorities, greatly to their own advantage. In Essequebo and Demerara they were kept down by subsidising Arawak Indian trackers, who hunted them from savannah to forest, and from forest to swamp, killing and capturing them almost as fast as they ran away. In the smaller and more settled islands the runaways were generally re-captured at once and severely punished as a warning to others. There the more daring plotted insurrections which often caused much trouble for a few days until suppressed. They did not last long, for the negroes were wanting in the power of combination, because they all wanted to be leaders. Then there was generally some faithful slave or white man's mistress to give the warning, which sometimes caused such prompt action that the outbreak did not occur at all. Yet with all that the danger was serious, and one that could hardly be coped with by forts and batteries.

As early as the year 1649 a plot for a general rising in Barbados was discovered through the information of a bond-servant. All the whites were to have been murdered, but fortunately the ringleaders were arrested before the time fixed and eight of them condemned to death. Then in 1676, under the leadership of a Coromantee, it was arranged that on a certain fixed day, at a signal to be given by blowing shells, all the cane-fields should be set on fire, the white men killed, and their women retained by the negroes as their wives. This also was frustrated by information received from a house negress. Hearing two men talking of the matter, she made inquiries, and learnt of the plot in time to inform her master. Six of the prisoners were burnt alive and eleven beheaded, while five committed suicide by hanging themselves before the trial. The story was told in a pamphlet entitled, "Great Newes from the Barbados, or a true and faithful account of the great conspiracy." Yet again in 1693, after a fearful epidemic had much reduced the number of the whites, a third conspiracy was set on foot. The Governor was to have been killed, the magazine seized, and the forts surprised and taken. When the plot was nearly ripe two of the leaders were overheard conversing about it and instantly arrested. They were hung in chains for four days without food or drink, promises of pardon being made if they revealed their accomplices, which they did at the end of that time, with the result that some were executed and others cruelly tortured. We might go on to tell also of the abortive insurrection of 1702 and several others, but as there were never any very serious risings in Barbados, we must proceed to other colonies.

In Jamaica several abortive attempts at general insurrections were made, some of them assisted by the maroons, who continually received accessions to their numbers from desertion. These people also made incursions on their own account, which led the Government to offer £5 a head for every one killed, the reward being payable on the production of his ears. In 1734 they destroyed several plantations and killed a hundred and fifty white men, which led to an attempt at suppressing them altogether. Captain Stoddart therefore took a detachment of soldiers into the mountains to the maroon town of Nanny. Arriving at night he planted a battery of swivel guns on a height that commanded the collection of huts, before the negroes were aware of his coming. They were rudely awakened from their sleep to find the place surrounded, and in alarm many flung themselves over precipices in their hurry to escape. Some were killed, a few captured, and the town utterly destroyed. About the same time a party of maroons from another place were so bold as to attack the barracks at Spanish Town.

Two years later, under Captain Cudjo, the maroons became so formidable that two regiments of regular troops besides the island militia were employed to reduce them. The Assembly also ordered a line of block-houses or posts to be erected as near . as possible to their haunts, at which packs of dogs were to be kept as part of the garrison. Then they sent to the Main for two hundred Mosquito Indians whom they engaged as trackers. This brought matters to a crisis, and Captain Cudjo was compelled to sue for peace, which was granted. A treaty was therefore made with them in 1738 at Trelawny town, by which they were to be considered as free on condition that they captured runaway slaves, assisted in repelling invasions, and allowed two white residents to remain in their towns. Thus peace was restored for a time, and the Mosquito Indians were allowed to go back to their country.

However, Jamaica was not to be free from slave insurrections apart from the maroons, for in May, 1760, at St. Mary's, the slaves of General Forrest's plantation fell suddenly upon the overseer while he was at supper with some friends, and massacred the whole company. They were immediately joined by others, and commenced a career of plundering and burning all the plantations in the neighbourhood. Business in the island was at once suspended, martial law proclaimed, and every white man called out to assist in putting down the revolt. The negroes, however, tried to avoid an open conflict, trusting to hide in the forest, where, however, a large body was discovered and defeated. The maroons had been sent for, but did not arrive until this action had taken place, when they were sent in pursuit of the flying rebels. This they pretended to do, and in a few days returned with a collection of ears which they said had been taken from those whom they had slain, and for which they were paid. The story was found out afterwards to have been a falsehood, as instead of pursuing the fugitives they had simply cut off the ears of those who had been slain before they arrived. This led the authorities to think the maroons in league with the revolted slaves and afterwards to look upon them with distrust. However, by the aid of a body of free negroes, the rebels were at last captured, to be punished in the cruel manner so characteristic of the time. Some were burnt, some hung alive on gibbets, and about six hundred transported to the Bay of Honduras. Two were hung alive on the parade at Kingston, one to linger for seven days and the other for nine, during which time it was said "they behaved with a degree of hardened insolence and brutal insensibility." In the course of the whole insurrection about sixty whites and four hundred negroes were killed, and damage done to the amount of one hundred thousand pounds.

In 1736 a slave revolt took place at Antigua, or rather it was discovered and anticipated. Five negroes were broken on the wheel, six hung in chains and starved to death, one of whom lived for nine days and eight nights, fifty-eight were burnt at the stake, and about a hundred and thirty imprisoned. These horrible punishments were intended as a warning to the others, and no doubt they had such an effect on that generation.

Few of the early insurrections met with any success, notwithstanding that the negroes largely outnumbered the whites in every colony. At the most the blacks had a few days' liberty to murder, burn, and pillage, after which came the terrible retribution. There was, however, one conspicuous exception : poor Berbice was actually taken over, and every white man driven from the plantations.

The Dutch were noted nigger drivers, and although the English were unable to boast much of their humanity, they stigmatised the Hollander as a cruel master. If a negro was obstinate, the Englishman threatened to sell him to a Dutchman or Jew, but the worst threat of all was to give him to a free negro. Whether this bad character was deserved or not is doubtful, but it is quite certain that the criminal law of the Netherlands permitted "the question" when a prisoner would not admit his guilt. This, however, was applicable to white as well as black, there being no particular slave code in the Dutch colonies.

What was the immediate cause of the great rising of 1763, in Berbice, was never exactly ascertained, but vague complaints were made of ill-treatment by certain planters. It commenced on the 27th of February, on an estate in the river Canje, and from thence spread like wildfire over the whole colony. The population consisted of, besides the free Indians, 346 whites, 244 Indian slaves, and about 4,000 negro slaves. The garrison was supposed to consist of sixty soldiers besides officers, distributed at several forts and posts, but owing to sickness only about twenty were fit for duty when the rising took place.

An epidemic of fever and dysentery had prevailed for two years among both whites and slaves, weakening the former in such a manner that they had no courage to contend with the revolted negroes, but mostly ran away to Fort Nassau when they heard of the rising. Almost out of their senses from fright, they urged Governor Hoogenheim to abandon the fort and colony at once. Only one of the councillors stood by the Governor, and it was as much as these two could accomplish to prevent even the soldiers from running away. As for moving against the rebels, this was impossible, for not one of the colonists would follow Councillor Abbinsetts in his attempt to do something. Their fright even affected the officials and soldiers in such a manner that the Governor could hardly escape their importunities to be allowed to leave.

Four vessels lay in the river, two merchant ships and two slavers, but even their crews were sick, and the captain of one so utterly broken down that he could not attend to his duties. The Governor tried to get them to go up the river and do something, but they were almost as frightened as the colonists. Only in one place were the negroes opposed ; a few whites taking refuge in the block-house at Peereboom, some distance above the fort, where their way of escape was cut off. But for want of a little assistance they were compelled to make terms with the negroes. Under the agreement the whites were to be allowed to go down to the fort in their own boats, but as soon as they began to embark the negroes fell upon them, men, women, and children, massacred some and took others prisoners, a few only managing to get across the river.

Among the fugitives was a lad named Jan Abraham Charbon, whose story-gives a graphic picture of the alarm and consternation produced by the insurrection, and of its results on himself.

He was the son of a planter, and the alarm was brought to the estate at night by a faithful slave. The plantations below were all in the hands of the rebels, who were burning and murdering on both sides of the river. The whites from several neighbouring estates gathered together and decided to make a stand at Peereboom, hoping for assistance from Fort Nassau. They got to the block-house early in the morning, to the number of thirty whites, with a body of faithful slaves, who had not yet deserted them, although they did so later.

Soon after their arrival the insurgents surrounded the house and attacked it, the whites making a successful defence until seven o'clock in the evening. Then one of Charbon's slaves came forward and asked if they wanted peace. On receiving a favourable reply the leaders on both sides came to the agreement above-mentioned. Next morning the whites were fired upon as they went to embark, and Charbon was wounded. However, he jumped into the river and swam across, hiding himself in the jungle, where he came upon another fugitive named Mittelholzer.

For eight days the two wandered about the forest, losing their way and almost dying from hunger and thirst. They dared not approach the river for fear of the negroes. Once they came upon the back of a plantation and hurriedly gathered a few cobs of Indian corn, immediately afterwards running back into the bush to eat them. While lying down a negro with a sabre passed quite close without seeing them, but presently another with a gun peeped into the bushes and caught sight of them. On this Mittelholzer ran out with his drawn sabre and so furiously attacked the rebel that he cut off one of his hands, captured his gun, and put him to flight. However, this audacity did not save him, for he was captured soon afterwards, Charbon managing to escape into the forest. Alone the boy wandered about for six or seven days, until, again becoming desperate from hunger, he returned to the same plantation, to fall into the hands of the negroes. He was stripped of his clothes, put in the stocks, flogged, and threatened with death, but was finally spared on account of his youth, and because the rebel chief, " King " Coffee, wanted a secretary to write letters to Governor Hoogenheim, proposing terms.

Meanwhile the poor Governor hardly knew what to do. He sent to Surinam and Demerara for assistance, but while awaiting this the military officers informed him that the fort was untenable against even a single assault. The wooden palisades were so rotten that a strong man could pull them down easily, and then the building was of wood and could easily be fired. He was ultimately obliged to destroy it and retire down the river, where he at first took possession of the lowest plantation, Dageraad, hoping to remain there until assistance arrived. But even here the rumours of an attack by the rebels made the people clamorous to be allowed to leave, and Hoogenheim had to retire to the mouth of the river, where there was a small guard-house, or signal station, near the site of what is now New Amsterdam. Thus the last hold on the plantations was given up, and the whole colony abandoned to the negroes.

A month passed before the first arrival from Surinam. All that time the Governor and a few whites waited day after day, sometimes almost in despair. The vessels had, at the request of their captains, been allowed to leave, carrying with them some of the people, while others had gone off to Demerara. This desertion was almost necessary, as the food supply was very limited and of a poor quality—cowards were useless, and therefore no objection was made to their departure. Hoogenheim was at last somewhat relieved by the arrival of the English brigantine *Betsy* with a hundred soldiers from Surinam, and with this small contingent he at once began to retrace his steps with a view to recover the colony. He went back to Dageraad, and in a day or two after was attacked by seven hundred negroes, who fought from early morning to noon, when they retired after suffering a great loss in killed and wounded. It was after this battle that young Charbon arrived with a letter bringing "greetings from Coffee, Governor of the negroes of Berbice." The rebel chief said that as the negroes did not want war, he would give His Honour half the colony, while he himself would govern the other half and go up the river with his people, who were determined never again to be slaves. No notice was taken of this, and Charbon, who had been warned to bring back an answer at his peril, was too pleased to get back to his white friends to again wish for his post of secretary.

Even now the Governor's situation was not only perilous, but most pitiful. St. Eustatius sent two vessels, but almost as soon as they arrived the men were attacked by sickness, and instead of being a help they had to be nursed, even the Governor himself taking his part in the necessary attendance. At one time there were not enough healthy soldiers to relieve guard, but fortunately Coffee had no means of knowing this, or all would certainly have been over with them.

It was not until December that a fleet arrived from the Netherlands, and then a horrible vengeance overtook the rebels. There was not much difficulty in subduing them, especially when a large contingent of Indians was sent overland from Demerara to drive them from the forest. In March, 1764, the trials began with a hundred ringleaders, fifty of whom were sentenced to death. Fifteen of these were burnt, sixteen broken on the wheel, and twenty-two hanged. The following month they executed in similar ways thirty-four, and later again thirty-two. The chiefs were burnt at slow fires, punishment which they bore with the utmost stoicism. One named Atta, however, told the bystanders that he only suffered what he deserved. Finally, in December a general amnesty was proclaimed, which made the negroes cry out with joy, *Dankje ! Dankje !*

Berbice was of course utterly ruined for a time. The plantations were overrun with weeds, the buildings in ruins, and many of the slaves missing. Of the whites only 116 remained; the rest were dead from sickness, had been killed by the negroes, or had fled from the colony. The loss in killed was small, as the general fright prevented any show of resistance. What would have happened if the whites had fallen into the hands of the rebels was shown in one or two flagrant cases. One of the colony surgeons was said to have been flayed alive on the ground that he had poisoned the slaves by forcing them to take medicine. One poor girl who had been captured at Peereboom was compelled to submit to the embraces of King Coffee and driven mad, while another committed suicide to prevent a similar degradation. About eight hundred slaves were missing, most of

MARCH THROUGH A SWAMP.
(*From Stedman's "Surinam."*)

whom had been killed, as very few managed to escape to the bush.

Behind the coast of Guiana is a long stretch of swamp, which in slavery times was the general resort of runaways. For miles extends a grassy plain like a meadow, the sedges entirely covering the two to four feet of water which would otherwise give it the appearance of a great lake. Except through the various streams that drain it, access is almost impossible during the rainy season, and even the Indians care little to explore its recesses beyond fishing in the canal-like creeks. However, here and there are little islands or sand reefs, and on these the runaway slaves took refuge. First, perhaps, a murderer would escape and hide himself for a time until the hue and cry had abated, returning now and again to the plantation at night for the purpose of getting provisions from his friends. Then others would follow, until a party of twenty to a hundred, with their wives, had established a little village. Towards the end of the last century a number of these communities of bush negroes had been formed in Demerara, and their depredations became so common that regular expeditions were sent against them, guided by Indian trackers. In 1795 they joined with the slaves to raise a general insurrection, but special measures were taken so that they were almost suppressed for a time.

Before this they had formed a line of stations for seventy miles from the river Demerara to the Berbice. Every camp was naturally surrounded by water, and by driving pointed stakes in a circle, and leaving the entrance to wind through a double line under water, they were made almost impregnable. To reach them the attacking party had to wade up to their middles through perhaps a mile of ooze and water, to be cut with razor grass, and all the time at the mercy of the negroes. Only during the dry season was anything like success possible, and even then the negroes generally saved themselves by flight.

Many of the slaves were friendly with the runaways, but they were much feared by the more timid. On one occasion a negro went to cut wood at the back of a plantation in Demerara and came suddenly upon the outpost of a camp, probably the entrance to the concealed path which led to the little sand reef. In walking along he stepped upon a bush-rope, and immediately after heard a bell ring above his head. Before he could get away a ferocious bush negro stood before him and demanded his business, but the poor slave was so frightened that he ran home and reported the occurrence to his master. Some of the slaves went so far as to enjoy hunting runaways—in fact, there was little love lost between the two parties. One of these was offered his freedom as a reward for the assistance he had given in an expedition, the Government engaging to purchase him of his owner provided they both consented. Tony, however, did not wish to leave a good master, and refused, stipulating, however, that he should retain the right to accept the kind offer at some future period. When his master ultimately left Demerara, some years afterwards, Tony claimed his promised freedom and got it.

While the bush negroes in other parts of Guiana

were kept within reasonable bounds, those of Surinam, like the maroons of Jamaica, had never been conquered. Treaties were agreed to by them in 1749 and 1761, but disputes continually occurred, with the result that the colonists were always more or less in fear of their raids. Then they carried off most of the slaves whenever they attacked a plantation, until their number became so great as to be a real danger. In 1773 the authorities in the Netherlands resolved to make a special effort to conquer them, and for this purpose raised a corps of all nationalities which was put under the command of Colonel Fourgeaud.

That soldiers should be brought from Europe for such a service shows the utter ignorance of the Dutch authorities. If the colonists themselves could not put down the bush negroes, how could it be expected that this would be effected by fresh troops from a cold climate, who had no knowledge of the country, the mode of fighting, or the difficulties of travelling through the bush and swamp?

Commissioners had visited them at different times to arrange the treaties, but there was generally something wrong with the presents (virtually blackmail), or else they were given to the wrong parties. In 1761 the chief Araby had insisted on the commissioners binding themselves by his form of oath. This was done by each party tasting the blood of the other. With a sharp knife a few drops were drawn from the arm of each person into a calabash of water with a few particles of dry earth. After pouring a small quantity of this mixture on the ground as a libation, the calabash was handed round from one to another until all the company had taken a sip. Then the gado-man (priest) took heaven and earth—exemplified by the water and clay—to witness the agreement, and invoked the curse of God upon the first who broke it, the company and crowd of negroes around calling out *Da so !* (that is so, or amen).

Yet, after all this solemnity, quarrels soon arose again. One chief with his sixteen hundred people had come to terms, but these did not bind his neighbour, who perhaps had half as many. The different chiefs were not united in any way, and it followed, therefore, that, after thousands of guilders had been spent on one, the others made incursions to get a share of the good things for themselves. To the colonists they were all bush negroes, but among themselves they were as distinct as if they had been different nations. Even when at peace, and when the chiefs had received gold-headed canes as symbols of authority, they would often call at the outlying plantations and demand rum or anything else they fancied, which the whites dared not refuse.

The immediate occasion for the special corps from the mother country was an insurrection of the slaves in 1772, who, after plundering and burning some of the plantations, and murdering their owners, fled in great numbers to join the bush negroes. The whole colony was a scene of horror and consternation—the colonists expected the rising to become general, and took refuge in Paramaribo, thus leaving their plantations unprotected. However, it was soon checked, mainly by raising a body of three hundred free negroes, called rangers, who were expert bush-fighters, and therefore thoroughly well fitted to cope with the rebels.

One of the chiefs named Baron had settled on an island in the swamp, such as we have described, where he defied the whole colony. There were no means of communication except hidden tracks under water, and in addition to the palisades the chief had érected a battery of swivel guns which he had stolen from the plantations. Thus triply defended by water, stakes, and guns, it is no wonder if he thought his position impregnable. However, he was discovered by a party of rangers, and assaulted by them and a large body of white soldiers. Camping first on the edge of the swamp about a mile away, they could see Baron's flag waving in defiance on the little island, while they were at their wits' ends to find a means of getting at him. A great many shots were wasted by both sides before they found the distance was too great, even for the swivel guns, and then the rangers began to act. Several weeks were passed in attempting to make a causeway by sinking fascines, but when the workers had come within range, so many were killed that it had to be abandoned. In despair of ever effecting anything, they were about to retire, when some of the rangers discovered the hidden pathway under water. A feint was now made of attacking one side by one party, while another crept along the track, and thus at last the fortress was stormed. A terrible hand-to-hand fight took place, in which many were killed on both sides, but even then Baron managed to escape with a good number of his followers.

This defeat made little impression, for soon afterwards the slaves on three plantations killed their white masters, and, like the others, went off to join the bush negroes. It was now felt that something must be done or the colony would have to be abandoned. The bush negroes had to be hunted from their recesses, however difficult the task might be, otherwise there would be no safety even in the town itself. The expeditions could only move in Indian file, exposed to ambushes in the most difficult parts of the track, and firing from behind trees everywhere. There was no possibility of bringing the party together if attacked; it followed, therefore, that the long string of men went forward with the utmost caution. In front came two powerful blacks with machetes or cutlasses to clear the way, and immediately behind them the vanguard. These were followed by the main body alternating with ammunition bearers, and, finally, a long line of carriers with food, medicines, utensils, and kill-devil (rum) with the rearguard. Sometimes the party would flounder through a swamp for hours, holding their firearms above their heads to keep them dry. Then drenching showers would fall, and give the greatest trouble to prevent the powder from becoming useless. Creeks had to be passed on fallen trees, or the party would be detained until a trunk was felled and trimmed to afford a passage. Exposed to malaria, mosquitoes, bush ticks, and maribuntas, they went on day after day, only to find, on reaching the village of the bush negroes, that they had gone elsewhere, to perhaps turn up at some unprotected plantation. The European troops died off in great numbers, while the enemy were in their element. It followed, therefore,

TRELAWNY TOWN.

(From Edwards' "West Indies.'

that little was done, and that the old system of conciliation had to be adopted, with the same unsatis-
factory results.   Finally, by utilising their mutual
jealousies, about 1793 they were driven so far away
from the settlements as to become almost harmless.
Their descendants still exist almost as savages, with
curious manners and customs, partly inherited from
their African forefathers, and partly adopted from
their neighbours the Indians.

We must now return to the maroons of Jamaica,
who had not been conquered, although a nominal
treaty existed, and the white residents remained at
their posts. In July, 1795, two of them were flogged
for pig-stealing, and this was considered a disgrace on
the whole community.   On the return of the pig-
stealers to Trelawny they raised a great outcry, and
the resident was at once ordered to leave on pain of
death. Efforts were made to pacify them, but they sent
a written defiance to the magistrates who had ordered
the flogging and declared their intention to attack
Montego Bay.   The militia were called out and
soldiers applied for, but before the preparations were
completed, a body of maroons appeared and asked for
an interview with four gentlemen whom they named.

Hoping the matter might be prevented from going
farther, these and several other whites went to the
rendezvous, where they were received by three hundred armed men. The maroons complained of the disgrace on the whole body, through the flogging having
been performed by a negro overseer in the presence
of felons, and demanded reparation.   They wanted,
first, an addition to their lands, and, second, a dis-

missal of the then resident in favour of one they had formerly. Promising to forward their requests to the Governor, the gentlemen left, the maroons appearing as if pacified.

However, this interview was only applied for to gain time, and especially to allow the departure of the British fleet which was then on the point of leaving, and might be detained if they moved too quickly. On the report that there was a probability of a settlement of the matter the fleet left, when the maroons immediately began to plot with the slaves for a general rising. Reports of this had been received by the Governor before, but just after the men-of-war had departed more definite news arrived, which induced him to send a fast-sailing boat to bring them back. Fortunately this was successfully accomplished, and at once confidence drove out the fear of murders, fires, and plundering which had alarmed the inhabitants. The slaves were correspondingly disheartened and left the maroons to fight alone.

But even the maroons themselves became divided in opinion on the return of the military and naval force. The Governor taking advantage of this, issued a proclamation calling upon them to submit, but only thirty-eight old men came forward, the others being determined to fight. They set fire to their own town and commenced hostilities by attacking the outposts. This led to a pursuit in which the whites fell into an ambuscade, many being killed, without as far as was known doing any harm whatever to the enemy. Now commenced a series of raids on the plantations, in which even infants at the breast were massacred.

PACIFICATION OF THE MAROONS.
(*From Edwards' "West Indies."*)

The matter becoming serious, the General Assembly resolved to hunt the rebels with dogs, as had been intended before the treaty. They accordingly sent over to Cuba for huntsmen with their powerful bloodhounds, the descendants of those which had once worried the poor Indians, and afterwards assisted the buccaneers. Times had changed however, and a feeling grew up that hunting men with savage beasts was not quite the thing. This led to some expressions of opinion adverse to the action of the executive, but they excused themselves on the ground that the safety of the island demanded extreme measures. If war was justifiable at all, any and every means, they said, was allowable; in fact, "all was fair in war."

Meanwhile the maroons had been driven to their strongholds in the mountains, where they had little to eat, and were virtually compelled to ravage the plantations for food. On the arrival of forty *chasseurs* with their hundred dogs, however, they became alarmed, and began to sue for mercy. It does not appear that there was any real necessity for using the animals, their presence being enough for the purpose. They were led *behind* the troops, and on their appearance the maroons surrendered in great numbers, this putting an end to the insurrection.

Now came the question of what was to be done with them. It was argued that no country could suffer people to live in it unless they could be controlled by law, and that obedience could not be expected from these people. To expect it was entirely out of the question; it was therefore resolved to transport them from the island. Accordingly, in June, 1796, six hundred were sent to Halifax, Nova Scotia, where lands were granted them and a subsistence allowed until crops could be raised. Not liking the climate, they were ultimately established in Sierra Leone, where they became the nucleus of the present colony. Those who had submitted remained in Jamaica, where their descendants are still well known.

XI.

THE SOVEREIGNTY OF THE SEAS.

BY the middle of the eighteenth century Spain had fallen behind, and even Holland had lost her prestige. It followed, therefore, that the only Power that could rival Great Britain was France, and she was an enemy that could never be despised. The struggle in the West Indies between these two Powers now became, if possible, more intense; and if the result gave the sovereignty of the seas to Britons, they have mainly to ascribe it to their naval training in this part of the world. The mistakes of Admiral Vernon were lessons which, being borne in mind by later admirals, tended to prevent similar disasters in the future.

There was a short intermission in the struggle between 1748 and 1756, when the "Seven Years' War" commenced; but before the actual declaration hostilities had commenced between the two rivals in India and North America. Now arose one of England's great admirals, Rodney, who gained his laurels in the Caribbean Sea, and was mainly instrumental in putting France in the background as a naval power. He first came to the front in 1759, when he bombarded Havre, and later, with that other great seaman, Sir Samuel Hood, he became a "household word" in the West Indies.

Before they appeared, however, the British captured Guadeloupe, and commenced a general raid upon the French shipping. But, as usual, our gallant foes were by no means despicable, for in 1760 they claimed to have taken 2,539 English vessels, against a loss of only 944. On the 5th of January, 1762, Rodney sailed from Barbados for Martinique, in command of eighteen ships of the line, and on the 4th of the following month the island capitulated. Then Grenada was taken, to be followed by Dominica, Tobago, St. Vincent, and St. Lucia, thus giving the whole of the French Caribbees into the possession of Great Britain. Spain being also involved, Admiral Pococke attacked Havana in May, and, after a siege of twenty-nine days, took the Morro Castle, a fort hitherto considered impregnable. A fortnight later the Governor of Cuba was compelled to capitulate, thus giving the town also into the hands of the British. These exploits made France and Spain sue for peace, which was signed at Paris in February, 1763, when Grenada, St. Vincent, Dominica, and Tobago were ceded to Great Britain, the other captures being restored.

After this war positive orders were sent to the British West Indies to break off all trade and intercourse with the French and Spanish settlements, with the result that contraband and other traffic was thrown into the hands of the Dutch and Danes. Then the Dutch islands of Curaçao and St. Eustatius began to flourish more and more, and those of the Danes, St. Thomas and St. John, became free ports. During the wars these islands rose to a pitch of prosperity hardly possible to any of those belonging to the combatants, on account of their neutrality. Naturally they were almost barren and of little account as plantations ; but as *entrepôts* they were exceedingly useful, not only to their owners, but to the belligerents as well. Here alone could French, Spanish, and British ships meet without fighting, and for them they could run when pursued by the enemy.

The island of St. Thomas was first colonised in 1666, but for a long time it made little progress. It became useful to the pirates, however, mainly from its being a safe place at which to dispose of their captures. Then merchant vessels found it sometimes convenient to go in to escape these rovers, perhaps to be followed by them, and yet remain safe until an opportunity occurred for escaping their vigilance. Prizes were brought here and sold, the prospect of good bargains leading to the settlement of a number of rich merchants, and especially Jews. What with all this, and a little contraband traffic, the people of St. Thomas did very well, and soon the harbour became one of the busiest in the West Indies.

And here we must mention that the Jews were a very important factor in the development of the early settlements. It will be remembered that large numbers of these people were driven from Spain after the conquest of Granada, and how they went to Portugal and the Netherlands. A large number also went to Brazil, where at first they had a measure of freedom in the exercise of their religion not granted in the mother country. When the Dutch captured Brazil, perfect freedom followed ; but after Portugal took her own again, this was withdrawn, and in consequence many left for Surinam and the West Indian islands. Here they were joined by some of their co-religionists from Holland, and in time became a powerful body of planters, but more especially traders. To them were due many improvements in the manufacture of sugar, and even the introduction of the cane into some places. In every colony there was a small community, often with a synagogue, and their connection one with another, as well as their virtual neutrality, made their transactions more safe than those of other traders. As may be supposed, they had no love for the Spaniard, and consequently were the main financiers, not only of privateers, but even pirates.

St. Thomas, Curaçao, and St. Eustatius lived by the misfortunes of others. No longer could the jolly buccaneer sell his prizes and booty at Jamaica ; he must go elsewhere, and let other places reap the advantage of his free and easy bargains. For it was " easy come, easy go " with him, and the fortune he made was soon wasted in riotous living. This was all to the advantage of the wily Jew, who first haggled about the price of a cargo, and then got his money back by charging enormous profits on the supplies. The rover was as careless as the proverbial " Jack ashore," and could easily be induced to spend his last piece of eight on the luxuries so temptingly laid before him, utterly regardless of the consequences. He had only to go out and capture another vessel to be able to return and renew his jollification.

In war time these harbours were crowded with the shipping of all nations, and many a fortune was made that enabled the merchant to go to Europe as a West Indian nabob. Then there was a great demand for neutral vessels, in which goods could be transhipped for conveyance to colonies where the belligerent flag might bring a crowd of privateers before the vessel got safely into harbour. Even physicians and surgeons made their piles, for there was always more or less sickness on board the vessels, and a hundred dollars a visit was a common fee.

In 1774 began the dispute with the American colonies of Great Britain, and four years later France joined them, thus bringing trouble again upon the West Indies. The first important move was made by the French, who, in September, 1778, took Dominica, on which the English retaliated by capturing St. Lucia. Then a fleet was sent out from England under Admiral Byron, and another from France under Count de Grasse. The French took St. Vincent and Grenada, and every island of either nation was in a state of alarm and consternation. In July, 1779, Spain joined the others against England, on the ground that her flag had been insulted. To this it was replied that she harboured American privateers, and furnished them with false documents, under which they carried Spanish colours. Thus

England had her hands full, for the Yankees alone gave her quite enough work, without the addition of these old rivals.

As yet Rodney had not come out, but in the years 1778 and 1779 he pressed his claim on the Government to have a command in the West Indies. The seas were well known to him, and he had his views as to the proper mode of carrying out operations ; but for some time his application was refused. Finally, however, in October, 1779, he was appointed to replace Admiral Byron, with supreme control over the operations in the Caribbean Sea, as well as freedom to intervene if necessary on the American coast.

Rodney was at last satisfied, and he left in December with a convoy, the whole fleet numbering three hundred. In the centre were transports and merchant vessels, and on either side men-of-war. Off Cape Finisterre he captured a convoy of sixteen Spanish vessels, and beyond Cape St. Vincent fought with another squadron, and captured four men-of-war, including the admiral. On then to the relief of Gibraltar, from whence he sent part of the fleet into the Mediterranean, and where he remained until February 13, 1780, when he sailed for the West Indies.

Arriving off St. Lucia on the 28th of March, he came upon the French fleet under De Guichen, which he attempted to engage, but was prevented from the want of skill in his captains. The result was that both fleets sailed away from each other without much damage to either, both stating that the other refused to fight. As, however, the French had thirty vessels to the English seventeen, they could have compelled an action ; so that, although the affair was not creditable to either, it was perhaps a little more disgraceful to the larger fleet. Rodney was in a great rage. He attributed his failure to the incompetency of his subordinates, who had not been properly trained to make combined naval evolutions. Every captain, he said, thought himself fit to be Prime Minister of Britain.

However, he continued his cruise, barring the way of the French, and driving De Guichen to St. Eustatius to refit. Now he began to teach his captains those naval manœuvres in which he considered them so much wanting, which his assistant admiral, Sir Hyde Parker, did not altogether like. Rodney, it appears, treated all his subordinates as if they were raw recruits, and, while he gained obedience, created a great deal of ill-feeling. But, with all their training, they could not bring De Guichen to fight, even when they encountered him a second time ; yet we may presume that the training was by no means wasted.

As if Great Britain had not enough enemies, in December, 1780, she declared war with the Dutch, on the ground that they assisted the American colonies. What a formidable array—the Colonies, France, Spain, and Holland ! Yet, somehow or other, she managed to cope with the whole.

St. Eustatius was the great offender among the Dutch colonies. Notwithstanding that the home Government had sent out strict orders to all her settlements not to honour the flag of the revolted

British colonies, or to supply them with contraband of war, there is no doubt that they were very loose in inquiring into such transactions.   As we have said already, this and other islands were very useful to the belligerents ; and, as we have just stated, De Guichen went to St. Eustatius to escape Rodney and refit.   This was no doubt a sore point with the British admiral, who barred the enemy's passage to his own islands only to see him get what he needed from the Dutch.

When the news of the declaration of war came out, Rodney was ready at once to pounce upon the offender ; and on the 3rd of February, 1781, before the authorities of St. Eustatius had heard the news, he appeared in the harbour.   The Governor could hardly believe his ears when an officer appeared to demand the surrender of the island to His Majesty of Great Britain, but being entirely unprepared, and quite unfitted to cope with such a force, he was obliged to surrender at discretion.

Here was the opportunity for revenge, and Rodney embraced it.   Even his best friends could hardly excuse the arbitrary doings which followed, and which were stigmatised as unworthy and almost dishonourable to a British admiral.   Being determined to root out this nest of contrabandists, he confiscated all the property of the inhabitants, and ordered them to quit the island.   The harbour was filled with shipping, and the stores with goods, the vessels numbering two hundred and fifty, and the contents of the stores worth about three million pounds.   Here was indeed a disaster to the Jews, not only of St. Eustatius, but even of British islands, for they were all in correspondence. Rodney went so far as to say that many of the English merchants ought to have been hanged, for it was through their means, and the help of this neutral port, that the enemy were able to carry on the war.

The people were astonished at such unheard-of treatment. Never before had such a thing happened, except in the raids of buccaneers and pirates. The Jews petitioned Rodney and General Vaughan to rescind their decision. They had received orders to give up the keys of their stores and inventories of the goods in them, as well as household furniture and plate ; then they were to prepare themselves to quit the island. Such orders from British commanders, whose principal characteristics were mercy and humanity, had distressed them in the extreme, so that their families were absolutely in despair.

This appeal had no effect, even when it was supported by some of the British officers, and such an auction now began as was never known before. The news reached Barbados and the other islands, and down came a horde of speculators, prepared to make their fortunes at once if possible. Such a haul did not occur every day, and they intended to take advantage of it. Thousands of bales of goods were brought out and sold, without either seller or buyer knowing anything of their contents. They might contain rich silks and velvets or the cheapest slave clothing. It was a grand lottery in which every bidder got a prize, although they were in some cases of little value. No one needed to despair of a bargain, however, for there was so much to sell as compared with the number of purchasers, that everything went cheap. Some few got bitten, but in the end hardly a tithe of the value of the goods was obtained.

While this was going on at St. Eustatius, some Bristol privateers got information of the outbreak of hostilities, and pounced upon Demerara and Berbice, where they levied blackmail and captured most of the shipping. As usual with these plunderers, they had no authority to capture the colony, nor had they in this case even commissions against the Dutch. However, they put the inhabitants in a state of consternation, until, a few days later, two men-of-war arrived from Barbados to receive the capitulation, which was demanded on the same terms as that of St. Eustatius, although neither party knew what these terms were. Nothing was left but submission, although the authorities protested against such an unheard-of manner of dictating unknown terms. The Governor of Barbados had heard from one of the inhabitants of that island that the Directeur-General of Demerara had expressed, at his dinner-table, his fears that in case of a war the river would be plundered by privateers, and of his preferring to surrender to one of the king's ships : for this reason he had sent the men-of-war. This was considered a bit of " sharp practice " by the Demerarians, but perhaps turned out for the best.

Two commissioners were appointed by the colony to go in one of the English vessels to St. Eustatius and arrange the articles of capitulation, which were fortunately on altogether different lines from those of that island. Surinam, St. Martin's, Saba, and St. Bartholomew's also surrendered on the same unknown terms, but the admiral said that he and General Vaughan thought they ought to be put on a different footing. They would not treat them like the other, whose inhabitants, belonging to a State bound by treaty to assist Great Britain, had yet nevertheless assisted her public enemies and the rebels to her State, with every necessary and implement of war as well as provisions, thus perfidiously breaking the very treaties they had sworn to maintain.

The treatment of St. Eustatius caused a great stir, not only in the West Indies, but in England as well. A remonstrance was sent to Rodney by the merchants of St. Kitt's, who claimed that a large quantity of their goods had been seized. Some of these were insured in England, and they considered their Excellencies responsible for their losses, for which they would seek redress by all the means in their power. It was impossible, they said, for many of them to be more utterly ruined than they then were, and they asked that certificates in reference to their property should be sent to England, in demanding which they were claiming a right rather than a favour. In reply, Rodney said he was surprised that gentlemen who called themselves subjects and merchants of Great Britain, should, when it was in their power to lodge their effects in the British islands to windward, under the protection of British laws, send them to leeward to St. Eustatius, where, in the eyes of reason and common sense, they could only be lodged to supply their king's and country's enemies. The island, he continued, was Dutch—everything in it was Dutch—all was under the Dutch flag. As Dutch it should be treated, and this was his firm resolution as a British admiral, who had no view whatever but to do his duty to his king and country.

Two merchants from St. Eustatius went to London, where they were examined by the Attorney and Solicitor-Generals. They clamoured for justice, and got it, for one of them was committed on a charge of high treason for corresponding with the American agent at Amsterdam, and for furnishing the Americans with military stores and ammunition. Several attempts were made to injure Rodney with the king, but the blow on the enemy was so severe that His Majesty would not listen to the detractors. It is said that a cry of rage went up from the French and American colonies, and that Rodney gloried in his triumph. He was undoubtedly inclined to ride rough-shod over everybody and everything, but as long as he was successful, only the enemy complained.

But the trouble was not yet over, for the merchants of St. Kitt's sent lawyers to file their claims in the Admiralty Courts. Then St. Eustatius was re-captured for Holland by the French, and the tide turned against the admiral. Now was the time to attack him, and his enemies took advantage of it. The mob that threw up their caps and shouted for joy at the glorious news of the capture, now lifted their hands in horror at Rodney's misdeeds. Even his friend Hood was guilty of the meanness of charging his comrade with carrying off vast sums of money, and never accounting for them. Rodney was recalled to England, where he arrived on the 19th of September, 1781, in ill-health, and rather downspirited. In December Burke moved the House of Commons for a committee to inquire into the affair, but although he pressed the motion with all his powers of oratory it was rejected.

Meanwhile the French were turning the tables upon the late victors and having their revenge for the disasters which had fallen upon them. This led to Rodney being again consulted, with the result that on the 19th of February, 1782, he arrived in Barbados with twelve ships of the line. This was the most critical period during the whole war. On the 19th of October previous, Lord Cornwallis had surrendered to the Americans at Yorktown, and this disaster was followed not only by the loss of the West Indian captures, but of the British colonies of St. Kitt's, Nevis, Montserrat, Dominica, and St. Vincent. It was by the special request of the king that Rodney had been again sent out, and before his departure he declared that either the French admiral or himself should be captured. Lord Sandwich, to impress him the more, on the eve of his departure said: "The fate of this Empire is in your hands, and I have no wish that it should be in those of any other."

Meanwhile the Count de Grasse was at Martinique, preparing a large fleet for the final reduction of the British by conquering Jamaica. He was expecting large reinforcements of French vessels and troops, which Rodney tried unsuccessfully to cut off. On the 8th of April the French were reported as having sailed for Hispaniola, where they were to be joined

by a Spanish contingent, and Rodney at once sailed
in pursuit. The result was that, at last, on the 12th,
a decisive victory was gained off Dominica. Admiral
de Grasse was captured, many of his fleet destroyed,
and the whole expedition broken up. The British
West Indies were thus saved, and the people of
Jamaica erected a statue to the gallant admiral.
Rodney, in concluding his despatch giving the
account, said it was his most ardent wish that the
British flag should for ever float in every part of the
globe, and there is no doubt that this triumph con-
duced to such an end. It stands prominently forth
as the greatest sea fight of the age, and was only
eclipsed by those of Nelson, who we may state
received much of his naval training in the West
Indies.

In January, 1783, peace was again restored. Great
Britain lost her American colonies, restored those
she had taken from France and Holland, and got
back her own, except the island of Tobago, which
was ceded to France. From Spain she got the right
to cut logwood between the rivers Hondo and Belize,
on the understanding that all other places on the
coasts of Central America should be abandoned, and
that no forts be erected on the concession.

For ten years there was peace, and during that
time the planting colonies were developed to a
wonderful extent, while those dependent on the
contraband traffic became much depressed. The
English settlements increased in value so much, that
in 1788 they were calculated to have under cultivation two million and a half acres, with five hundred

and sixty thousand slaves. These were the palmy days of the slave-trade, when the importations leapt up year after year, with a corresponding increase in the export of produce. The property was valued at over eighty-six millions sterling, Jamaica coming first, but nearly every other island flourishing to an extent hardly credible to those who have only seen them after their downfall.

What Jamaica was to the English, the western portion of Hispaniola became to the French, and even Spain increased her productions, now that things had become settled, and treasure seeking less remunerative. Altogether, the period from this time, to the end of the century, may be considered as the planter's best days, and the "good old times" of which we hear so much but find it so difficult to precisely indicate.

On the 1st of February, 1793, peace was again broken by the French Convention, the declaration of war being made against England and Holland. Thus began that struggle which seemed interminable at the time, and which actually lasted twenty-two years. As usual the West Indies suffered, but this time they were not quite so much the scene of contention as they had been formerly. Tobago was captured from the French on the 15th of April, but during the remainder of the year little was done. In January, 1794, however, Admiral Sir John Jervis arrived at Barbados, and in the following month took Martinique after a severe struggle. Then he went on to St. Lucia, which also surrendered, and before the end of April Guadeloupe fell. Then came reverses ; a French fleet arrived, and all were recaptured.

Meanwhile France had invaded Holland, and established a sister republic on her own lines, rendering it necessary for the Stadtholder, the Prince of Orange, to fly off to England. From Kew, where the king had given him a residence, he wrote letters to all the Dutch colonies, asking the authorities to place them in the hands of the British, and treat people of that nationality as friends and allies. With these despatches British fleets were sent to all the possessions of Holland, but only one or two obeyed the command, the result being that the others had to be taken by force, until hardly a Dutch colony existed in any part of the world.

In October, 1796, Spain joined France on the ground that the British, in their operations against the enemy, had injured her in several ways. One of the reasons given was so absurd that we can hardly conceive it to have been put forth seriously. Great Britain had captured Demerara, and this put her in a situation to possess positions of greater importance. Spain, however, got nothing by her taking up the quarrel, for her trade was absolutely swept from the seas, and communication with America almost cut off. This state of things became so troublesome that for the first time in her history neutral vessels were permitted to trade in her American colonies. She also lost the island of Trinidad, which had remained in her possession since the days of Ralegh.

Soon the whole of the West Indies and Spanish Main were virtually under the control of Great Britain, little opportunity being given to her enemies of crossing the Atlantic. No longer could the Caribbean Sea be the scene of the great struggle—the forces of the combatants were wanted nearer home. Now again came the harvest of the little island of St. Thomas, until Denmark was also numbered among the enemies of the " Queen of the Seas." Then the United States came to get her pickings as a neutral, which gave such an impetus to her ship-building and commerce, that later the seamen trained under such auspices became formidable rivals to the British.

The colonists did not altogether dislike this great war. True, freights and insurances were very high, but then the prices of produce were high also. There was a spice of danger in every voyage, but after all the risk was not so very great until the vessels came into the Channel. Then there was a convoy to protect them, and they might even get prize money by capturing traders of the enemy. Every vessel went armed, and many a privateer of the enemy got severely beaten by a gallant body of merchant seamen and passengers. This was a glorious time for the British navy, but the fleets in the West Indies had little to do after the beginning of the war. There was a great disturbance on the island of Hispaniola, a riot in Grenada, troubles in the French islands, and a few skirmishes here and there, but nothing of much consequence to the British.

There were many small difficulties of course, and the navigation laws had to be relaxed generally in favour of neutrals, as otherwise provisions would have been scarce. The Dutch were not altogether displeased with British rule, for Curaçao, which had not been conquered, was captured from its French garrison in 1800, at the request of the inhabitants, whose trade had been entirely stopped. Then the Spanish colonies came to an arrangement by which much of their produce went through British hands, and this prevented the neutrals from getting everything.

In 1802 the peace of Amiens gave France a rest for about ten months, when she got back her own and the Dutch colonies, leaving Trinidad as an addition to those of Great Britain. Hardly, however, had they taken possession, when the treaty was broken, and the British were again in their midst. A great deal of the work which had been undone by the peace had now to be undertaken afresh, but it was ultimately accomplished, so that things went on much the same as before.

The year 1805 was notable for Nelson's trip across the Atlantic in search of the French fleet, which however fled before him and got back to Europe. The same year also saw the heroic defence of " H.M.S." Diamond Rock, which however was not a ship, but an improvised fortress, which after a long struggle was obliged to capitulate. Hundreds of gallant exploits were performed in the West Indies by both English and French, and thus the war went on year after year, until it became something to be calculated for in commercial transactions. People began to look upon it almost as a natural state of things, and fathers told their children that they had peace on one occasion long ago for as many as ten years.

The British had undoubtedly become very arrogant. Their position on the sea was so supreme that they did much as they pleased with the few neutrals. This sort of thing did not suit the North American traders, who were Englishmen also, and like their forefathers resented any interference whatever. It resulted, therefore, that the United States declared war in January, 1813, and made the planters understand what took place "when Greek met Greek." Almost immediately every colony was pestered and worried by a number of fast-sailing schooners, as dangerous in a sense as had once been the fly-boats of the buccaneers. The heavy sugar boats going from plantation to port were captured in great numbers, and some of the harbours actually blockaded by the "Saucy Jack," the "Hornet," and other audacious Yankee craft with names as suggestive of their characters. Then, indeed, the West Indies were roused from their apathy—war was actually at their doors. However, peace came at last, and after 1815 it might be expected that the islands would go on prospering and to prosper.

Such, however, was not the case. In 1807 a great difficulty had come upon them by the abolition of the slave-trade, which at once put a stop to all extensions, either in the way of new plantations or of the acreage under cultivation. This was the first great check, and with the fall in prices, which ensued when Britain became the consignee of almost every settlement, caused a cry of "Ruin!" to arise, which has continued with short intermissions down to the present day.

XII.

DOWNFALL OF HISPANIOLA.

BEFORE the abolition of the slave-trade had affected the British islands the French colonies were distracted by the results of their great revolution. Hispaniola, or rather that portion now known as Hayti, had become, as we before said, the most important colony; we must now give the story of its downfall. If this had happened by the fortune of war it would perhaps not have been so deplorable, but to be utterly ruined as it was, until even now, after the lapse of a century, it is behind its neighbours, is very sad.

But, in the struggle for existence the straining after liberty has to be reckoned with, and although the process causes intense suffering to both lord and serf—master and slave—the fight is sure to come at some time or other. Miss Martineau uses the title, "The hour and the man," for her romance of the liberation of this once flourishing island. The hour had come, but we are afraid *the man* has not yet appeared on Hispaniola.

When the French people took the government from the hands of their king and summoned the States

General, revolutionary ideas had already come to a head, and the matter of slavery received much consideration. In all the colonies were numbers of free coloured persons, who had been manumitted by their fathers, and in many cases sent to Europe for their education. In Paris they were brought into communication with a kind of anti-slavery society, called *L'Amis des noirs*, before which they had opportunities of ventilating their grievances. These consisted of civil disabilities which kept mulattoes in the background, and prevented their taking what they believed to be their proper positions in society. The time was fitted for such an agitation, the people were there, and it was only to be expected that their complaints would come in the long catalogue of charges against the aristocrats, among whom were included the West Indian planters. However, although there was little sympathy with the colonists, nothing particular was done as yet, except the issue of the celebrated declaration that all men were born, and continued to be, free and equal as to their political rights. It might be said, perhaps, that this alone gave freedom to the slave and civil equality to the mulatto, but as it did not specially apply to them, little trouble ensued. The planters, however, were sufficiently acute to see the logical outcome of the declaration, and were correspondingly troubled, as they felt that if published among the negroes it might convert them into implacable enemies, and bring on dangerous insurrections. They were soon pacified, however, by orders to convene provincial assemblies, and send representatives to Paris : this they thought would prevent mis-

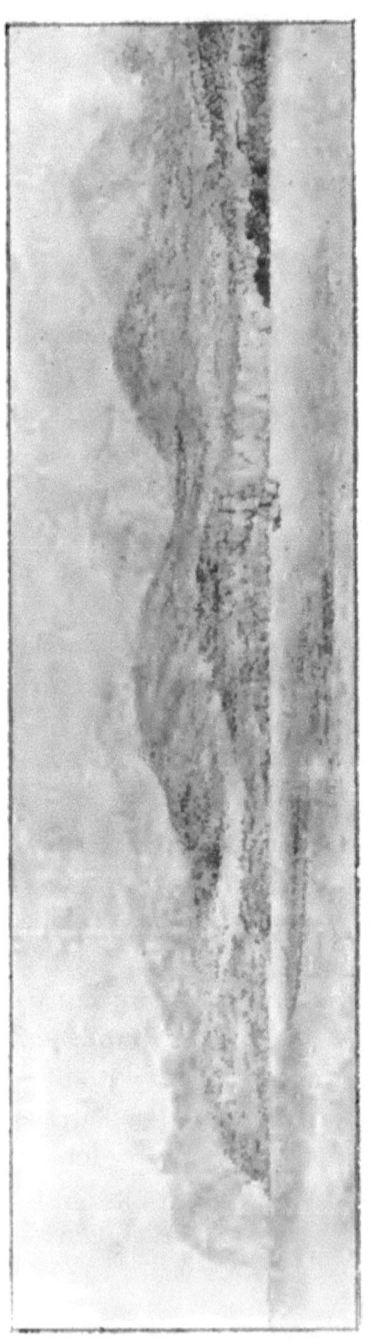

VIEW OF PART OF HISPANIOLA.
(*From Andrews' "West Indies."*)

chief, as their interests could be made known and promoted in France.

The free coloured people soon heard the news, and at once began to claim their rights as citizens, which the planters were by no means prepared to grant. On this refusal they began to arm themselves, and make demonstrations in various parts of Hayti, but at first were easily put down by the authorities. As yet there was little ill-feeling; the demonstrations were only alarming from their significance and their possible consequences. It followed, therefore, that little was done beyond a demand for submission, the mulattoes being allowed to disperse on promising to keep the peace. A few whites, however, who had been leaders in the agitation, were severely punished, and when a certain Mons. Dubois not only advocated the claims of the coloured people, but the slaves as well, he was banished from the colony.

Mons. de Beaudierre, a *ci-devant* magistrate, also helped to add to the trouble. He was enamoured of a coloured woman, who owned a valuable plantation, and wanted to marry her, but at the same time wished to see her free from all civil disabilities. Accordingly he drew up a memorial to the committee of his section, claiming for the mulattoes the full benefit of the national declaration of rights. This roused the authorities, who at once arrested him, but so strong was the feeling of the whites that they took the prisoner from gaol and put him to death.

The agitation in Hayti as well as in Martinique led to petitions and remonstrances to the National Assembly, and on the 8th of March, 1790, the majority voted that it was never intended to comprehend the internal government of the colonies in the constitution of the mother country, or to subject them to laws incompatible with their local conditions. They therefore authorised the inhabitants of each colony to signify their wishes, and promised that, as long as the plans suggested were conformable to the mutual interests of the colonies and the metropolis, they would not cause any innovations.

This of course raised a clamour among the friends of the blacks and mulattoes, who considered it as sanctioning the slave-trade, which they wanted to put down. In Hayti the General Assembly met and made some radical changes, which were opposed by many of the old colonists, and this brought discord among the whites. The Governor dissolved the Assembly, but this only brought more trouble, for the subordinate Western body took the part of the General Assembly, and went so far that the Governor tried to suppress it by force. But the members put themselves under the protection of the national guard who resisted the troops sent against them, and after a short skirmish drove them off. Thus all authority was put at defiance by the whites, when if they wanted to keep down the coloured and black people, it was of the greatest consequence that union should exist. The General Convention called the colony to arms, but, before actually commencing hostilities, they resolved to proceed to France, and lay the whole matter before the Convention. Accordingly to the number of eighty-five they sailed on the 8th of August, 1790, the authorities also agreeing to await the result.

Among the coloured residents in France was a young man named James Ogé, the son of a mulatto woman by a white man, whose mother owned a coffee plantation. He was a regular attendant at the meetings of the friends of the blacks, where, under such men as Lafayette and Robespierre, he had been initiated into the doctrine of the equal rights of men. On hearing of the vote of non-interference with the colonies, Ogé, maddened by the thought that the civil disabilities of people of his colour would be continued, resolved to go himself to Hayti. He was confident that the people there would join him, and going out by way of the United States he obtained there a good supply of arms, with which he arrived in October of the same year.

Six weeks after his arrival he wrote to the Governor, demanding that all the privileges of the whites should be extended to every other person, without distinction. As representing the coloured people he made this request, and if their wrongs were not at once redressed, he said, they were prepared to take up arms. He had already been joined by his two brothers, and they were busy calling upon their friends to insist, assuring them that France approved of their claim. But with all his efforts he could get but few followers, the same difficulty cropping up here as in most of the slave insurrections—a want of the power of combination under one of their own race. However, he at last got together two hundred, and, receiving no answer from the Governor, they commenced a series of raids on the plantations. Ogé cautioned them against bloodshed, but the first white man that fell into their hands was murdered, and others soon met with the same fate. Even mulattoes, who refused to join the insurgents, were treated the same way; one man who pointed to his wife and six children, as a reason for his refusal, being murdered with them.

The Governor now sent out a body of troops and militia to suppress the revolt, with the result that Ogé was defeated, and obliged to take refuge with the remnant of his followers in the Spanish colony of St. Domingo. The whites were now roused, and began to cry out for vengeance upon the coloured people in general, whether they had sympathised with Ogé or not. In self-defence they had to take up arms in several places, but by conciliation on the part of the authorities a general insurrection was averted for the time. A new Governor now arrived, and one of his first acts was to demand the extradition of Ogé by the Spaniards, which, being done, he was executed by breaking alive upon the wheel. In his last confession he is said to have stated that a plot was then hatching for the destruction of all the whites, but little notice was taken of this information. The whites believed that now the leader was dead things would go on in the old way, but, unfortunately for them, they were mistaken.

Meanwhile the delegates had arrived in France, where they were honourably received. After an interview with a Committee of the Convention, however, they were informed that their decrees were reversed, the Haytian Assembly dissolved, and they themselves under arrest. This, when the news reached the colony, put the whites into a state of consternation, and for awhile it appeared as if Hayti would be the scene of a civil war. Captain Mauduit, who had led the force against the assembly, was murdered by his own troops, and preparations were made to resist the authorities.

The planters thought these arbitrary measures of France very oppressive, but they had yet to learn how far the revolutionists might go. In May, 1791, the matter of equal rights for the coloured people came up before the National Convention, and their claim was strongly advocated by Robespierre and others. It was now that the words, "Perish the colonies rather than sacrifice one of our principles," were uttered by that bloodthirsty revolutionist, to afterwards become a stock quotation of the extremist in every country. The result of the discussion was the decree of May the 15th, that the people of colour resident in the French colonies, and born of free parents, should be allowed all the privileges of French citizens ; to have votes, and be eligible for election to the parochial and colonial assemblies.

This brought on a crisis in Hayti. The coloured people were determined to obtain their rights, and the planters equally resolved that they should remain as before. The Governor was so much alarmed that he at once sent to France for further assistance, at the same time asking for the suspension of the obnoxious decree. Hearing of this, the mulattoes began to assemble and take up arms, and the Governor hardly dared to take action pending the result of his application.

On the morning of the 23rd of August, 1791, the people of Cape François were alarmed by reports that the slaves in the neighbourhood were in open revolt, plundering the plantations and murdering the whites. The disturbance had commenced with the hewing in pieces of a young white apprentice on Pin. Noé, which murder was followed by a general massacre of every white man, except the surgeon, who was spared that he might become useful. From one estate to another the revolt spread, until the whole neighbourhood was a scene of murder, fire, and rapine. The white townspeople put their women and children on board the ships, and then united for a stubborn defence, but the coloured men wanted to remain neutral. This roused such a strong feeling that even at that critical time the whites had to be prevented by the authorities from murdering the mulattoes. By thus protecting the mulattoes their good-will was gained, and they volunteered to go out against the rebels.

Amidst the glare of a hundred conflagrations a strong body of men was collected and sent against the negroes. They defeated one body of four hundred, but accessions were continually made to the side of the rebels, until their overpowering numbers compelled the whites to retreat, and do their best to save the town. The revolt had been continually spreading, and now extended over the whole country, coloured people joining the negroes in their work of destruction. One planter was nailed to a gate, and then had his limbs cut off, one after another; a carpenter was sawn asunder, on the ground that this mode of execution suited his trade; and two mulatto sons killed their white father, notwithstanding his prayers and promises. White, and even coloured children, were killed without mercy at the breasts of their mothers, and young women were violated before the eyes of their parents. Here and there the horror was relieved by kind actions on the part of faithful slaves, who, while joining in the revolt for their own safety, saved their masters and mistresses.

The inhabitants of the town did all they could by

sorties, but this was very little. The rebels would run away at the first onset, but only to return in overpowering numbers. A few were taken and broken on the wheel, others fell in the skirmishes, but the insurrection still went on. It spread to the neighbourhood of Port au Prince, but, on the inhabitants of that town agreeing to enforce the obnoxious decree, the rebels retired. This action was at last followed by those of Cape François, and a partial truce ensued. In two months, it was said, a thousand plantations were destroyed, and ten thousand blacks and two thousand whites killed.

The news of this great disaster caused a revulsion of feeling in Paris, and the decree which had caused so much trouble was annulled on the 24th of September, before the results of the insurrection and the truces were known. The arrangement had been come to at Port au Prince on the 11th of the same month, and on the 20th at Cape François. Thus almost at the time when it was being repealed the colonists were promising to see it enforced.

It is hardly necessary to say what could be the only result of the arrival of this revocation. The struggle was renewed, and all hopes of reconciliation were at an end. The coloured party charged the whites with treachery and duplicity ; now they would fight until one or the other was exterminated. They captured Port St. Louis, but got a severe repulse from Port au Prince. Both sides were desperate, and although there were fewer massacres in cold blood the rebels fell in thousands. But as they were so numerous this slaughter made little impression.

Even when the prisoners were tortured with a refinement of cruelty hardly credible, no good resulted from such examples. The time for all that had passed, yet the whites nailed one poor mulatto by the feet in a cart, and had him driven round the neighbourhood as a spectacle, before breaking him on the wheel.

In January, 1792, three commissioners arrived from France to attempt a reconciliation, which they commenced by publishing the decree revoking the rights of the coloured people. Then they proclaimed a general amnesty for all who should surrender within a given time. Such utter ignorance as was thus shown has hardly been equalled in any age ; we can only ascribe it to the fact that the scum had risen to the top. The mulattoes were roused to fury, and the whites equally exasperated. At Petit Goave the rebels held thirty-four white prisoners, and at once they were brought forth to be broken on the wheel, previous to which the proclamation of amnesty was read to them, their executioners mockingly claiming it as a pardon for the cruelties they were exercising.

This sort of thing, however, could not go on very long. Most of the plantations and provision grounds had been destroyed, and both parties felt the want of food. Unless something were done they would all be starved ; for without means of buying supplies even the whites could hardly exist, while the blacks did nothing to raise further crops in place of those they had eaten or destroyed. France again made an attempt to put matters straight by declaring, on the 4th of April, 1792, that the people of colour and free negroes ought to enjoy equal political rights with other citizens. New assemblies were to be called, in the election of which they should be allowed to vote ; a new Governor of Hayti was appointed, and new commissioners sent out to inquire into the whole matter.

The Governor and the commission arrived at Cape François on the 13th of September, and finding everything in confusion, they sent the late administrator to France as a prisoner, and called a new assembly. Then the commissioners put themselves in communication with the rebels, which made the whites think them about to emancipate the slaves. This was followed by a dispute between them and the Governor, and the appointment of yet another head, who arrived in May, 1793. He refused to recognise the commissioners, but they were not so easily set aside, for having the whole power of the colony under control, they took possession of Port au Prince, Jacmel, and Cape François, afterwards ordering the Governor to leave. This led to another war, in which the coloured rebels and even negroes were utilised by the commissioners, who thus, in a way, sanctioned the revolt. Similar atrocities to those formerly enacted were renewed, and again the colony was distracted in every part.

The ruined planters now lost all hope, and began to leave for the United States, Jamaica, and other colonies. Some went to England, especially those Royalists who attributed all their disasters to the revolution. Here they began to urge the British to conquer Hayti, although as yet war had not been declared with France. In September, 1793, an expedition was sent from Jamaica, and on its arrival at Jeremie the British were apparently welcomed by the whites. But the colony was so utterly distracted that little could be done, and although they took Port au Prince they were repulsed at Cape Tiberon. Then sickness fell upon them—" Yellow Jack "—and this, with the delay of reinforcements, made all prospects of success quite hopeless. With a foreign enemy at hand the commissioners did all they could to reconcile the parties, and to this end, just before the landing of the British, proclaimed complete emancipation of all the slaves, which was ratified in Paris on the 4th of February, 1794. This brought the whole body of rebels together, and the position of the enemy became untenable. Finally came the cession of the Spanish part of the island to France, and now it might be supposed that something could be done to restore peace.

This repulse of the British was greatly due to the influence of a very remarkable personage, Toussaint L'Ouverture, a pure negro, and lately a slave. He had joined the revolt from its commencement, and had succeeded in gaining such an influence over his race as had hitherto been unknown in any slave insurrection. As soon as the general emancipation had been declared, he was so grateful that he joined the French, heart and soul, drove out the British, put down the mulattoes, and was appointed commander-in-chief of the united forces. In 1801 he became virtually Dictator of the whole island, and was made President for life, with the result that many plantations were re-established, and the colony was making slow progress towards recovery.

Napoleon Buonaparte has been much lauded for his diplomacy, but he certainly knew nothing of the West Indies. After the peace of Amiens he had a little time to look after the colonies, and Hayti was among the first to receive attention. Toussaint was then almost at the height of his power, and had prepared a Constitution which was laid before Napoleon, on reading which the First Consul said it was an outrage on the honour of France, and the work of a revolted slave, whom they must punish. It was true that the black President was virtually independent. He lived in the palace at St. Domingo, and, with his councillors of all colours, enacted the part of a little sovereign. To crown his audacity, he, in July, 1801, proclaimed the independence of the island, and himself as supreme chief.

This roused the anger of Napoleon, who retaliated by a proclamation re-establishing slavery in the island —a measure so foolish that even the planters themselves saw the impossibility of carrying it out. To reduce the negroes again to servitude was utterly impossible, even with all the power France could then bring into the island. However, it was attempted with a force of thirty thousand men and sixty-six ships of war. When this immense fleet arrived at Cape François the town was commanded by the negro Christophe, who, finding himself unable to cope with such a force, burnt the palace and withdrew. The French landed and sent two sons of Toussaint, who had been sent to France for their education, and to whom they had given a passage to their father, bearing a letter from Napoleon, offering him great honours if he would declare his allegiance. All that Toussaint said in reply was that he would be faithful to his brethren and his God, and with that he allowed his sons to return.

As yet the declaration that slavery was to be re-established had not been published, and the negroes were working the plantations on a share of the crop, with penalties for idleness. The French tried to put the negroes against Toussaint, in which they succeeded to some extent, the result being that civil war was renewed, and that the power of the black chieftain was broken. Then the general thought it time to issue the proclamation, which fell upon his negro allies like a thunder-clap, and made them again rally round Toussaint. Thus almost everything which had been gained was utterly and for ever lost.

Now the French tried a little double-dealing. The general stated in a new proclamation that ignorance had led him hastily to fall into error, and that to prevent anything of the same kind, and to provide for the future welfare and liberty of all, he convened an assembly of representatives of all the inhabitants, regardless of colour. This won over the leaders, and finally peace was concluded with Toussaint. The fallen president wished to retire to his estate and into private life, but having been cordially invited to meet the general to discuss with him the welfare of the colony, he was seized at the interview and put on board a French frigate, which immediately sailed for

France. Here he was imprisoned for life without trial, and finally allowed to starve by withholding food and water for four days.

The negroes again rose, and the soldiers were by this time so weakened by yellow fever, which even carried off the Governor, that little could be done against the rebels. Yet everything possible was attempted. Bloodhounds were brought from Cuba to worry the rebels to death; they were shot and taken into the sea to be drowned in strings. Dessalines had now become their leader, and on the 29th of November, 1803, he with Christophe and Clervaux, the other rebel chiefs, issued the St. Domingo declaration of independence. Restored to their primitive dignity the black and coloured people proclaimed their rights, and swore never to yield them to any power on earth. "The frightful veil of prejudice is torn to pieces, and is so for ever; woe be to whomsoever would dare again to put together its bloody tatters." The landholders were not forbidden to return if they renounced their old errors and acknowledged the justice of the cause for which the blacks had been spilling their blood for twelve years. As for those who affected to believe themselves destined by Heaven to be masters and tyrants, if they came it would be to meet chains or to be quickly expelled. They had sworn not to listen to clemency for those who dared to speak of the restoration of slavery. Nothing was too costly a sacrifice for liberty, and every means was lawful to employ against those who wished to suppress it. Were they to cause rivers and torrents of blood to flow—were they to fire half the globe to maintain it—they would be innocent before the tribunal of Providence.

This declaration was followed on the 30th of March, 1804, by an address of Dessalines, in which he said that everything that reminded them of France also reminded them of the cruelties of Frenchmen. There still remained, he said, Frenchmen on their island—creatures, alas! of their indulgence; when would they be tired of breathing the same air? Their cruelty, when compared with the patient moderation of the blacks—their difference in colour—everything said that they were not brothers, and would never become so. If they continued to find an asylum, troubles and dissensions would be sure to continue. "Citizens, inhabitants of Hayti, men, women, girls, children, cast your eyes upon each point of the island! Seek in it, you, your wives; you, your husbands; you, your sisters!" Their ashes were in the grave, and they had not avenged their deaths. Let the blacks learn that they had done nothing if they did not give the nations a terrible but just example of the vengeance of a brave people, who had recovered liberty, and were jealous to maintain it.

They were again roused, and from the 29th of April to the 14th of May an indiscriminate massacre of the whites took place, as many as 2,500 being killed during the fifteen days. On the 28th of April Dessalines issued a manifesto congratulating them on their success. At length, he said, the hour of vengeance had arrived, and the implacable enemies of the rights of man had suffered the punishment due to their crimes. His arm had too long delayed to strike,

but at the signal, which the justice of God had urged,
they had brought the axe to bear upon the ancient
tree of slavery and prejudice. In vain had time and
the infernal politics of Europe surrounded it with
triple brass. They had become, like their natural.
enemies, cruel and merciless. Like a mighty torrent
their vengeful fury had carried away everything in
its impetuous course. "Thus perish all tyrants over
innocence and all oppressors of mankind!" Where
was that evil and unworthy Haytian who thought he
had not accomplished the decrees of the Eternal by
exterminating those bloodthirsty tigers? "If there
be one, let him fly—indignant nature discards him
from our bosom—let him hide his shame far from
hence! The air we breathe is not suited to his gross
organs—it is the pure air of liberty, august and trium-
phant." Yes, they had rendered war for war, crime
for crime, outrage for outrage. He had saved his
country—he had avenged America. He made this
avowal in the face of earth and heaven—it was his
pride and glory. Black and yellow, whom the
duplicity of Europeans had endeavoured to divide,
now made but one family—he advised them to maintain that precious concord and happy harmony. In
order to strengthen the tie let them call to remem-
brance the catalogue of atrocities—the abominable
project of massacring the whole population, unblush-
ingly proposed to him by the French authorities. Let
that nation which was mad enough to attack him,
come—let them bring their cohorts of homicides. He
would allow them to land, but woe to those who
approached the mountains! "Never again shall a

colonist or a European set his foot upon this territory with the title of master or proprietor."

On the 8th of October the writer of these bloodthirsty addresses was crowned as Jacques the First, Emperor of Hayti.

In 1808 an attempt was made on the part of Spain to regain her old colony on the eastern part of the island, where France still maintained a nominal supremacy. Spain was now an ally of Great Britain, and, with the aid of British troops, she took St. Domingo and retained this part of the island until 1821, when a revolution took place and it became independent, to be almost immediately united with its sister republic.

Meanwhile the Emperor Jacques did not long enjoy his throne in peace, for he was murdered by his coloured soldiers on the 17th of October, 1806. A republic followed, under the presidency of General Petion, who was at the head of the mulattoes, but did not agree with the blacks. This led to a division, the north, with Cape François as the capital, coming into the hands of the negro Christophe, who got himself crowned as the Emperor Henry the First; the southern district, with Port au Prince, forming a republic under President Petion.

Henry was a man of good common sense, but like most negroes, much inclined to ape the whites. One of his toasts at a dinner was characteristic: "My brother, the king of Great Britain, and may he be successful against Buonaparte, and continue the barrier between that tyrant and this kingdom." He created a legion of honour, called the Order of St. Henry, built a palace, and began to acquire a fleet; he gave balls and encouraged operas, had a great seal, gave titles of nobility, and procured a set of regalia and jewels, with velvet robes and all other appendages of royalty. Under his rule the country flourished, for he would have no idlers. Yet he was a tyrant, and at last, in 1820, he was attacked by his own guard, and committed suicide to prevent falling into their hands. President Boyer, who had succeeded Petion, now took advantage of the confusion to incorporate the two districts, and two years later he added the revolted Spanish portion, thus bringing the whole island under one rule, the presidency of which he held for twenty-two years.

XIII.

EMANCIPATION OF THE SPANISH MAIN.

THE influence of the French Revolution was felt in most of the other islands, but nowhere did it lead to such disasters as befel Hispaniola. In 1795 there was an insurrection in the island of Grenada, where the coloured people, under French influence, nearly drove the English out of the colony. Even when defeated they held their own in the mountains for about a year, committing many atrocities on the whites who fell into their hands. In most of the French islands there were insurrections more or less dangerous, some of which were put down by the British conquerors, who thus helped to keep the peace. It could not be expected, however, that small places like Martinique and Guadeloupe would ever have made such stubborn resistance as the great island of Hispaniola.

A very great impression was made on the Spanish colonies, who during the war, owing to the distracted condition of the mother country, attained to a degree of freedom hitherto beyond their reach. This led to unfavourable comparisons between past and present, and the feeling that grew up was fomented by the

British, who now had many opportunities from the measure of free trade which resulted from the peculiar circumstances of that period. Secret societies were then common all over Europe, and in Spain they were not wanting. In the early years of this century one of the most energetic members was Francisco Miranda, a native of Caracas, who had been a soldier under Washington, and had distinguished himself by his prominence in many of the revolutionary projects of the time. He was the prime organiser of the creoles of South America, and under his auspices the "Gran Reunion Americana" was founded in London. Bolivar and San Martin were initiated into this society, and took its oath to fight for the emancipation of South America. Miranda did his best to ensure the co-operation of Great Britain and the United States, but failing in this, determined to get up one or more insurrections without their assistance.

On the 27th of March, 1806, he sailed with three vessels and two hundred men from Jacmel, Hayti, and on the 11th of April arrived at the Dutch island of Aruba, from whence the little company proceeded to Puerto Cabello. The demonstration, however, was nipped in the bud, for two of his vessels being almost immediately captured by the Spaniards, Miranda was obliged to fly in the other to Barbados. Here he met Admiral Cochrane, with whom he entered into an arrangement for British assistance. Conceiving that it might be mutually advantageous to Great Britain and the Spanish provinces that the latter should be freed from the yoke of Spain, the admiral agreed to support him in a descent on Venezuela, between the coasts opposite Trinidad and Aruba. The only stipulation was for free trade with Great Britain as against her enemies, and with that Miranda went off to Trinidad.

Here he hoped to gain recruits from among the Spanish people of the island, to whom he issued an address. The glorious opportunity, he said, presented itself of relieving from oppression and arbitrary government a people who were worthy of a better fate, but who were shackled by a despotism too cruel for human nature longer to endure. Groaning under their afflictions they hailed with extended arms the noble cause of freedom and independence, and called upon them to share the God-like action of relieving them.

This stirring address made little impression, and consequently few followers were enrolled. However, he got eight armed vessels and two traders, and sailed from Trinidad on the 25th of July, 1806, for Coro on the Main. The fort and city were taken, but the people, instead of joyfully welcoming their deliverers, ran away and could not be induced to return. Miranda, finding the place untenable, went over to Aruba, of which he took possession as a basis for further operations. But the British authorities looked upon his scheme as impracticable, especially as it tended to injure their trade, and in November Miranda was compelled to disband his little company of less than three hundred at Trinidad.

The time for a revolution had not yet arrived, but it was fast approaching. It could not be expected that Great Britain would assist filibustering against her ally, which Spain now became, and without some outside assistance Miranda found it impossible to do anything. However, the people themselves were at last aroused, and on the 19th of April, 1810, the city of Caracas deposed the captain-general and appointed a Junta to rule in the name of the king. This body invited the other provinces to join and form a league for mutual protection against the French, who now had virtual possession of the mother country. Other provinces took the Government side and prepared to suppress the revolt, which led Caracas to ask the assistance of Great Britain and the United States.

Among the Venezuelans was Simon Bolivar, who afterwards became the most important personage in the struggle for independence. Like Miranda, he was a native of South America, and like him had imbibed revolutionary ideas in Paris. He was a planter, and had taken no part in the overthrow of the captain-general, but from his principles being well known, he was appointed with others to proceed to London in the interests of the Junta. On their arrival they were answered cautiously, the authorities not wishing to commit themselves under the circumstances. Here Bolivar met Miranda, and took the oath of the "Gran Reunion," promising to work for the independence of South America, notwithstanding his nominal position as an advocate of the king of Spain against Napoleon.

Meanwhile the Spanish Regency had proclaimed the leaders of the movement to be rebels, declaring

LA GUAYRA ON THE MAIN.

(From Andrews' "West Indies.")

war against them and blockading their ports. The Central Junta responded by raising an army, which was defeated with considerable loss at Coro and had to retire on Caracas. This caused some discouragement, but Miranda now arrived, was welcomed with an ovation, and appointed lieutenant-general of the army. He was also asked to draw up a constitution and to become one of the deputies at the first congress of Venezuela to be held in March, 1811.

No longer was there any question of the French, the struggle was for entire independence. A civil war began, which raged with varying fortunes for twelve years, in the course of which were enacted scenes more worthy of the days of buccaneers than the beginning of the nineteenth century. In 1812 Caracas was destroyed by an earthquake, and in another locality perished the greater portion of a thousand men, marching against the Spaniards. It was reported that those provinces where the revolution had most influence suffered greatest, while those more loyal almost escaped. This was due to the fact that the mountainous region, in which Caracas is situated, felt the full effect of the earthquake, but the priests, who were mostly loyalists, told the ignorant peasantry that it was a judgment on the Patriots. The result was that large bodies deserted, until the whole Patriot army became disorganised. Miranda was captured and sent to Spain, where he died in prison in 1816, but Bolivar managed to escape.

New Granada had revolted before Venezuela and was more successful. It was to this province that Bolivar retired after the downfall of the Patriot cause in Venezuela. Then the Spanish captain-general, Monteverde, who was called "the Pacificator," commenced his work by imprisoning so many Patriots that the gaols were choked, and many died of hunger and suffocation. In the country districts he let his troops ravage and plunder like hordes of banditti. Even his superiors were at length compelled to recall him on account of the numerous complaints and petitions. At last the people were again fairly roused, until there came a war of extermination, in which both parties tried to outvie the other in murder and rapine.

Off the peninsula of Paria lay the small island of Chacachacare, and on it forty-five fugitives took refuge, where they consulted as to the renewal of the war. With only six muskets and some pistols, they landed on the coast on the 13th of March, 1813, surprised the guard of Güiria, took their arms and marched into the town, where they were joined by the garrison, making their number two hundred. Thus began the second war, in which the Patriots, assisted by the return of Bolivar and a body of troops from New Granada, again took possession of a large part of the province. On the 15th of June Bolivar proclaimed extermination to the Royalists, and named the year, the third of independence and first of the war to the death. This severity created many enemies in Venezuela, as well as in other countries, and even Bolivar himself afterwards said that the proclamation had been issued in a delirium. However, the result was that both sides became more ferocious than ever, especially when the Indians were induced to join the Patriots.

On the 6th of August Bolivar entered Caracas in triumph. The bells rang, cannons roared, and the people cheered him as their liberator. His path was strewn with flowers, blessings were called down upon his head, and beautiful girls, dressed in white and the national colours, led his horse and crowned him with laurel. The prison doors were opened, the Patriots set free, and, in spite of his proclamation, no act of retaliation sullied his triumph. Two days later he re-established the republic and proclaimed himself Dictator as well as liberator.

There were now two Dictators in Venezuela, Marino in the east and Bolivar in the west, but the Spaniards were by no means conquered. Bolivar published another decree on the 6th of September, that all Americans who were even suspected of being Royalists were traitors to their country, and should be treated as such. Ten days later twelve thousand men arrived from Spain, and Bolivar, who had been besieging Puerto Cabello, was forced to retire. This encouraged the Royalists, who got the llaneros of the Orinoco on their side by promises of freedom to kill and plunder in the cause of the king, and threats of punishing by death all who disregarded the call to arms.

Bolivar was captain-general, but he shared his power with Marino, the rights of both resting on force alone. To put an end to this, an assembly of notables was convened at Caracas, to whom he resigned his office, and then accepted it again at their request. But the Patriots, even when united, were as yet unable to stand before the Spanish army, and very shortly afterwards their flag was only visible on the island of Margarita. Bolivar again took refuge in New Granada, where he was elected captain-general, and entitled Liberator and Illustrious Pacificator. He, however, quarrelled with the Governor of Carthagena, and was forced to fly to Jamaica, saying before his departure that Carthagena preferred her own destruction to obedience to the federal government.

In 1815, after the great peace, Marshal Morillo came out with 10,600 men selected from the army that had fought against Napoleon. He was to reduce the whole of the Main from Spanish Guiana to Darien, dealing first with Margarita. In the course of a year he did this, committing such atrocities as made his name a byword over the whole of South America. In the siege of Carthagena, which lasted about three months, the Patriots suffered greatly, hundreds dying of starvation; but at last, on the 6th of December, 1815, it was captured. An amnesty was proclaimed, but in spite of that four hundred old men, women, and children who surrendered were all killed, while most of the stronger men who survived managed to escape.

The remnant of the Patriots was now scattered over the country as guerillas, and while Morillo was subduing New Granada a fresh signal for a general revolt was given. The Royalist Governor, in November, 1815, ordered the arrest of Arismendi, who had been pardoned, and at once the Margaritans rose, took possession of a part of the island, captured the fort, and killed the whole garrison. At the same time the guerillas united under Paez, who now came to the front as a llanero and leader of his class. Thus the struggle was resumed with all its former virulence.

Bolivar, when he heard of the fall of Carthagena, went over to Hispaniola to meet President Petion, who was an ardent supporter of the revolution. Here he received assistance of arms and money, with which he began to fit out an expedition to recover his lost position. There were many refugees from the Main on that island, but they were not altogether friendly with the late Dictator, however Petion managed to secure their co-operation. It followed, therefore, that on the 16th of March, 1816, three hundred Patriots left for Margarita, where they captured two Spanish vessels and united with their fellow-countrymen under Arismendi. Going over to the Main they soon got together a powerful force which overran the whole country and ultimately achieved its independence.

But before this happened the Patriots met with many reverses. Sometimes it appeared as if they would be utterly exterminated ; then the tide turned in their favour and they were again successful. The country was devastated by both parties, until cultivation was abandoned in many districts. Provisions for the armies were often unattainable, and this drove the soldiers to plunder wherever there was an opportunity, no matter that the sufferers were of their own party.

The struggle was watched with sympathy by the people of England, and Canning went so far as to make a declaration of neutrality favourable to the Patriots. Then came a systematic attempt to raise British volunteers, and, as there were many officers and men who had been disbanded since the great peace, a considerable force was raised. Carried away by enthusiasm they would hear nothing of the difficulties and dangers they had to encounter, but rushed to fight in the ranks of a people striving to liberate themselves from the grossest oppression. The country was represented as a perfect paradise, and the officers were promised grants of land in this delightful Eden, while the men had offers of double the pay of the British army. A similar call was also made in Germany with good results, and it was expected that what with the British Legion and this other contingent the result would be no longer doubtful.

On their arrival at Margarita, however, they at once began to perceive that poverty reigned everywhere, and that no provision whatever had been made for them. The Patriots foraged for themselves, and anything like a commissariat was virtually unknown; but British soldiers were not accustomed to such a state of things. Then the food supply was at the best only live cattle, which they had to kill for themselves, cassava bread, and a few roots such as yams. The rations were so irregular, that one or two days would pass without any supply whatever, and this ultimately led to complaints and something like a mutiny, which was put down with the "cat."

After some delay the British Legion was sent on to the Main, where they were worse off than in Margarita. Instead of welcoming them, the Patriots seemed to be jealous, and did not even give them the opportunity of fighting as they wished. When posted before Cumaná they were exposed to the burning sun and drenching rains, without tents or any other shelter; their drinking water was stagnant and brackish, and for rations had only a pound of beef per day for each man, from oxen which they had to butcher. They were also greatly shocked at the enormities of the Patriots, who carried on the struggle in a manner suggestive of the Middle Ages rather than modern days. Prisoners were indiscriminately massacred, their murderers enjoying the work as if it were a recreation. It is true that in the then condition of the country large bodies of prisoners could neither be fed nor guarded; still the British could not but feel that the cause they had joined was not altogether what it had been represented. Want of proper food led to sickness, and soon they became quite broken down. Many died of fever and dysentery, some deserted and got away as best they could, the general result being that little benefit was derived from the British Legion by Venezuela.

If such was the experience of the foreigners, what must have been that of the Patriots? They were certainly more used to the country and its food, and therefore suffered less from sickness; but this advantage was lost when it came to actual starvation. With the men engaged in the struggle, only the women and children were left to cultivate enough cassava to keep body and soul together. Even this little was often stolen by a foraging party, who did not hesitate to murder the whole family if any objection was made. Fugitives, if not cut off, made their way in canoes to Trinidad and Demerara, often arriving almost dead from the privations they had endured.

Delicate Spanish ladies and little children sometimes arrived—their pitiable condition causing an outflow of sympathy from the planters, and a feeling of detestation for their persecutors.

At the commencement of the year 1820 the Columbian Republic had become an accomplished fact, and on the 25th of November an armistice was concluded between Morillo and Bolivar, which virtually ended the struggle. The United States had looked upon it with favour, and Lafayette in France said that opposition to the independence of the New World would only cause suffering, but not imperil the idea. In 1823 the celebrated Monroe doctrine was formulated, and Canning said in the same year that the battle was won and Spanish America was free.

Central America had not suffered like Venezuela and New Granada. From Mexico to Panama was the old captain-generalship of Guatemala, but little interest was taken in the province, Spain leaving it almost entirely in the hands of the Catholic Missions. It was not until Columbia had gained her independence that Guatemala moved in the same direction, although there were slight disturbances in Costa Rica and Nicaragua from 1813 to 1815. At first there was a project to found a kingdom, but this gave way to the proposal for union with Mexico under the Emperor Iturbide, which was carried out, but did not last long. In 1823 Central America established a Federal Republic, and at once abolished slavery and declared the slave-trade to be piracy—a decision to which the other revolted colonies came about the same time.

XIV.

ABOLITION OF SLAVERY.

NEGRO slavery, although it formed the sinews and backbone of the plantations, was, as we have seen, considered unjust by the French republicans and immoral by a large section of the benevolent in Great Britain and the United States. In both countries the Society of Friends, or Quakers, commenced to influence public opinion against its continuance as early as about 1770, and had it not been for the French Revolution it is probable that emancipation would have taken place early in this century. The premature and inconsiderate action of the French in Hayti lost to France her most valuable plantation, for some years giving such an example of what might happen were emancipation to be granted elsewhere, that those in favour of the system could always point to it with the finger of warning. Yet with all that the friends of the slave were undaunted ; and as a beginning, in 1807, they procured the abolition of the slave-trade as far as Great Britain and her colonies were concerned, and then went on to get the traffic prohibited by other nations. Denmark had led the van by declaring it unlawful as early as 1792, but little impression was made until the nation most concerned took action.

This was a great blow to the British West Indies. The labour question had always been of the first importance, and to put a sudden stop to the supply meant a check to all progress. For twenty years before a great impetus had been given to planting, which was much assisted by the downfall of Hayti and consequent reduction of her produce to such an extent that she no longer affected the market. Now that the planters could get no more negroes, anything like enlargement of the acreage under cultivation was impossible. Latterly, also, produce had diminished in price, which made cheap labour all the more important. They had great difficulty in making their estates pay, and when sugar fell to half its former value a cry of "Ruin!" went forth all over the West Indies. It is interesting to note that the panacea which they expected would save them was free trade. At that time the British warehouses were filled with sugar and other tropical produce, while every continental port was closed by Napoleon, and the United States by the navigation laws. Not only did Great Britain store the produce of her own colonies, but that from those of the French and Dutch as well. In 1812 it was stated that the sugar consumption of Great Britain amounted to 225,000 hogsheads, while the production of her colonies was 150,000 in excess of this. The Southern States had just taken up cotton cultivation, and brought the price of that article too low for the West-Indian planter, and, as if that were not enough, coffee also fell in price to an alarming extent.

Sugar paid best, and was therefore fostered to the exclusion of the other products ; and now began the plantation system which became so obnoxious to the anti-slavery party. Hitherto, with a full supply of labour, the negroes did little work as compared with their capabilities—now something like the factory system of the mother country was introduced. The old methods would no longer enable the planter to get a profit, and he must make the best of his labour supply. Great administrative ability, more careful management, attention to economy, and concentration, were all necessary to prevent losses, and that these were not wanting can easily be seen from the results. The slaves were driven into the field in gangs, and kept at work by the threat of the driver's whip, while the overseers and manager gave most careful attention to the whole system.

Not only did the negroes work, but the whites also ; in fact, on the part of the latter there was a continual strain after a fortune on which to retire from this tiresome and harassing work of nigger-driving. Where one succeeded, ten failed ; many died of the exposure and of the *anti-malarial* drinks they imbibed so plentifully. So great was the mortality that the colonies became proverbial for their number of widows, some of whom, however, were not above managing their own plantations. It was a race for wealth, to which everything else was secondary.

The slaves diminished every year in the absence of additions from outside; as the whites would have

done under similar circumstances. That there was
no natural increase was mainly due to the fact that
the sexes were unequal, and then, again, maternal
affection was sadly wanting in the women, who
seemed to care less for their children than some
domestic animals. This state of things was mainly
the outcome of the system, which was undoubtedly
immoral, but the mental disabilities of the race must
also be taken into consideration. The anti-slavery
party considered that environment was everything,
if they could only free the negro from compulsory
servitude he would at once become an industrious
labourer. Yes, in their opinion, if he had the in-
centive of wages, it would make him a credit to himself and his community. The slaves, they said, were
worked to death, yet as free men they would do more
and perform their tasks better. Their experience with
free workmen led to these conclusions, but this could
not apply to the West Indies nor to the negro
race.

The anti-slavery party was very strong, and
although it is not stated that they took "Perish
the colonies!" for their motto, it is very certain that
they cared little about the future of either white or
black as long as they carried their object. To this
end every possible case of oppression and ill-treatment was exaggerated, and spoken of as if it were
common, notwithstanding that the case only came to
their notice through the trial and punishment of the
offender. The fact was the planter could not afford
to ill-treat his slave—no other animal of his live
stock was of so much value. If a valuable horse

were killed another could be obtained to replace him, but this was almost impossible in the case of the negro. Formerly, when he cost about £20, it might have paid to work him to death; now that his price was five or six times as much, self-interest alone prevented ill-treatment. There was a strong public opinion in every colony which prevented cruelty, and there were societies in some which gave prizes to those in charge of estates who raised the greatest number of children in proportion to their negroes. This breeding of negroes was necessarily very slow work, and did little to make up for the stoppage of importation. It followed, therefore, that every year the amount of available labour became less.

In 1815 the anti-slavery party commenced a further agitation, in favour of the negro, with the result that a Registrar of slaves was appointed for each colony, and ultimately a Protector. By obtaining an annual census they hoped to have some check on the decrease, and at the same time see if any Africans were surreptitiously imported. In some places there was already a slave registration for the purpose of adjusting the head-tax; here the planters did not oppose the measure, although they resented interference. Others, like Barbados, protested against the innovation as something quite unnecessary, or, even if desirable, not to be imposed upon them from outside. This led to a great deal of discussion at the planters' tables, where the slave waiters listened to what was said, and from thence carried garbled reports to the others.

In every colony were numbers of free negroes and

coloured people, some of whom were loafers and spongers on the slaves, while others went about the country peddling. Having nothing to do, they became the news-carriers and circulators of garbled reports. In 1815 there lived in Barbados a free coloured man named Washington Franklin, who, like many negroes, was possessed of a good memory and a great power of declamation. Getting hold of the English and colonial newspapers, he would read the speeches of Wilberforce and others, and after putting his own construction on them, retail them in language tending to rouse the slaves. To him was due an impression that prevailed in Barbados, probably from a misunderstanding of the Registry Bill, that they were all to be free at the beginning of the year 1816. When New Year's Day had passed they became dissatisfied, believing that their masters had received orders to set them free, but would not execute them. They had heard of the successful rising in Hayti, and were determined to attempt a similar revolt in Barbados.

After waiting for the expected freedom until the 14th of April, they determined on that day to have a general rising, which was signalled by burning heaps of cane-trash in the parish of St. Philip. Soon the fields were set on fire, and frenzied mobs, continually increasing in numbers, went from one plantation to another seeking arms. This went on for two days, but on the arrival of the militia they dispersed, leaving a waste behind. As usual a great many of the negroes were executed, although it does not appear that any whites got killed in the revolt.

However, the **Registry** Act was delayed for two years, **to** be ultimately **passed** in January, 1817.

Towards the **end** of the last century a new class of men appeared in the West Indies—the Protestant missionaries. Catholic missions had been established in the Spanish possessions since the time of Columbus, but hitherto, **with** the exception of **a** few Moravians, no other Church had done anything to convert the slaves in the British **colonies**. Between 1780 and 1790, Methodist societies were established in most of the islands, notwithstanding **the** opposition of **the** planters, who in some cases appear to have **thought** that **baptized** Christians could **no** longer be **held in** slavery. This vulgar error, however, was not the **real** cause of the antagonism to these teachers, **but rather the** feeling natural to a master which **makes him** resent any outside interference between himself and his servants. **The** best and kindest were the first to feel **this. The slaves** were their children, and to them **they applied, in** all their troubles **and difficulties, as to** a great father. **It** followed, therefore, that when the missionaries came and proclaimed themselves **friends** to the slaves, giving them advice in secular as **well as** religious matters, the cordial feeling was **broken.** "Massa" **was much** put out, **for he** liked **to hold** the position **of a little god** to these poor ignorant creatures over whom he held such power. The slaves were sometimes **whipped as bad** children when they did wrong, **and as** children they cared little for a flogging. It **is** easily conceivable that a humane missionary might feel more pain at witnessing such a punishment than the culprit himself, but it is a fact that cruel punishment was never mentioned by the slaves as an excuse for a revolt.

The missionaries were shocked at the apparent nakedness and destitution of the negroes, as a visitor to the West Indies will be even now. They did not remember that their clothing and houses were well suited to the climate, and that a home in the English sense of the word would not have been appreciated by them. These things were reported to the societies at home, the members of which knew no more about the tropics than the merchant who once sent a consignment of warming-pans to Barbados. Those who wanted to raise a cry of cruelty to the poor slave, circulated these facts, and put their own construction upon them, one going so far as to state that there were no chimneys to the houses, as if this omission were a slave disability or oppression, although any visitor to the colonies could have told him that these conveniences were hardly found anywhere.

The negro willingly listened to his friend the missionary, and felt eager to perform the rites and ceremonies of the little congregation. The Established Church was that of England, and although in some places there were special services for the blacks, in others "slaves and dogs" were refused admission. This exclusiveness threw the slaves into the hands of the Moravians, Baptists, Methodists, and the agents of the London Missionary Society. The Church government of some of these was in the hands of the congregation, and as this was a sort of playing at "Massa," the slave took to them all the more readily.

No doubt these ministers were very good men, and

animated by a **great love for** the negroes, but this did
not prevent their being misunderstood by both **master**
and slave.   Then many of them were connected with
the anti-slavery **society**, and however careful they
might be not to offend local prejudices, **by speaking**
against the obnoxious system, as conscientious men
they could not help showing their bias.   The established clergymen, **on the** contrary, when they preached
to the slaves, told them **to " be subject** to the powers
that **be**," and to remain content in the condition where
Providence had **placed them.**

At first most **of the** planters only **sneered at these**
attempts to **convert the slaves**, but when **they saw**
what an attraction the chapels became, they opposed
them **openly.   Gangs** of young fellows would attend,
and **sometimes break up** the meetings by jeering at
the preacher.   In 1807 an **ordinance** was passed **in**
Jamaica " for preventing the profanation of religious
rites and false worshipping **of God, under** the pretence
of preaching and teaching, by illiterate, ignorant, and
ill-disposed persons, and of **the** mischief consequent
thereupon." Considering **it the** first duty of all magistrates to encourage **the solemn exercise of** religion,
and whereas **nothing** tended more to **bring it into**
disrepute than **the** pretended preaching **and ex-**
pounding of **the Word** of God by ignorant persons
and false enthusiasts, to persons of colour and
slaves, **it was** enacted that, after the 1st of July, no
unauthorised **person** should presume to teach, preach,
offer public prayer, or sing psalms to any assembly
of these people, on **pain of a fine** of a hundred
pounds, imprisonment for six months, **or** whipping.

Similar punishments were also to be inflicted on any one preaching in an unlicensed building, as well as on the owner of a house or yard in which it had been permitted.

Another way of stopping the assembly of slaves was to pass a law against their meeting at night, and punish them if they left the estate without a written permission. There were always excuses for this apparent harshness, as plots had been arranged at nocturnal meetings, some of which had given a great deal of trouble. Even if a pass were granted to attend chapel, the estate's authorities could hardly be expected to follow and see that the slave did not go elsewhere. The missionaries took it that all this was done to hamper their work, but such was not the case altogether.

The anti-slavery party became very strong about the year 1820, and every obnoxious regulation was a text for discourses on the infamy of the whole system. If a planter were punished, the case was trumpeted over the country to promote a greater antagonism. How absurd this really was could only be seen by the West Indians themselves, and if they attempted to say anything they were put down as liars, becaused they were biassed in favour of the other side. One writer pertinently remarked that, among the hundreds of military and naval officers stationed in the West Indies, not one had borne out the statements of the missionaries, and we may call attention to the curious fact that Captain Marryat, who was well acquainted with every colony, speaks always of the negro as a happy fellow. The genial novelist does not mince matters when he speaks of oppression on board ship, and it is not to be supposed that he would go out of his way to screen the planters.

Some of the colonies passed laws against indiscriminate manumissions, and these were declaimed against as tyranny. Yet their wisdom was so patent that, under the system, they could only be heartily approved by every one competent to judge. There is one little fact that stands out most prominently as a redeeming point, if such a thing be possible—under slavery there was no poverty—there were no tramps nor beggars. The owner of the plantation had to feed his people in sickness and in health, in childhood and old age. If manumissions could be given by the mere stroke of a pen, many a poor sick or broken-down creature would have been cast adrift to become a burden upon the community. Now and again we yet hear some old woman complain that if this were slavery time, she would not be half-starved as she is to-day, notwithstanding the poor relief.

It may perhaps be thought that we are attempting the defence of slavery; we only wish to show that it was not quite so black as it has been painted. It had its dark side; but, on the other hand, many a bright gleam can be perceived by those who have seen some who were born into servitude and heard their stories. They were well fed, had as much clothing as they really required, were as a matter of policy well treated as a rule, and were quite as happy as they are to-day. Magistrates, policemen, and gaols were almost unknown; the planter gave the negro a slight flogging now and then, and this ended the tale of his misdemeanours. A bad master might be cruel as a bad husband may be also, but we should not condemn marriage on account of its abuses. The great argument against slavery was the degradation it produced on the minds of both parties. However, we are not writing the history of slavery, but the story of the West Indies, and must apologise for the digression.

In 1823 the House of Commons, on a motion of Fowell Buxton, " that the state of slavery is repugnant to the principles of the British Constitution, and of the Christian religion," resolved to ameliorate the condition of the slave by giving him civil rights and privileges. As a result of this, orders were sent out to abolish the flogging of women, and discontinue the use of the whip in the field.

Already the West Indian planters were alarmed at the interference of the British Government, and the overriding of colonial laws by Orders in Council. In 1819 they had petitioned against being compelled to manumit their slaves in cases where they wished to buy their freedom, but their protests went for nothing. Now also they had to submit, although they did so with a bad grace. The British Government left the carrying out of the provisions of the resolutions to the colonial legislatures, but at the same time giving them to understand that there was no option.

In 1811, when the Governor and Court of Policy of Demerara neglected to issue a proclamation allowing negroes to attend chapel in the evening, they received a sharp reprimand, and the Governor was superseded ; now they knew that nothing was left but to obey orders.

When, therefore, the despatch containing these resolutions arrived in Demerara, a meeting of the legislature was at once convened to prepare the necessary ordinance. There was no attempt to evade this duty or delay compliance, but such a radical change required great consideration, especially in regard to the control of females without the use of the whip. Negresses were, as a rule, less amenable to discipline than the men, and it was thought that something must be done to prevent insubordination. Several meetings took place from the 21st of July, 1823, to early in August, at which the ordinance was prepared and passed, but up to the 18th of the latter month it had not been published. Such a delay, however, did not imply any intention of evading the duty, for three or four weeks often elapse from the time of passing to the publication of a Bill.

Meanwhile the negroes got an idea that something had been done in England for their benefit. Like the slaves in Barbados and other colonies, they heard discussions at their masters' tables, and supposed that the something which had taken place meant their total emancipation. " The king had freed them, but the planters refused to carry out the order." On the East Coast of Demerara there was then a small chapel belonging to the London Missionary Society, under the charge of the Rev. John Smith. This chapel was a rendezvous for the negroes of the neighbouring plantations, who not only came to service, but met afterwards for a little gossip.

Some who could read gave their ideas of what they had gleaned from their masters' newspapers, while others told what had been said at the dinner-tables. It does not appear that Mr. Smith had told them anything of the new resolutions, nor is there evidence that the deacons of the chapel knew of them. It followed, therefore, that all the information they had was these garbled reports of their own people.

On Sunday, the 17th of August, a number of the bolder spirits met after service and discussed a plot which had been already under consideration, for a general rising at eight o'clock next evening. Their idea was to put their masters in the stocks, arm themselves, and, when the Governor came, demand their supposed rights.

On Monday morning a coloured servant informed his master of the plot, on which he at once rode off to Georgetown and interviewed the Governor. Warnings were sent to most of the planters, and preparations made to suppress the revolt if it took place, but such reports were not uncommon, and although the whites looked after their weapons they did not feel much alarm. As a matter of policy it was better to assume indifference, as anything like desertion of the estates, even so far as the sending away of women and children, would have encouraged the negroes.

The signal was given by a fire near the chapel, on which the slaves assembled in great mobs, over-powered their masters, put them in the stocks, and took all the firearms and other weapons they could find. The Governor was already in the neighbourhood with a small party of cavalry, and on seeing the signal proceeded to inquire into its meaning. On the way he was met by an armed mob, who, on being asked what they wanted, answered, " Our right ! " He told them of the new law, and promised a full explanation on the morrow if they would disperse and come to him at a neighbouring plantation. There was a slight hesitation for a few moments, but presently, with cries of " No ! no ! " and the blowing of shells, they drowned his voice. Then some of the more moderate advised him to go away, which he was obliged to do, as his whole company numbered hardly a dozen.

Bearing in mind the disasters of the Berbice insurrection, the people of Georgetown were much alarmed. Placing their women and children on board vessels in the river, the men prepared to resist to the death. Martial law was proclaimed, and every person, without distinction, called upon to enrol at once in the militia, all exemptions being cancelled. They responded heartily, and soon the town put on an appearance as if deserted, except at those places where guards were stationed. The stores were closed, the slaves kept indoors, and, save for the arrival and departure of mounted orderlies, not a sound could be heard. Even the negroes themselves, in their kitchens and outbuildings, were overawed, and hardly spoke above a whisper.

The Methodist ministers came forward and enrolled themselves in the militia, but they were not called upon to perform any duty. The Rev. John Smith, however, took no notice of the proclamation, although he admitted having seen it. On the evening of the revolt he went for a walk with his wife, and on his return found that the manager's house was being attacked by a mob of slaves. He succeeded by expostulation in preventing their doing much injury, and even rescued the manager from their hands, but instead of sending notice of the rising to the neighbouring estates he went quietly home. As far as he knew no one had been warned of the revolt, and he was certainly remiss in his duty when he did nothing whatever. When, on the following day, he was visited by a militia officer, and ordered to enrol himself in accordance with the Governor's proclamation, he refused on the ground of his exemption, although he knew that all exemptions had been cancelled.

As usual the rebels had no proper leaders, and for some reason or other—the missionaries ascribed it to religious teaching—they did not burn the houses or destroy the crops. One or two whites who resisted were wounded, one at least fatally, but here again the insurgents were forbearing. Fortunately they were soon suppressed, and this no doubt prevented such atrocities as had been committed elsewhere. What with the soldiers, the militia, and crews of vessels in the river, the force brought against them was overwhelming. Only one attempt was made to fight, but the first volley of the troops sent the rioters scattering into a cotton field. In about two days the insurrection was over, and then came the hunt for fugitives, who as usual took to the swamp at the back of the estates. A large body of Indians was employed, and in the end most of them were captured, some to be hanged at once and others after sentence by court-martial.

Mr. Smith's behaviour was considered as something more than suspicious—he was believed to have had knowledge of the plot, and charged with an intention to side with the negroes if he saw any prospect of their success. On his refusal to take part in the defence of the colony he was taken prisoner, and after the negroes had been tried and sentenced, his case was brought before a court-martial. He was charged with promoting discontent among the slaves, conspiring to bring about a revolt, knowing of the plot the day before and not reporting it, and holding communication with one of the leaders after it had broken out without attempting to capture him. The case created a great stir, public opinion being universal that he was the prime mover in the whole affair.

His trial lasted over a month, at the end of which he was found guilty and sentenced to be hanged. This sentence, however, seems to have been given to satisfy the people ; it was not published, nor was it intended to be executed without reference to the home Government. This is proved by the report in the "Royal Gazette" of the colony, which stated that the trial was over, but the nature of the proceedings was such as to render it imperative on the Governor to transmit them for His Majesty's consideration. The public were not informed of the verdict, but it is not to be supposed that they were ignorant of the result of the trial ; on the contrary, the sentence met with their approval, and they complained of the delay in carrying it out, as compared with the hasty executions of the negroes. Mr. Smith was ultimately reprieved, on the understanding that he removed himself from the West Indies, and engaged never to come back to Guiana or go to any of the islands. But the poor missionary was sick, and under treatment before the insurrection, and it may be presumed that the worry of the trial hastened his end. He died in prison before the king's answer arrived, and was buried at night to prevent a hostile demonstration.

We have been thus particular in giving the facts of the Demerara East Coast Insurrection, because it made such an impression in England. The anti-slavery party used the case of the " Martyr " Smith as a watchword, and it was a prime factor in hurrying on emancipation. The immediate result was an Order in Council to enable slaves to contract legal marriage, to hold property, to buy their freedom on a valuation by disinterested parties, and to put them under a Protector, whose duty was to see that their rights were not infringed. They were now citizens, their only civil disabilities being compulsory labour and a tie to the plantation or their masters.

This, however, did not satisfy the anti-slavery party, and they went on with their struggle for total emancipation, in which they at last succeeded. In 1833 an Act of Parliament was passed, by which, after the 1st of August, 1834, slavery was to give place to an apprenticeship of four or six years, according to the status of the slave, the former term

for house-servants and the latter for labourers on
the plantations, or "predials." Every child born
after that date was to be entirely free, and here
came in one of the greatest blemishes of the law.
These poor infants belonged to nobody; their
mothers cared little for them, and it could not be
expected that the planters would pay to keep up the
old system of superintendence. Even those who
had been instrumental in getting the law passed now
began to make comparisons between the position of
the child-bearing woman under the old and new
systems. Hitherto they were unable to find words
harsh enough to use in condemning slavery—now
they began to find that it had its good points. Then
the new system required new administrators, and, to
prevent any suspicion of bias, magistrates were
brought from England. Yet these very same un-
biassed gentlemen ordered flogging for the men
and the treadmill and dark cell for the women.
The Quaker delegates sent out to inspect the result
of their work were horrified. They said that the
cat was worse than the old whip, and that the
apprenticeship system caused ten times more suffering than slavery.

And such was really the case. The negroes could
no longer be kept under subordination—they even
claimed entire freedom at once. Several disturbances
took place before they could be made to understand
that they had to work seven and a half hours every
day, to pay for their homes, provision grounds, and
other allowances. In Demerara the Governor addressed them as erring children, telling them that

THE FIRST OF AUGUST.

(*From Madden's "West Indies."*)

they could not all be masters, and that every one must work. They had never seen a white man handle the shovel or the hoe—he was free—now they had attained to the same condition, the same coveted freedom from hard labour must be theirs also. True, there were free negroes, some of whom had learnt trades, but even they were above working in the field. Why should free negroes work? Certainly not for their wives and children. The women got their allowances, and the planter had hitherto looked after the children. The negro had no house rent to pay, his two suits of clothing came regularly every year, and if he was sick the doctor attended to him. Except to deck himself with finery, he had no use for money ; a few would work overtime when they wanted something of that sort, but the majority did as little as possible.

In 1838, when the house servants were to be freed, while the predials must serve two years longer, the difficulties of such an arrangement became insurmountable. A daughter or wife might be entirely free, and the father or husband an "apprentice." Then came the difficulty of classification, which the commissioners appointed to arrange the divisions necessarily decided against the opinion of one or the other disputant, driving him to appeal. All this rendered a continuance of the system impossible, and slavery was terminated altogether on the 1st of August, 1838, the planters receiving from the British people twenty millions sterling as compensation, being about one-third of the estimated value of the slaves.

The French had received such a lesson from the

revolt of Hayti that they did little for their negroes. However, after the downfall of Louis Philippe in 1848, the revolutionary Government abolished slavery throughout the colonies, without compensation.

After freedom had been secured in the British

A RELIC OF THE SLAVERY DAYS—OLD SLAVE BUYING FISH.

colonies the slaves in neighbouring places naturally became discontented. There were not many desertions from the islands, but in Guiana, where the Dutch negroes were slaves on one side of the river Corentyne, and the British free on the other, the runaways from the former caused a great deal of trouble to the Dutch. Whenever an opportunity occurred, a party of slaves stole a boat and made off to the British side, until the Surinam planters became much alarmed. Ultimately a Dutch gunboat was stationed at the boundary river, and this put an end to the migration.

Some of the islands were much affected, especially those of the Danes, which were frequented by British vessels, and were largely English in their sympathies. Here the negroes soon learnt what had happened, and began to express dissatisfaction with their own position. However, Denmark saw that something had to be done, and in 1847 enacted laws for gradual emancipation in her islands. From the 28th of July of that year all children born of slaves were to be free, and at the end of twelve years from that time slavery was to cease altogether.

This did not satisfy the negroes, who became more discontented, and in 1848 an insurrection took place on the island of St. Croix. On the 2nd of July it was rumoured that the slaves would refuse to work next day, and in the evening the whites were alarmed by the ringing of bells and blowing of conch shells. At first it was considered as an alarm of fire, but on inquiry the whites found that the negroes had revolted, and were demanding their freedom. Later, people came in from the country districts with the news that there were noisy demonstrations, but that as yet no actual violence had been committed. So little alarm was as yet felt that no precautions were taken, although some persons became uneasy.

Next morning the negroes streamed into Christiansted in great numbers, and commenced to demolish the police office. An officer coming into town was attacked by a woman with an axe, which fortunately missed him, but the crowd was so good-humoured that, on his treating the matter coolly, he was allowed to pass: this apparent good feeling made the authorities hesitate in taking extreme measures, even when the mob came round the fort, shouting and calling for freedom. Now, however, they began to collect trash for the purpose of setting fire to a house, and the Stadthauptman and a Roman Catholic priest went among them to try remonstrances. All the answer they got was that the slaves could not fight the soldiers, but they intended to burn and destroy everything if freedom were not given them. One of the mob carried a British flag as an emblem of liberty, and several English sailors were reported as forming part of the crowd. Soon all their good-humour was gone, and they commenced plundering the stores, the whites running away to vessels in the harbour.

About three o'clock in the afternoon the Governor arrived from St. Thomas, and went among the crowd telling them that they were free, at the same time ordering them to disperse quietly. For a few hours there was a lull, but next morning they reassembled in the country districts as if in doubt whether the Governor really meant what he had said. Some planters now brought their families to town, leaving their houses to be plundered. Parties of soldiers were sent out, and hundreds of prisoners were taken, the mobs, which in some cases numbered two or three thousand, dispersing at their appearance. Martial law was declared, Porto Rico sent six hundred Spanish troops, the insurrection was at last quelled, and peace restored. The Governor stood his trial in Denmark, to be acquitted, and to have his declaration of complete emancipation confirmed.

Slavery still continued in the Dutch possessions until 1863, and even then it was only replaced by compulsory labour for ten years, leaving the final emancipation until 1873. Yet with all that there were no disturbances to hurry on the process or cause trouble. In Cuba a law was passed in 1870 to give freedom to all above the age of sixty, as well as to children born after the passing of the Act. This, however, was not enforced on account of internal dissensions, and although Porto Rico gave her slaves their liberty on the 23rd of March, 1873, the Cuban Emancipation Bill was not passed by the Spanish Senate until February, 1880, and under that law slavery only came to an end on the 6th of October, 1886.

XV.

RESULTS OF EMANCIPATION.

THE slave emancipation was a terrible blow to the West Indies, and one from which many of the islands have not yet recovered. It was, the planters said, the second attempt to ruin them, the first having been the abolition of the slave-trade. The party who brought it about looked to see their *protégées* become a contented, hard-working peasantry, in place of driven cattle, as they called them. The planters, on the contrary, were morally certain that as free men they would not work, and without a labour supply their estates would be utterly ruined. The British taxpayer grumbled at having to pay twenty millions, but this was a mere sop for the estate owners. With the loss of their human chattels the plantations in many cases became utterly valueless; for the negroes congregated round certain centres, leaving most of the outlying places without enough people to keep up the cultivation. Labour had been degraded by the system, and now the full effects of such influence began to be felt.

The compensation money, in many cases, went towards paying off mortgages and other claims, the

holders of which saw the impending ruin and hastened
to save themselves as far as possible. But it was not
enough even for that, for many plantations had liens
of half the appraised value of the land, buildings, and

NEGRESS, GUIANA.

slaves. The last security being entirely gone the
others became worthless, and, as no one cared to
advance money on such risks, the nominal owners
could not even get as much as to pay wages. A
plantation valued at perhaps £60,000 a few years

before, and easily mortgaged for half that amount, received £16,000 for compensation with which to pay off the claim, and then wanted cash to carry on as well. Banks were established, but only solvent estates could get help from them, and consequently

NEGRESS FISH-SELLERS, GUIANA.

hundreds were abandoned in the larger colonies, and hardly one, with the exception of those in Barbados, could produce as much sugar as formerly. West Indian Nabobs, who had been getting their ten thousand a year and living in England, went out to see what could be done. Their incomes were entirely gone, and with them all hopes for the future. Widows and children lost their only means of support, and ruin fell on hundreds of families in England as well as in the West Indies. But not only did this

CHINESE WOOD-CARRIER.

downfall affect the owners and their relations, but merchants as well. Old firms shook to their very foundations, while many became bankrupt, to bring suffering to the homes of thousands who had hardly known of the sugar colonies beyond the invectives of the anti-slavery society. Many who had been strong advocates of emancipation now wished they had never said anything about it, but the die was cast,

EAST INDIAN COOLIE.

and there could never again be anything like the shilly-shallying of the French at Hayti.

The negroes would not work, and there were no means of forcing them to do so. The anti-slavery party still had their delegates in the West Indies to see that the "poor negro" was not oppressed in any way, and their representatives in Parliament to call the Government to account if they allowed any vagrancy laws, or even the shadow of a coercive

EAST INDIAN COOLIE FAMILY.

measure in the colonies. One ordinance after another for this purpose was disallowed, until every planter was in despair.

To retain their labourers was a matter of life or death. Some continued the old slave allowances to put them in good humour, but as these made the negroes independent of wages, the privilege was abused. They took everything and did nothing in

COOLIE BARBER.

return. Some went so far as to say that the Queen had promised that their late masters should supply them as usual, entirely regardless of the amount of work they did. This made the planters sore. What with one trouble and another the few who survived the wreck hardly knew how to act. They must not do anything to drive their people away, for there

EAST INDIAN COOLIE GIRL.

were many inducements offered by others in the same predicament. The negro was master, and he knew it. So much depended on him that he was enticed to labour, by high wages and greater privileges, until this bidding of one against another produced the very result which it was intended to avoid.

Something had to be done.   First, the allowances

COOLIE WOMEN, BRITISH GUIANA.

of those who would not work were stopped ; then their houses and provision grounds were taken away. Thousands of fruit-trees were destroyed to prevent their living on mangoes and bananas during the season.   Then the planters attempted to combine

to bring wages to a paying level, and this led to
strikes of the negroes. Everything tended to further
estrangement until employer, and labourer drifted far
apart. In British Guiana the negroes bought some

COOLIE VEGETABLE SELLERS, BRITISH GUIANA.

of the abandoned plantations and established villages ;
in some cases they even attempted to carry them on
as sugar estates, but as all wanted to be masters they
in every case failed,

As if this were not enough, the British Government went in for free trade, and allowed foreign slave-grown sugar to compete with that of the colonies. It seemed as if the French revolutionary cry of " Perish the colonies ! " had now been introduced into the British Parliament.   From one point of view the

EAST INDIAN COOLIES, TRINIDAD.

planters had been amply paid with the compensation money. Some went so far as to say that twenty millions could have bought all the estates in the West Indies, implying that the colonists had no further claim upon them. Even the anti-slavery party would not see that they were encouraging the slave system in other countries by opening their markets. This completed the ruin begun by emanci-

EAST INDIAN COOLIE, TRINIDAD.

pation, but as long as the principles were adhered to it did not matter.

Most of the remaining plantations now fell into the hands of those who had liens upon them, and they, not liking to lose their money altogether, commenced the uphill work of again bringing them into cultivation. Even a few colonists continued the struggle in hopes of better times. In Demerara there were two cases where eminent lawyers—the legal profession, by the bye, doing well when everything else was on the verge of ruin—spent all their profits in keeping

TRINIDAD COOLIES.

their sugar estates from utter abandonment. One of these got so heavily in debt that at one time he could not pay his house rent, and as the landlord dared not sue him, he had metaphorically to go on his knees and beg him to quit.

However, the sturdy English spirit survived in a

few, and they set to work to obtain labourers from other parts of the world. At first they thought of Africa, but the anti-slavery party would not hear of immigration from the "dark continent," for fear of abuses. Then India was tried, with the result that a few coolies were brought over by private parties, notably to Demerara by John Gladstone. But again the cry of slavery went forth, due to the managers leaving the new-comers in the hands of their head-men or sirdars. It was charged against them that they beat their underlings, and of course the planters had to bear the responsibility. The result was that East Indian immigration was prohibited for a time. After a hard struggle on the part of the planters it was renewed, and in the end prevented Trinidad and British Guiana from utter abandonment.

Besides Hindoo coolies, Chinese were also imported, as well as Maltese, Madeirans, and a few Germans. At first the negro thought little of this competition, but when he gradually dropped into the background, with his missionary friends, he commenced to protest against it. His friends said, and it was the truth, that there was enough labour in the colonies to carry on the estates, but the difficulty was that it could not be depended upon. Then the wages demanded by the negroes was entirely beyond the means of the planters—the price of sugar would not admit of them. It was a case of cheap labour or the alternative of giving up the struggle, and with the East Indians, British Guiana, and Trinidad recovered from the brink of ruin to become more flourishing in some respects than in the years immediately preceding emancipation.

Jamaica, the greatest of the British colonies, suffered the most as she got but few immigrants, and it is only during the last decade that she has again begun to hold up her head. Without healthy competition with other races, the negroes sunk back, until they became even more degraded than those of British Guiana and Trinidad.

In Barbados, on the contrary, the population was so dense that the freedman must either work or starve. There were no waste lands and few absentee proprietors, nor were any of the estates abandoned. Labour was plentiful and cheap ; it followed, therefore, that the island soon recovered from the check and went on prospering. The compulsion of the whip gave way to the force of circumstances, and the struggle for existence which ensued has made the Barbadian negro the most industrious in the West Indies. Not only is he this, but he is, like his former masters, intensely loyal to Great Britain and " Little England." All the black, coloured, and white people in the other islands call themselves Creoles, but he is " neither Crab (Carib) nor Creole, but true Barbadian born."

In the French, Danish, and Dutch colonies labour laws were enforced after emancipation, and generally with good results. They felt the change, but not to such an extent as their neighbours, and recovered all the sooner. Then they were not utterly disheartened by the unhealthy competition of slave-grown products like the English. Possibly, however, the British freedman would not have borne coercion, for even the Danes resented it.

We have seen already that the negroes of the island of St. Croix were by no means willing to submit to what they considered injustice, and how they forced on their own emancipation. However, down to 1878 they were bound to the soil as it were under annual engagements, from which they were not released without proper notice, even after the term had expired. They had houses, provision grounds, allowances, and very low wages, and were bound to work five days a week. The engagement expired annually on the 1st of October, and on that day those who did not renew their contract assembled in the two towns of the island for a jollification, where something like the old " mop " or hiring fair of England took place.

In 1878 they somehow got the impression that the labour law was about to be relaxed, but there does not seem to have been any combination among them to obtain such an end ; they were dissatisfied, and that was all. About the same time the Government were so assured of their peaceable disposition that they reduced the garrison of Christiansted, the capital, to sixty men. When the 1st of October arrived the negroes assembled as usual in Frederiksted, round the rum shops, appearing good-humoured, although noisy, as such a crowd always must be. Nothing particular happened until, at about three o'clock in the afternoon, a cry went up that one of their number had been beaten by a policeman, on which they attacked the peace officers, and drove them into the fort, which was police-station and barracks. Some of the principal whites came out and remonstrated with them, and at first they seemed as if they would dis-

BARBADOS.
(From Andrews' "West Indies.")

perse, but just then the police-master, his assistant, and two soldiers rode into their midst, brandishing swords and ordering them to move off at once. Infuriated by this, the mob attacked the horsemen with stones, and drove them back into the fort, which they now stormed. The British Vice-Consul then went among them, and, after a little parleying, induced them to go with him to the outskirts of the town. Here he got a statement of their grievances, which were —first, that their wages were too low (only ten cents a day); second, that the annual contract was slavery; third, that the manager of the estate could fine them at will; and fourth, that if they wanted to leave the island they were obstructed. Having promised to do all he could for them, the Vice-Consul begged them to disperse.

ST. LUCIA.

(From Andrews' "West Indies.")

They were apparently leaving the town, when a woman came running up with the report that the man who had been beaten by the police had just died in the hospital. This made them furious, and all further hopes of their pacification had to be given up. They invaded the hospital, knocked down the sick-nurse and a patient who inquired their business, and demanded to see the murdered man. They were informed that he was not dead but only dead drunk, and would soon recover if left alone. On being convinced of this, they again went off and attacked the fort. The defenders, when assailed with stones, fired over their heads, but this only made them all the more violent. The outer gate was broken down and some of the negroes were shot. Just at that moment a planter came up, intending to enter the fort, and at once they beat him with sticks until he was nearly killed.

However, the bullets checked them, but only to throw the attack on other parts of the town. Stores were pillaged and set fire to, until a great portion of the town was in flames. From some of the stores they took weapons in the shape of cane-bills, and in one were alarmed for a few moments by an explosion of gunpowder. The whole of Bay Street was soon in flames, and like troops of fiends the negroes went dancing round the fires, in some places pouring on them cans of petroleum if the houses did not blaze up fast enough. Then the rum casks began to burst, and streams of burning spirit ran down the gutters, adding to the horror of the scene. The women were always the most reck-

less—they danced and howled with mingled joy
and rage. The men added to the din by clashing
their sticks together or against the burning stores,
some blowing shells as a sort of rallying signal.
"Our side!" was the watchword, and all who could
not or would not repeat it were severely beaten.
Most of the whites, however, had fled, leaving them
entirely unchecked in their destructive work.

Meanwhile the police-master had sent to Christiansted for assistance, and while he waited the mob
again assailed the fort and again without success.
All through the night the disturbance continued, and
it was not until six o'clock in the morning that a
small band of twenty soldiers arrived. At their first
volley the mob dispersed, flying precipitately from the
town to carry the riot all over the island. Two soldiers
left in charge of a waggon were killed; and on learning
this the soldiers were roused to a state of fury almost
as great as that of the rioters. They hunted them from
one plantation to another, invaded their huts, stabbed
through the mattresses, and killed every negro who
came in their way, without taking the trouble to
inquire whether they had been concerned in the affair
or not. Three hundred prisoners were taken, and on
the 5th of October a proclamation was issued calling
on all the negroes to return to their houses or be
treated as rebels, after which the disturbance was
quelled. Twelve hundred were sentenced to death,
and a Commission of Inquiry was sent out from
Denmark, the result of their report being that the
obnoxious labour law was repealed.

We have been thus particular in our account of

this riot, because it exemplifies the character of the negro and is a type of such disturbances in other colonies. There is generally some ill-feeling at the bottom, but as a rule no conspiracy beforehand. When the dissatisfaction reaches a certain point, little is required to raise the passions of the black man, and that little thing is almost sure to occur. Unlike the European, he does not proclaim his grievances, except in a general way, among his own people—he has not yet arrived at that stage where civilised man uses the platform and press. It follows, therefore, that his passions smoulder for weeks and months, until some trifle—often a misunderstanding —brings them to the surface.

At St. Croix there does not appear to have been anything like race prejudice, or that envious feeling which makes the negro think himself down-trodden by his rivals; but that is a characteristic of most riots, and is strikingly exemplified in two that have taken place in Demerara.

After the emancipation the negro in British Guiana became of less and less importance as more and more immigrants arrived, until he grew quite sore. No longer could he demand extortionate wages, for the labour market was virtually governed by the current rates paid to the coolies. These people, however, were quite able to hold their own, and the negro knew this; it followed, therefore, that he vented his spite upon the most inoffensive people in the colony.

The Portuguese from Madeira came to British Guiana absolutely destitute just after the failure of the vines on their island. They found the negro more prosperous than perhaps he has ever been since, for this was the time when, if he worked, he could always save money if he chose. In fact, many did so, and bought land which is still in the hands of some of their descendants, on which houses much superior to those now in existence were erected. The Portuguese could not endure the hard labour of sugar-planting, but soon found openings as small shopkeepers or pedlars. Hitherto there was little competition in these businesses, but the few who carried them on were negroes or coloured persons. These were soon ousted out, and the Portuguese became almost the only small trader in the colony. This was a grievance to the negro, who could not see that he himself reaped the benefit—certainly he took advantage of the reduced prices while abusing the sellers.

At the beginning of the year 1856 the negroes of Georgetown were excited by the arrival of an anti-Popery agitator, who had become notorious in England, Scotland, and the United States. John Sayers Orr, known as "the Angel Gabriel," because he blew a trumpet to call the people together, was a native of Demerara, and soon found out what a strong antipathy to the Portuguese existed among the people. This suited his ideas exactly, for were they not Roman Catholics—the very body which he had been declaiming everywhere against?

Soon his horn-blowing brought crowds into the market square every Sunday, where his harangues roused his hearers to such a pitch of fury that the authorities became alarmed. He was therefore arrested, brought before a magistrate, charged with convening an illegal assembly, and committed for trial. This committal of the popular hero was the spark which set all the negroes' passions in a blaze, but, strange to say, they did not attack the authorities. Their spite was against the Portuguese, and soon almost the whole colony was the scene of a general raid upon their shops. Hardly any escaped, but one after another was broken open and the goods either carried away or destroyed. Some went so far as to use the Governor's name, as if he had authorised the raid, and in this way got ignorant people in the country districts to help them to seize boats, provisions, and even the produce of the farms of the obnoxious Portuguese.

The riot was ultimately quelled, but not before the damage amounted to over a quarter of a million dollars. Hundreds of prisoners were captured, but beyond the shooting of one policeman there does not appear to have been any serious casualties, neither were there any executions. It is interesting to note that the idea of poisoning, which is connected with Obeah superstition, was conspicuous here as in the Berbice slave insurrection. One black man charged a Portuguese with threatening to poison his customers with the provisions he sold them ; but all the satisfaction the negro got was a reprimand from the magistrate.

The second great riot in Georgetown is notable for its similarity to that at St. Croix. The feeling of antipathy to the Portuguese still continued, and the negro had a special grievance on account of the reprieve of a murderer of that nationality. If he had been black he would have been hanged, they said—it was colour prejudice. However, no disturbance took place for several months, and even then it only came about through a misunderstanding. A black boy buying a cent roll of bread in the market, snatched one of the penny rolls instead, when the Portuguese stall-keeper struck him down with a stick. The boy was taken up senseless and carried to the hospital, while his assailant through some misunderstanding was not arrested. At once there was a cry of " Portugee kill black man ; Binney (the clerk of the market) let he go," and they began to assail the clerk with sticks and stones.

The police arrived, dispersed the mob, and shut up the market, but this only led to their scattering throughout the city. The report that the black boy was dead was carried into every yard, and at once swarms of women and boys, with comparatively few men, began to smash the Portuguese shops. The authorities did next to nothing, beyond sending out a few special constables, armed only with sticks, to fight against overpowering crowds better provided with weapons than themselves. The consequence was that for two days Georgetown was in the power of thousands of negroes, and damage resulted to the amount of nearly fifty thousand dollars. The disturbance was finally checked by arming the police, and issuing a proclamation that they were authorised to fire on the rioters. Not a single shot was fired, however : the threat was quite sufficient for the purpose.

It will be seen from these cases that of late years

the negroes have not **perpetrated** such massacres as **once** characterised their insurrections, but the insurrection at St. Thomas-in-the-East in Jamaica seems to show that the old spirit was not dead in 1865.

For **several years** previous Jamaica had **been much** depressed—in fact, she had **hardly begun to recover** from the ruin which followed emancipation. Then came a two years' drought, which **caused** some distress among the people, who had **no** other means of support than what was **derived from their** small provision fields. The Baptist **connexion was** very strong in the island, and Dr. Underhill, the Secretary of its Missionary Society, **went out, and on** his return published reports **blaming the Government** for the distress, **which** he **appears to have highly** exaggerated. This tended to produce **more** dissatisfaction and to give the negroes an object **on which they could** vent their feelings. In one **of Dr. Underhill's letters** he said the people seemed **to be** overwhelmed **with** discouragement, and that he feared they were **giving** up their **long struggle with injustice and** fraud in despair. Thus a **feeling was** produced **which** only required some little incident to bring **on a** serious disturbance.

On the 7th of October a black man was brought up for trial before the Custos of St. Thomas-in-the-East, when a somewhat **orderly mob** marched into the town to, if possible, release the prisoner. They crowded round the court-house **and made** such a disturbance that one of them **was taken** in charge, only, however, **to be** rescued at once by his friends. Nothing more was done on that **day,** but warrants having been issued or the arrest of the leaders, their execution was forcibly resisted. The negroes now seem to have planned a general rising and issued notices calling their people to arms. " Blow your shells, roll your drums ; house to house take out every man ! War is at us ; my black skin, war is at hand. Every black man must turn at once, for the oppression is too great." They were, they said, ground down by an overbearing and oppressive foreigner, and if they did not get justice would burn and kill.

On the 11th of October a mob assembled at the same court-house, and being resisted by a small body of volunteers, they killed the Custos, and every white man who opposed them, to the number of twenty-eight, released all the prisoners and burnt the building. Immediately afterwards there was a general rising in the district, which spread for about fifty miles.

Governor Eyre, when he heard the news, at once determined to suppress the insurrection before it affected the whole island. Martial law was declared, a body of maroons employed, and within a few days the riots were suppressed. Many of the negroes were shot as they tried to escape, others taken and hanged at once, their villages burnt to the ground, and altogether they received such a lesson as effectually put a stop to anything of the kind in the future. It was stated that 439 people were killed and 600 flogged ; a thousand houses were burnt and a great deal of property destroyed by both parties.

The severity of Governor Eyre caused a great outcry in England, especially among the Baptists.

Among those who were executed was Mr. Gordon, a member of the Assembly, who no doubt fell a victim to the feeling aroused among the whites. He was charged with being a prime instigator of the revolt, but it does not appear that he went beyond what is generally allowed to a political agitator. Such agitation, however, amongst ignorant people, who are easily excited, is particularly dangerous, and likely to recoil on the heads of those who initiate it, who must be prepared to risk the consequences.

Governor Eyre was recalled, and prosecuted without success. He undoubtedly saved the island, and, although such executions as were committed can hardly be excused, yet when we consider the alarm and excitement, we must make some allowances. And, after all, it must be remembered that the loss of life would probably have been much greater had not the insurrection been nipped in the bud.

Barbados is unique in several respects, and as may be supposed there is something remarkable even about her riots. The patriotism of the inhabitants, both black and white, is proverbial all over the West Indies. There is no place in the world to equal Barbados—no colony but what has been conquered by the enemy at some time or other. "Little England" was said to have offered an asylum to King George the Third when Buonaparte intended to invade England, and no doubt if such an offer was ever made it was done in all sincerity. Barbadians are proud of their constitution, and jealous of its infringement in the slightest degree. This feeling led to a disturbance in 1876, which was the nearest approach to an insurrection on that island in late years.

It has often been suggested that a confederation of the British West Indies would be advantageous in many ways, and in 1876 the Secretary of State was of opinion that a closer union of Barbados and the other Windward Islands was desirable. The Governor of all the islands was then Mr. Pope Hennessy, who had lately been appointed, and who had been directed to obtain the consent of Barbados to a partial union. The measures proposed were of little importance, consisting only of the amalgamation of the prisons, lunatic asylums, and lazarettos, and the extension of the powers of the Chief Justice, Auditor-General, and the police force to cover the whole of the islands.

An outsider would suppose that there was nothing offensive in these changes, but that, on the contrary, they would be beneficial in many ways, but most of the Barbadians opposed them strongly. Barbados, they said, was solvent, while some of the islands were on the verge of bankruptcy—their island should not be taxed to support paupers. They held meetings at which six points were agreed to, and on which the leaders harangued crowds throughout the island. These were, first, that their Court of Appeal would be abolished ; second, that all the mad people from other islands would have to be supported by them ; third, that all the lepers would come there ; fourth, that the officials of other islands would live on them ; fifth, that the power would be taken from the people and given to the Governor ; and sixth, that as the

House of Assembly had always been faithful they resented any interference with it.

The Governor was desirous of carrying his project, and possibly went farther than was consistent with his instructions, which were to bring about the arrangement in an amicable manner. He did all he could to create a party in its favour, and was charged by the other side with using underhand means to this end. The main point, however, on which he laid stress, and which seems to have caused the trouble, was the advantage to the Barbadians of having the other islands so close as to become virtually like their own parishes, so that the surplus population would be able to take up lands that were then useless, and lying waste.

Barbados is densely populated. All the lands are occupied, and it is very difficult to procure even a small lot—this makes the people all the more eager to get possession of a little freehold. Yet, with all this, they will not settle in other islands, where they can get a piece of ground for next to nothing.

Somehow or other the more ignorant people seem to have got the notion that the Governor was promising them land in Barbados, and this made them enthusiastic for his project. Something like communism would, they thought, follow if the Confederation Act were passed, and this was the reason in their opinion why the other party fought against it. The planters spoke as if Mr. Hennessy had laid himself open to such a misunderstanding, and that made them all the more virulent against him.

The anti-Confederation party said that it had

always been the pride and glory of Barbados to have a separate political existence, and if under their own institutions they had achieved a success which made them the envy of their neighbours, why should they change? The majority of the House of Assembly were on their side, and it is difficult to understand why the Governor pressed the matter in the way he did. The opposition was no doubt foolish, but still, if the people chose to be silly, he could not overcome their prejudices. Party feeling ran high, only the mob shouting for Hennessy and Confederation. Those on one side would hiss him as he appeared— the others took the horses from his carriage and drew him along in triumph. It was reported that he never went out without a guard, and that even his wife lived in continual fear. She had been threatened with the abduction of her child, and one ruffian went so far as to pelt the little one as he was driven along the street, for which he was prosecuted.

At last, on the 18th of April, 1876, when the party feeling had existed over six weeks, matters came to a crisis. A man went into the yard of Byde Mill plantation, flourishing a cane-cutter, and bearing a red flag. He was, he said, a Confederation man, had just come from the Governor, and wanted some liquor (cane juice). Getting nothing he went out and brought his brother who bore a sword, and the two quarrelled with the man in the boiling-house, the one with the sword attempting to stab him. They defied a constable who came to arrest them, and one blew a shell which brought a mob of women and children, who went into a field of sweet-potatoes and began to carry them off. Three mounted police arrived, but they were pelted with stones, and one who attempted to arrest the man with the sword got wounded. A magistrate then came and read the Riot Act, but the mob refused to disperse. As usual there were grievances, some complained that their pay had been stopped, which the manager said was because they could not work the mill full time for want of wind.

Two cane-fields were now set on fire, and the disturbance spread, its great characteristic being raids upon the potato fields. In several places live stock were killed, dwellings broken into, and everything chopped or broken to pieces. A few shots were exchanged, but no one appears to have been killed, although many got wounds and bruises from sticks and stones. Everywhere the mob declared they had the authority of the Governor for what they were doing, and the sufferers from their depredations charged Mr. Hennessy with delay in putting down the disturbance. This, however, was probably due to the effect of the persecution of Governor Eyre, which has made every West Indian Governor hesitate before going to extremes. However, when the people from the country districts began to fly to Bridgetown he sent out a few soldiers who very quickly dispersed the mobs. A sensational telegram to London stated that five hundred prisoners had been taken, forty people killed and wounded, rioting was suspended, but their position was threatened, and that confidence in the Government had entirely gone. This was highly exaggerated, but a great deal of property was destroyed or injured, fifty estates pillaged, and probably over fifty persons received more or less serious blows.

Quite a storm fell upon Hennessy, who on the 26th of April had to issue a proclamation threatening to direct the law officers to take prompt measures against those who libelled him, by saying that he had sent emissaries through the island to mislead the people, and that he countenanced and abetted the disgraceful and lawless acts of the marauders.

XVI.

THE ISTHMUS TRANSIT SCHEMES.

BY the second half of the last century the supply of gold and silver from Peru had much diminished, and the road across the isthmus almost fell into disuse. In 1780, during the great war, the British appear to have had some vague notion that it would be good policy to secure the track across Nicaragua, for which purpose an expedition was fitted out. Early in that year Nelson sailed from Jamaica with five hundred men, and after getting a number of Indians from the Mosquito shore and a reinforcement of British troops, the party made the difficult ascent of the San Juan river, and captured the fort of the same name. But, through ignorance, the whole affair proved disastrous—the fort was useless, and the losses through sickness very great. Of eighteen hundred men only three hundred and eighty survived, and Nelson himself nearly lost his life. He was obliged to go home to recruit, and it was only after spending two or three months at Bath that he recovered to continue that glorious career which made him so famous.

However, it was not long afterwards that a project

for utilising the isthmus was brought under the consideration of the British Government by General Miranda, of whom we have spoken in another chapter. He wanted Pitt to assist him in his projects for the emancipation of the Spanish colonies, and, as a means to this end, in 1790, proposed that the British should take possession of Darien, and thus further their commerce in the Pacific. Nothing was done at that time, and a few years later Miranda made a second proposition that the United States should join with Great Britain, and open roads and canals for both nations.

Mr. Pitt seems to have agreed to this, and was only prevented from attempting to carry it out by the delay of President Adams. The United States were to furnish ten thousand men, and Great Britain money and ships. In 1801, under Lord Sidmouth, an expedition was actually set on foot, only to collapse at the Peace of Amiens. Again, in 1804, Pitt tried to carry out the project with Miranda, but the condition of Europe stood in the way of expeditions to the Spanish Main.

In enumerating the advantages likely to accrue from the emancipation of South America, a writer in the *Edinburgh Review* of January, 1809, laid great stress upon a passage across the isthmus. It was the most important to the peaceful intercourse of nations of anything that presented itself to the enterprise of man. So far from being a romantic and chimerical project, it was not only practicable, but easy. The river Chagré, about eighteen leagues westward of Porto Bello, was navigable as far as Cruzes, within

ATLANTIC ENTRANCE TO DARIEN CANAL.
(*From Cullen's "Darien Canal."*)

five leagues of Panama. But there was even a better route; at about five leagues from its mouth the Chagré received the river Trinidad, which was navigable to Embarcadero, from which Panama was only distant thirty miles through a level country. The ground had been surveyed, and not the practicability only, but the facility of the work *completely ascertained.* Further north was the grand lake of Nicaragua, which by itself almost extended the navigation from sea to sea. The Governor of St. John's Castle

(Fort San Juan) had been instructed by the king of Spain to refuse permission to any British subject desirous of passing up or down this lake, " for if ever the English came to a knowledge of its importance and value they would soon make themselves masters of this part of the country."

But not only had the best places for a canal been selected at this early time, but the many advantages to be derived from its construction had been well considered. The same writer went on to say that from this splendid and not difficult enterprise, not merely the commerce of the western shores of America would be brought, as it were, to their doors, but that of the South Sea whalers, who would be saved the tedious and dangerous voyage round Cape Horn. Then the whole of the vast interests of Asia would increase in value to a degree that was then difficult to conceive, by having a direct route across the Pacific. It would be as if, by some great revolution of the globe, they were brought nearer. Immense would be the traffic which immediately would begin to cover the ocean—all the riches of India and China moving towards America. Then also the commodities of Europe and America would be carried towards Asia. As a result of this, vast depôts would be formed at the two extremities of the canal, to soon develop into great commercial cities. Never before had such an opportunity been offered to a nation as Great Britain had then before her, owing to a wonderful combination of circumstances.

Mr. Robinson, a United States merchant, in 1821, said that the most ardent imagination would fail in an attempt to portray all the important and beneficial consequences of such a work, the magnitude and grandeur of which were worthy the profound attention of every commercial nation. The powers of the old and new world should discard all selfish considerations, and unite to execute it on a magnificent scale, so that when completed it might become, like the ocean, a highway of nations, the enjoyment of which should be guaranteed by all, and be exempt from the caprice or regulation of any one kingdom or state.

Such were the views promulgated at the beginning of this century, but nothing was done until about 1850, when the pressure of circumstances again brought the isthmus into note.

Darien and Panama are in the Republic of New Granada, but north of these come the small states of Costa Rica, Nicaragua, Honduras, San Salvador, and Guatemala. All of these are inhabited by true Americans—native races who have to a considerable extent absorbed the slight admixture of European blood introduced by their conquerors. Some places are so inaccessible as to be virtually outside the pale of civilisation. The roads are nothing but mule tracks, full of quagmires where the animals have to wade up to their girths in mud—in fact, little better than the paths so well described by Lionel Wafer. The rivers are numerous, and, on account of the heavy rainfall, their currents are very strong, and all the more dangerous from the numerous sandbanks and rapids which obstruct their course. Since the states gained their independence they have passed through so many changes of government that at the beginning hardly a month passed without a revolution in one or the other. This went on until 1848 without interference from outside, but with the discovery of gold in California came an invasion of ruffians of all nations.

The old freebooters almost seemed to have come to life again. Hardy adventurers from all parts of the world rushed off to the new " El Dorado," woke the sleepy Nicaraguans on the San Juan river, and roused the people of Chagres. Over the isthmus of Panama or through the Nicaragua lake they flocked by thousands, necessitating the establishment of Transit Companies to provide them with mules, boats, and steamers. The easiest, although longest, route was through Nicaragua, which was controlled by the Vanderbilt Company, and during the time the " rush " lasted they took over two or three thousand per month. The Company had steamers on the lake to meet the throng of diggers as they arrived, and they passed through at regular intervals like a tide. The overland part of the route presented a strange spectacle, with their pack mules and horses. Men of all nationalities, armed with pistols and knives, which they were prepared to use on the Greasers (natives) at the slightest provocation, put these altogether in the background. A traveller has spoken of them as a string of romantic figures that could not be matched in any other part of the world. Some glowed with fervent passion, as if on fire, others were hard, cold, and rugged as the rocky passes they traversed, while a few were worn, old, and decaying, under the effects of the hardships and reverses of their stormy existence. Every line in their faces had a meaning, if it could only have been interpreted, telling of sin and suffering—of adventures more terrible than were ever portrayed by the pen of the romantic writer, and of experiences as fascinating as they had been dangerous.

Among the results of this rush through Nicaragua was the expedition of William Walker, the great filibuster of this century. With fifty-five men he went forth from California to conquer Central America, and in the end nearly succeeded. He got himself elected President of Nicaragua, but ultimately raised such a storm that he was brought to bay by some forces from Honduras and Costa Rica, and had to surrender to the captain of a British man-of-war, by whom he was handed over to his enemies to be shot.

With this wonderful traffic across the isthmus arose the old canal schemes, as well as a new one for a railway. Easy and rapid transit must be obtained in some way or other, and this time being in the age of steam, it naturally followed that the project for a railway gained immediate support. It was commenced in 1850, at which time the terminus on the Gulf side was settled, and the foundations of the new town of Aspinwall or Colon laid a few miles east of Chagres. The difficulties were enormous, on account of the marshy ground and the number of rivers to be crossed. The wooden bridges were almost immediately attacked by wood ants, floods carried away the timbers, but more distressing than all was the loss of life through sickness. Chinese labourers were imported in great numbers, only to fall victims to the same deadly climate which had given Porto Bello and the isthmus generally their evil reputation. However, the railway was completed in 1864, at the enormous cost of $7,500,000, although its length is only 47½ miles. Thus one part of the great project was carried out, and a good road provided for passengers and light goods, the annual value of which latter is now about £15,000,000.

But those in favour of a canal were not sleeping all this time. The old routes were again mooted, that through Lake Nicaragua being put down at 194 miles in length, while the other, since known as the Panama, was only 51. Dr. Edward Cullen, however, in 1850 went out and made some surveys, with the result that he advocated the old Darien line as the shortest and most practicable. He would start from the same Port de Escoces that witnessed the downfall of William Paterson's scheme, and which he said was a most commodious harbour for the terminus of a canal. The isthmus was here only 39 miles across, and free from many of the difficulties which beset the other routes.

As a result of Dr. Cullen's reports, in 1852 it was proposed to establish "The Atlantic and Pacific Junction Company," with a capital of fifteen millions sterling. The prospectus stated that the period had arrived when the spread of commerce and the flow of emigration to the western shores of America, Australasia, and China, demanded a passage more direct than those by way of the Cape of Good Hope and Cape Horn. Various projects had been formed for uniting the two oceans, but all these were open to the objection that they fell short of supplying a continuous channel from sea to sea, for vessels of all dimensions, by which alone transhipment could be obviated. Sir Charles Fox, Mr. John Henderson, Mr. Thomas Brassey, and Dr. Cullen had received a concession of territory from New Ganada to the extent of 200,000 acres, on condition that a deposit of £24,000 be made within twelve months. It was believed that the work could be completed for twelve millions.

The *Times* spoke disparagingly of the new Company, and this probably prevented its acceptance by the financial world. The line, it said, had not been actually surveyed, but only superficially examined, and, after all, if it were finished, it could only come into competition with the Nicaragua Canal, every foot of which had been the subject of precise estimates, and which would only cost *four millions.* Several letters from the projectors and supporters of the Company followed, with other leaders, the result being that the Darien Canal never went beyond a project. Presently also the rush for California abated, and the railway met the wants of the passengers; all the canal schemes were therefore again shelved for a time.

Then came an almost Utopian project for a ship railway, the cars of which would run down into the water, take up the largest vessel, and carry it over without trouble or difficulty. This met with little encouragement, and was soon dropped.

In 1879 Ferdinand de Lesseps, who had achieved such a glorious success with the Suez Canal, took up the matter of a canal between the two oceans, and summoned a congress of savants, engineers and seamen, to inquire into and discuss the questions of its possibility, and of the most suitable place for its excavation. A number of projects were considered, among them that of Dr. Cullen, brought forward by M. de Puydt, which, however, did not receive much attention, as there was a difference of opinion as to the reliability of the figures.

The schemes were ultimately reduced to two—those for the Nicaragua and Panama routes. The position of the great lake caused the former to be thoroughly discussed ; but there were several almost insurmountable difficulties in the way of its adoption. To clear the San Juan river, and make it into a great canal, would entail great labour and expense, and then seven or eight locks would be required. On the Pacific side locks would also be required for the Rivas, while the harbours of Greytown on the Gulf side, and Brito on the Pacific, were quite unsuited as termini for a canal. The total length would be $182\frac{1}{2}$ miles, and the time occupied in the passage four and a half days. There was also another great drawback : Nicaragua was and is subject to earthquakes, which would be likely at times to interfere greatly with such heavy works as were required. It followed, therefore, that notwithstanding the powerful support of the Americans, this line was abandoned in favour of that from Port Simon to Panama, not far from the railway.

Two French officers, MM. Wyse and Reclus, had explored the country, and proposed to carry the canal through the Chagres river, and thence, by means of a great tunnel, into the valley of the Rio Grande; but, on consideration, the tunnel was abandoned in favour of a deep cutting, which would not exceed 290 feet. The great objection to this was the floods of the Chagres river, which sometimes rose twenty-five feet in a single night; but this was got over by arranging for a separate bed for the canal. There were a few other difficulties, but propositions were made to obviate them; and at last the sub-commission reported that " the Panama Canal on the level technically presents itself under the most satisfactory conditions, and ensures every facility, as it gives every security, for the transit of vessels from one sea to another."

Now came the question of cost. The Nicaragua Canal was estimated at £32,000,000, and that at Panama £40,000,000. (The reader will compare these with former estimates, especially that of Nicaragua as stated by the *Times*.) The former was rejected absolutely, on account of the necessity for locks, and all further discussion was concerned with the latter. It was then calculated that, with transit dues of fifteen francs per ton, the net annual profit would be £1,680,000.

M. de Lesseps was elected to the Academy in 1885, when M. Renan said he had been born to pierce isthmuses, and that antiquity would have made him a god. Carried away by enthusiasm, the great projector saw no difficulties; he had already completed a work which had been declared almost impossible, now he would carry out a project similar to that proposed by William Paterson. However, Panama was not Suez, a rainless desert, but a place where floods, marshes, and quagmires took the place of almost level sands.

M. Wyse had vainly tried to start a Company; but when Lesseps, with all the prestige of his Suez Canal, joined him, there was comparatively little difficulty. Personally, Lesseps seems to have known little of Panama—all his knowledge was gained at second hand. The first public subscription was invited in July, 1879, the capital being 400,000,000 francs (£16,000,000), in 800,000 shares at 500 francs each. This large sum, however, was not obtained at once, only £3,200,000 being applied for. However, Lesseps was not discouraged, but determined to go on with the work, trusting that money would flow in as it was wanted, which ultimately proved to be the case, until the project appeared hopeless. He visited the isthmus, and made a triumphal progress over the line; he even witnessed one of the great floods of the Chagres river, which rose forty feet and covered the railway. Undaunted by this, he went over to Panama, and on the 5th of January, 1880, inaugurated the great canal with a ceremony and *fête*. He then stated that success was assured, and declared, upon his word of honour, that the work would be much easier on the isthmus than in the desert of Suez.

In March following he visited New York, where he was but coldly received, on account of American jealousy of European influence. The President said that the capital invested in such an enterprise by corporations or citizens of other countries must be protected by one or more of the great Powers, but no European Power could intervene for such protection without adopting means which the United States would deem inadmissible. This did not damp his enthusiasm ; if other countries would not assist, all the credit would go to France. The Company had a concession from the Columbian Republic for twelve years, and the United States would not be likely to interfere.

It will be interesting here to compare the estimates for the canal by different persons and at different times within two years :—

M. Wyse, 1879	£17,080,000
The Paris Congress, 1879	41,760,000
The Lesseps Commission, February, 1880 ..	33,720,000
M. de Lesseps himself, ,, ,, ..	26,320,000
Rectified estimate, September, 1880	21,200,000

Lesseps said he had an offer from a contractor to complete the work for twenty millions. Backed by the press and the deputies, the Company's shares sold freely, and on the 3rd of March, 1881, it was fully established. It was promised that in the course of that year the line of the canal should be cleared, and dredging commenced. Lesseps expected to finish in 1887, but in 1884 and the two following years he was obliged to advance the time to 1890. The canal was to be 47 miles long, 70 feet wide at the bottom, and 29 feet deep.

Little was done in 1881, but the work was divided

into five sections, and in the following year dredging and excavating were commenced. But, even thus early, it was found to be more difficult than had been expected. Up to March, 1883, only 659,703 metres had been excavated, which was reckoned to be about $\frac{1}{130}$th of the whole. This would not do, as it meant that over a century would pass before its completion. About seven thousand labourers, mostly Jamaica negroes, were employed at that time, and this number was increased until, in 1888, there were 11,500. In 1884 the average amount excavated was 600,000 metres per month, against Lesseps' estimate of two millions. Yet, with all that, it was calculated that in this year only $\frac{1}{140}$th of the material had been taken out.

The difficulties were enormous, First, there was trouble to find dumping places, where the earth would not be again washed into the excavations by heavy floods. Then came the rank vegetation, which was continually stretching from either side to choke the clearing. Weeds grew six to eight feet high in a rainy season, and these, with the straggling vines, kept a little army at work to clear them away from the embankments and tracks. The workmen suffered greatly from yellow and other fevers, and £600,000 was spent on hospitals and their appurtenances. Money was spent profusely on such things as grand offices and a magnificent house to lodge the President, if he should ever come to inspect the works. All along the route were ornamental bungalows, and the director-general at Panama had a salary of £20,000, besides a house and other allowances.   Even he suffered from fever, and his wife and daughter died of it.

Up to 1888 about fifty millions sterling had been spent, and hardly a fifth of the work was finished. Then financial difficulties led to an arrangement for merging it in a new Company, which proposed to complete the canal on a new plan.   Notwithstanding all the objections to locks, it was now proposed to save such an immense work of excavation by erecting four on either side, thus bringing the highest water level to 123 feet.   Eighteen and a half miles were said to have been completed, of which five were on the Pacific side and the remainder on the Gulf. To carry out the new plan, £36,000,000 more were required, but, as a matter of fact, only a third of the work necessary for this revised scheme had been done.

Then came the downfall, which has been compared to that of the South Sea Bubble.   When the Company went into liquidation, scores of shady transactions came to light.   Editors of newspapers and deputies had been bribed to gain their support, and money had been wasted in almost every possible manner. In February, 1893, M. Ferdinand de Lesseps and four other directors were prosecuted, with the result that he, MM. C. de Lesseps, Fontaine, and Cottin, were convicted of breach of trust and swindling, the two former being sentenced to five years' imprisonment and 3,000 francs fines each, and the latter two years and 20,000 francs fines.   M. Eiffel, the architect of the great tower of Paris, was found guilty of breach of trust, and sentenced to two years' imprisonment and a fine of 20,000 francs. Nine persons were then charged with receiving bribes, one of whom, M. Baïhaut, admitted that he got 375,000 francs. Three were found guilty, sentenced to imprisonment, fines, and to pay the liquidators of the company the amount of M. Baïhaut's bribe. Charles de Lesseps appealed against the charges of swindling, and these were quashed on the ground that the transactions had occurred more than five years before, thus getting the longer terms of imprisonment and fines of the three principals reduced.

Ferdinand de Lesseps hardly knew what was going on ; he was old, feeble, and in a state of apathy and stupor. Pity for his condition prevented the carrying out of the sentence as far as he was concerned, and he died on the 7th of December, 1894. The *Times,* in noticing his death, said the story was a most pitiful one. The blame of the Panama affair must be laid upon the people and the public temper. Bribery and corruption were symptoms of a thoroughly unhealthy state of things. An infatuated public provided enormous sums ; when these were spent, more went the same way, and to get these contributions everything possible was done. Lesseps was no engineer, but a diplomatist, planning great schemes and the means of carrying them out. He was the man of the moment in France. He was neither a financier nor an engineer, neither an impostor nor a swindler. He was a man of great originality, of indomitable perseverance, of boundless faith in himself, and of singular powers of fascination over others.

Meanwhile several attempts had been made to get

money to carry on the work, one of which was by means of a lottery. But the French people were discouraged, and were no longer prepared to throw good money after bad. It followed, therefore, that although in 1894 a new company, with a capital of sixty-five million francs, was proposed, and that it was announced in August that eight hundred workmen were engaged, it does not appear that anything is being done. If, as has been stated, only a third of the work has been accomplished for, say, thirty millions, allowing for waste of money, it can hardly be expected that double this amount will ever be obtained. What with the heavy floods and rank vegetation, a great deal will have to be done to recover lost ground ; in fact, some of the excavations must be filled up by this time. Those who know the country can easily understand that the handsome bungalows, hospitals, and workmen's houses must be overrun by woodants, and that the machinery is mostly spoilt by rust. Even if the canal is ever finished with locks, it is doubtful whether it could pay a dividend, as the work of keeping it open by dredging would be very expensive. No doubt it would be a boon to the world if it were finished, but capitalists expect profit, and will hardly be inclined to assist without such expectations.

The Nicaragua canal has been in course of excavation for several years past by an American Company. As finally adopted, it is to have a total length of 169.4 miles, of which $56\frac{1}{2}$ will be through the lake, and $64\frac{1}{2}$ through the San Juan river. There are to be three locks on either side, which may cause trouble in case

EUROPE SUPPORTED BY AFRICA AND AMERICA.
(*From Stedman's "Surinam."*)

of a violent earthquake; and then, again, the length of
the journey will be against it as compared with that
of Panama. It has been attempted in the United
States to make it a national work, and the sum of a
hundred million dollars is asked from the American
Government, or at least a guarantee on the issue of
bonds to that amount. We believe that very little
enthusiasm for the project has been shown. In
August, 1893, the Company was unable to meet its
obligations, and a receiver was appointed, since which
time we believe the work is being continued, and that
it has been decided to complete it as soon as possible.
M. de Varigny, in *L'Illustration* of June the 1st, 1895,
gives the following opinion on the work and its
political importance:—

"That the Washington statesmen take account of
the fact that the cutting of the isthmus is difficult,
costly, and, in case of a rupture with England, dangerous, we cannot doubt. But such is the fascination of great enterprises, of grand words and grand
theories, that senators and representatives hesitate to
oppose the current of opinion that is bearing along
the masses.

"The work has begun, and we can only hope that
it will succeed. There cannot be too many gates
of communication between different peoples. The
United States undertake to open this. Can they do
it, and doing it, will they give up the advantages they
will thereby acquire? The future will show."

INDEX.

"We have read Mr. Rodway's book with a good deal of pleasure. . . . It is well illustrated, and contains a large amount of really interesting observation, which may stimulate the general reader and which will recall many a half-forgotten scene to those who have themselves been travellers."—*Nature.*

"Mr. Rodway's book is delightful reading to the naturalist, more especially to the botanist ; and from the author's masterly and elaborate descriptions the untravelled reader can form some conception of the overpowering vigour of tropical vegetation."—*Scottish Geographical Magazine.*

"We have read Mr. Rodway's book with a good deal of pleasure ; . . . the book is worth reading."—*Nottingham Guardian.*

"Mr. Rodway . . . maintains the high standard of a goodly line of predecessors. . . . The illustrations to the book are excellent."—MR. EDWARD CLODD, in *The Academy.*

"Mr. James Rodway's 'In the Guiana Forest' conveys vividly the impressions made by the great forests of tropical South America upon a man who has acute artistic perceptions of Nature and a poetical way of describing what he has seen."—*Nation* (N.Y.).

LONDON : T. FISHER UNWIN.